Shadows 7

Shadows 7

Edited by
CHARLES L. GRANT

DOUBLEDAY & COMPANY, INC.
GARDEN CITY, NEW YORK
1984

520173

All of the characters in this book are fictitious,
and any resemblance to actual persons,
living or dead, is purely coincidental.

Contents

INTRODUCTION

by Charles L. Grant

Nostalgia, by its nature being often sweet, has a way of taking the sting out of how really miserable things used to be. Pain seldom lingers beyond its memory; heartbreak is an emptiness, and a numbness salved by violins and sighs; privation, once overcome, is a badge to wear as a reminder. At the moment of occurrence there is misery, perhaps even despair; yet given enough years, much of the worst of it can be recalled in conversation with only a bit of melancholy and a lot of "you think it's bad now, let me tell you . . ."

Fear is the same way. Nothing, not the most intense therapy or the most vivid nightmare, can ever completely recapture that one time, that one instant when nothing else mattered except that you were afraid. But there are those who try anyway, such as those in the pages of this book, because if nostalgia sometimes robs us of learning through sepia-memory, it also permits us to reexperience the worst times safely. Well, almost safely. Because pain can't really be relived, and heartbreak heals itself, and privation often becomes a technicolor miniseries where makeup takes the place of the real thing.

On the other hand, fear can be relived, and it can be reinduced when it's handled properly, and it can remind us that there are some things that are never overcome just because we will them to go away. When the full moon casts a shadow, turning your back won't make it disappear, which is why, so often, we often turn back, just to be sure we saw what we saw.

We did. And when we remember it, later, it has nothing to do with nostalgia and fond memory.

Charles L. Grant
Newton, New Jersey 1983

Shadows 7

Introduction

Being down on your luck is often portrayed in film and story as a somewhat romantic condition. Without ties one can become a wanderer, an observer, a minister without portfolio to what the world is "really" like. What the world is really like, however, is almost always much different than we ever imagined.

Joseph Payne Brennan is, quite simply, one of the masters. He is a poet; the creator of Lucius Leffing; the author of such classics as "Canavan's Back Yard"; and his latest book is a delightful hard-boiled detective novel, Evil Always Ends.

MRS. CLENDON'S PLACE

by Joseph Payne Brennan

It was late November; sleet driven by a north wind slanted down the dingy street. Shivering, I sought the meager protection of a tattered awning left unfurled above the window of an abandoned storefront, and considered my prospects.

I had exactly seven dollars in my worn wallet plus a few loose pennies in my pockets. My topcoat was threadbare and the stiff cardboard covering the holes in my shoes was thoroughly soaked. I had lost my job months before; I had been forced to give up my small but reasonably comfortable room. Luckily, I had managed to accumulate a little nest egg of fifty-odd dollars. By supplementing that with the proceeds of tireless trash-barrel scrounging (mostly nickels and dimes for cans and bottles), I had stayed unsteadily afloat.

But now I was down to seven dollars. The trash barrels were iced over with sleet and my wet socks were literally on the ground. Hunger pangs twisted my gut; my feet were growing numb; night was coming on. It was too late in the year to curl up in an alley or under bushes in a park.

The ripped awning was scarcely even an apology for a roof, but I left it reluctantly. Sleet raked my face like icy needles. After a block or two the numbness in my feet spread toward my knees.

I passed one gaunt, trembling street dog who glanced up with faint momentary appeal, but not a single pedestrian came into sight.

When I came abreast of the three-story brick tenement and saw the window sign reading *Rooms. Five Dollars in Advance,* I stopped. Five from seven left two and I needed food, but I felt that I had no choice.

I went up the ice-covered steps of a small wooden porch and rang the bell.

After I thought I might freeze to death on the porch, the frayed yellow curtain behind the top glass panel in the door was jerked aside. A wrinkled female face stared suspiciously out at me.

I lifted my disreputable canvas hat and forced a smile onto my frigid face. I suppose it came out a grimace, because a quick scowl spread over the wrinkled countenance beyond the yellow curtain. Surprisingly, however, the door inched open. A cold eye stared out at me, a nearly colorless eye, bleak and without pity.

As casually as possible, I said that I would like to look at a room.

The door opened wider. "Five dollars a day in advance. You can stay the night and through t'morra. Leave by six sharp or it's another five dollars. No noise, no trouble, or out you go."

I took an instant dislike to the hard-eyed harridan, but the sleet-laden wind was sweeping down the street with increasing force and my feet had gone entirely numb.

I followed the creature up a dimly lit flight of stairs on which the carpeting had been worn straight through to the wood. The house seemed warm in contrast to the outside, but it was drafty and actually only half-heated. A disagreeable odor filled the stale air. Far off in the house someone coughed steadily; otherwise there was silence.

Limping, the grim-faced landlady led me a short distance along a darkened hallway and opened a door.

The room, like its owner, looked coldly inhospitable: a brass bed, one chair, a battered dresser with one missing drawer. There was a half-drawn shade on the one small curtainless window. Greyish green paint had been plastered over wallpaper which was beginning to crack. One diminutive braided rug, badly raveled, lay in front of the bed. A dusty mirror hung above the dresser; otherwise the walls were bare. A naked low-watt light bulb dangled from the center of the ceiling.

Mechanically, I reached for my worn wallet and handed over my last five-dollar bill.

A quick, bony hand closed on it. "I'm Mrs. Clendon. Bath's two doors down, left." She started to leave and then turned. "Yer name . . . ?"

I didn't want to tell her my name. I'm not sure why. But of course, I did.

"Melson. William Melson."

With a half nod she left, closing the door behind her.

I took off my wet shoes and stretched out on the bed's tattered grey counterpane. A weak current of warm air seeped into the room through a tiny baseboard vent. It was enough to keep me from perishing from cold, but not much more than that.

After I had rested a few minutes, I got up, shivering, and explored the dreary little cubicle. The closet contained nothing save a few bent clothes hangers. The dresser drawers yielded two paper clips, one nail, and a stale milk cracker wrapped in tissue paper.

I went to the window and looked out. Sleet hammered the filmed-over pane with increased intensity. The storm was getting worse and now it was nearly dark.

Cold and exhausted as I was, I could not bring myself to go out again. I decided I could get through the night without actually starving to death.

I ventured down the hall to the bathroom, a freezing, clammy little cubicle complete with cracked sink and antiquated slate tub, and returned to my room carrying water in a used paper cup.

Supper consisted of the stale milk cracker, chewed very deliberately, and water, swallowed very slowly. It wasn't much, but it gave my stomach a little to work on besides its own lining.

After this banquet I undressed and got into bed. The blankets were thin and patched, but within recent weeks I had slept in far worse circumstances.

Although I ached with fatigue, I had trouble getting to sleep. Somewhere in the far depths of the house an occupant coughed and moaned continuously. When I finally fell asleep, I experienced vague but disturbing dreams. In my incipient nightmare the coughing and the moans seemed to emanate from all quarters of the house, an escalating, somehow menacing, wave of sound.

I awoke abruptly and sat up. The room was like a grave—pitch dark, cold, and silent.

I lay down again but sleep eluded me. Once I heard boards creak in the hall and thought someone had stopped outside my door. I was totally unable to recall whether or not I had turned the key.

I lay filled with apprehension until anger—anger at myself— overcame everything else. I got out of bed, crossed the room, and tried the key. The door was locked. I thought I heard someone shuffling off down the hall, but perhaps it was merely my imagination.

I went back to bed, but I remained awake until a semblance of grey light filtered through the filmy window. At that point I fell into a brief but dreamless sleep.

I awoke cold and ravenous but somewhat rested. Although sleet no longer struck the window, the morning remained grey and sunless. Wind rattled a loose shutter.

I dressed hastily, shivering. My damp, stiffened shoes pinched my feet as I stood up in them. I hated the prospect of tramping the windy, ice-covered streets, but I was getting weak with hunger.

I locked my room and went down the stairs. The house was silent. Every door I passed was closed.

I thought I had grown accustomed to rundown neighborhoods, derelict buildings, and neglected streets, but I found myself unusually depressed as I hunched along buffeted by the wind. Once I slipped on the icy walk and went to my hands and knees but, luckily, sustained no noticeable damage.

I still had two dollars firmly buttoned in the one good pocket of my tattered coat. Under the circumstances, its importance became magnified. I could get hot coffee, biscuits or toast, and possibly an egg. I didn't care to look ahead any further than that.

I was beginning to believe that the whole dismal area held not a single diner or restaurant when I saw a small sign: Eats. The place did not look prepossessing but neither did I. I went in and sat down at a counter stool, sighing gratefully. My feet felt frozen and my legs ached. Eats was a good ten blocks from Mrs. Clendon's clammy establishment.

An undersized man, black-haired and frowning, came down the counter. One other customer sat quietly a few stools away.

After carefully toting up the menu's total in my head, I ordered coffee, toast, and two soft-boiled eggs.

I could have eaten the breakfast three times over, but when it was paid for, only fifteen cents remained.

The scowling, undersized man watched intently as I picked up the fifteen cents. I shrugged inwardly. With the few loose pennies I could pick out of my pockets, I might buy another cup of coffee later in the day.

I started to leave, but remembering the soaked pasteboard inserts in my shoes, returned to the counter.

"Sir, would you have a small cardboard carton you could spare?"

Surprisingly, the small man grinned at me. "Soles gettin' thin, hah?"

I nodded. "So thin they aren't there!"

He gestured toward the rear of the room. "There's a storeroom back there. Lots of empties. Take what you want."

I found a couple of sturdy shoe-box-size containers in the littered room and tucked them under my arm. As I came out, I saw that my benefactor was standing in the doorway watching me.

"Up against it, hah?"

"That's for sure. Come six o'clock I'm back on the street for the night."

He studied my face. "You look honest. You want to earn a buck maybe?"

I set down the boxes carefully. "No maybe. You name it."

Two customers strolled in and sat down. He glanced out at them. "Sit down at the end of the counter. You can have another coffee on the house."

After the customers were served, he brought me a cup of coffee and leaned across the counter.

"I need somebody to clean up a little. And sometimes I go out for an hour in the afternoon. You wouldn't need to come in till eleven. Three dollars a day—under the counter!" He grinned at his little joke.

I accepted at once but added that I'd be happy to come in at opening time and stay till five-thirty—for a trifle more.

"How much more?"

I hesitated. "Well, five dollars—plus coffee and a sandwich or something."

He stood scowling, as if my suggestion infuriated him. When I decided all was lost, he grinned again.

"OK, we'll try it. But no shenanigans—or out you go!"

Triumphantly, I trudged back toward Mrs. Clendon's rooming house. I was to report to Eats at 6 A.M. and remain until 5:30 P.M. Mr. Karda, the scowling but apparently amiable owner, promised I could have coffee and sandwiches "on the house" after the lunchtime crowd thinned out. I would be required to sweep, scrub, wash and stack dishes, clear the counter, clean the coffee machine, etc. In the slow hours of the afternoon I might be required to fill in for Mr. Karda during his absence of an hour or so. I would be paid my five dollars daily before leaving at five-thirty.

Giddy with my good luck, I was back in my room before I remembered Mrs. Clendon's terms: "Leave by six sharp or it's another five dollars."

Sighing, I trekked down the stairs and sought out the charmer. The cold, sparsely furnished first floor appeared to be uninhabited. I wandered through darkened rooms, down icy corridors, calling out "Mrs. Clendon!" but there was no reply.

As I was about to return up the stairs, I heard the sliding sound of a bolt and the rattle of a chain. "Who's there?" someone called.

A sliver of light directed me to a door set almost under the staircase, a door I had passed without a second thought, assuming it was a closet or storeroom of some kind.

Mrs. Clendon's accusing eyes stared out at me. The door, ajar only inches, appeared to be studded with a glistening array of chains, locks, and alarm devices.

Behind the ill temper and impatience in those implacable eyes, I read something else—fear.

I explained my situation, promising that while I could not have the five dollars at six o'clock, I would definitely have it the next day.

The harsh voice was uncompromising. "Five dollars by six or you leave!" The door slammed. Chains rattled; bolts slid home.

Well, there was nothing for it. Cursing and shivering, I wended my freezing way back to Eats and asked Mr. Karda for the loan of five dollars "on account."

Understandably, Mr. Karda hesitated. The upshot of it was that I was told to take off my coat and get to work. Actually, I didn't mind. It was relatively warm in the small place. I dutifully swept, scrubbed, and scraped. During the afternoon I was allowed coffee and two ham-on-rye sandwiches. I was permitted to leave at five-thirty with five dollars, the understanding being that I had earned only three and that I owed Mr. Karda two.

At two minutes to six I knocked on Mrs. Clendon's door. After I had identified myself, and following a great rasping of bolts, clicking of catches, and clattering of chains, the door inched open.

I slid the five-dollar bill through the crack.

My payment was acknowledged with a nod. The grim eyes surveyed me. "Come a little earlier next time, Mr. Melson." The door closed.

Again, however, I read fear in those faded eyes. I shrugged wearily and went up the stairs. Probably, I reflected, the house had been burglarized a number of times, or possibly Mrs. Clendon had been injured by an intruder. Beyond that, anyone who operates a rooming house in a rundown neighborhood would at least occasionally encounter difficult customers. Well, it was no concern of mine.

I fell into bed trying to decide whether I was more tired than famished. Sleep soon decided the wearisome issue.

I'm not sure exactly how long I slept. About four hours, I estimated. I awoke suddenly, alert and apprehensive. Though the room remained cold, the air was peculiarly oppressive. It was not that it was merely stale; it seemed almost septic. In spite of the freezing weather, I was tempted to open the window.

I sat up, listening. From far areas of the house, I heard a continuous coughing, moans, and a kind of half-suppressed but frantic wailing. The sounds, though muted and at times intermingled, were unmistakable. It was no use for me to assure myself that it was only the wind, rattling loose shingles or sighing around outside the house.

I shoved the pillow back against the headboard, drew up my knees, and pulled the bedclothes around my shoulders.

What kind of a rooming house had I stumbled into? Was Mrs. Clendon running some kind of unlicensed home for the sick and dying? What human wrecks were shut away behind those closed doors along the corridor?

At intervals the disturbing sounds ebbed away into near silence, but every time I was about to slide back down and attempt sleep, they began again.

What I found especially puzzling was that I could not definitely place any one sound in any specific part of the house. I could not say for certain that a nasty, rasping cough came from across the corridor, nor that an intermittent groaning gasp had its origin in the cold and darkened rooms below. The strangely subdued but persistent cacophony appeared to emanate from different areas of the house, merging, shifting, at times swelling in volume, and then again fading away into a kind of febrile muttering.

As I crouched uncomfortably in the darkness, I finally came to the bizarre conclusion that I was lying in a pesthouse packed with the infirm and expiring, that the very walls of the building groaned with the grisly burdens which they hid.

At length, from utter mental exhaustion, if nothing else, I dozed off.

At once, frightening dreams took over my weary brains. Something hideous, something ultimately indescribable, stalked the stale corridors of the house. It moved ponderously from door to door, seeking mine. It was turning the knob when I awoke with a scream.

The wild pounding of my heart subsided as I saw that the door remained closed and that weak grey morning light was diluting the darkness.

After dressing hastily I walked down the worn stairs to the street door. The whole house was silent. Not a soul was in sight.

The cold had lessened a little, but I still shivered as I walked along.

Mr. Karda surveyed me with misgivings. "You been up all night?"

I shook my head. "No. Didn't sleep well. Nightmares."

The day seemed interminable, but as I worked, I consoled myself with the thought that at least I was warm and that I would have something to eat by midafternoon. Somewhat grudgingly, Karda had given me free coffee and toast for breakfast, but by lunch time I could have eaten boiled elephant ears.

Soup, sandwiches, and coffee at 3 P.M. revived me briefly; by five-thirty, however, I was exhausted. Gratefully, I accepted my five dollars and left.

A freezing rain was falling. In spite of my fatigue, I experienced a feeling of desolation as I approached Mrs. Clendon's rooming house. Well, at least it was a roof and a bed, I told myself. It would be an endless, miserable night for unfortunates huddled in doorways or crouched under highway bridges.

After the customary clatter and bang of bolts and chains, Mrs. Clendon extended a skinny hand for my five dollars. She merely nodded and shot the bolts again.

Sighing, I tramped up the stairs and sat on my bed. Although I was paying for my room, and eating enough to keep from starving to death, my situation remained precarious. After I paid Mrs. Clendon, not one cent remained in my possession. My clothes were disintegrating. The fresh pasteboard in my shoes was already mushy with moisture.

Pondering the price of new shoes, I stretched out on the bed. I must have dropped off to sleep within minutes. Just before exhaustion overcame me, I thought I heard a doorbell ringing and, later, the closing of a door.

Again my sleep was invaded by vile and frightening dreams. Moans, rattling coughs, sighs, and wails seemed to issue from all parts of the house. Abruptly, this discordant concert was succeeded by absolute silence.

After a short interval, something began shuffling, or sliding, down the corridor. As it moved, or breathed, it made a sound I find difficult to describe—a kind of weird, whistling bleat, almost a muffled scream, compounded of both agony and rage. It seemed as if every groan and sigh, every wail and whimper, which arose from inside the house, was somehow gathered together in that ghastly concentrated cry.

As before, I awoke with a wildly hammering heart and sat up in bed.

I listened. Something *was* moving down the hall, something that advanced slowly, gasping and wheezing. When it stopped, I was sure that it stood just outside my door.

As I crouched, petrified, I could hear an irregular breathing, an erratic breathing punctuated by rales. While I was staring through the darkness toward the door, whatever it was outside gave vent to a hair-raising squeal, whether of pain or fury, or both, I could not be sure. It was the most frightening sound I had ever heard.

While I waited, half expecting the door to crash inward, the shuffling, sliding sound resumed. Gradually, it grew fainter. I thought, or imagined, that whatever was prowling the corridor had reached the head of the stairs and started down, but I could not be sure.

I lay listening, filled with apprehension, but the shambler in the hall did not return. Even after silence settled down, I remained awake, feverish with fearful speculations. Just before dawn I dozed for a few minutes.

As soon as I awoke, I got up, dressed quickly, and hurried down the hall to the dingy bathroom. I was starting back to my room when a door burst open on the opposite side of the corridor and a glaring, disheveled figure erupted into the hall.

He stopped abruptly when he saw me. He drew back, his face twitching with agitation.

Towel-draped and tousled as I was, I halted and stared back at him.

"You—room here—mister?" he managed finally in a gravelly voice.

I nodded.

He shook his head in disbelief. "Don't know how you stand it! This was my first night—and my last! That old crone downstairs has the whole place packed with sick people! Some of 'em dying, I'll bet! Heard 'em moan and holler half the night! Roamin' the halls too, they was. I'm gettin' out!"

He turned, took a tight grip on the battered suitcase which he carried, and headed for the stairs. Half a minute later I heard the front door slam.

Thoughtfully, I returned to my room. Recalling the ringing of the doorbell just before I had fallen asleep, I now surmised that it had been the wild-eyed departed character inquiring about a room.

Well, at least I wasn't merely dreaming or hallucinating, I told myself. Someone else had heard the same sounds, or similar sounds, as I. Perhaps the fleeing one-night roomer was right: Mrs. Clendon was operating some sort of shady nursing home or last refuge for the senile and terminally ill.

But why were the occupants active and vociferous only at night? Why were the corridors always empty, the rooms always closed and quiet whenever I came or went? I couldn't answer my own questions. They raced around in my head like starving squirrels in a treadwheel cage.

In spite of the cold morning air and a brisk walk, I had developed a dull, persistent headache by the time I arrived at Eats.

I had lost my appetite. I nibbled sandwiches, but I got through the day thanks to extra cups of strong black coffee. On several occasions I caught Mr. Karda watching me with disapproving, suspicious eyes, but he made no complaint. I did the work assigned.

After he had paid me, and as I was about to leave, he approached me, frowning, and spoke. "You got trouble?"

I hesitated. I was tired and I didn't think he could be of much help in any case.

I shrugged. "Place where I room gets noisy at night. I don't get half enough sleep."

"Carousing? Women? Drunks? Stuff like that?"

"No, not any of those. Seems like a lot of sick people in there. I guess they get worse at night. Groan, yell, prowl around."

"Where you stayin'?"

I told him.

An odd expression crossed his face. I couldn't quite fathom it. He walked back to the counter and wiped it very carefully.

I had my hand on the doorknob before he looked up. "If I was you," he said, "I'd get a room somewhere else."

"What do you know about the place?"

It was his turn to shrug. "Oh, nothin', I guess. Rumors is all. I heard once that old bag takes in anybody for a quick buck. That's an old, old house too. Must be a lot of people died in there."

For some reason his comments exasperated me. "A lot of people have died in old rooming houses all over the city," I replied irritably. "And everybody's out for a quick buck these days."

He hung up the counter cloth and grinned. "Sure, sure. That's the truth! Just forget about it and try to get a night's sleep."

After the sordid ceremony of Mrs. Clendon's sliding bolts and clutching, bony hand, I ascended to my room and sprawled on the bed. As usual, I saw no one in the corridors. The doors of the rooms were all closed. Occasionally, a sporadic wind shook a broken shutter; otherwise the house was gripped in silence.

"Holding its breath," I told myself—and immediately regretted it. If I was to go on working all day, eating inadequately as I had been, it would be vital for me to get more sleep.

After minimum ablutions and perfunctory glances at a week-old newspaper which I had picked up, I undressed and got into bed.

Sleep would not come. Though I ached with fatigue, my brain remained active and alert. In my mind, Mr. Karda repeated his comment endlessly: *That's an old, old house. Must be a lot of people died in there.*

I finally got up and dressed. I had had enough, I told myself. I would take the initiative. I was tired of lying in bed, tense with fear, waiting for the sounds to start.

I stole into the corridor, locked my door, slipped the key into my trousers pocket and moved slowly down the hall. All doors were closed; all rooms quiet. Save for the tapping of the loose shutter, complete silence prevailed.

I went up and down the long corridor twice. I ascended carpetless stairs to a third floor, holding fast to a flimsy railing in the darkness. Two dim light bulbs created small islands of illumination along the second-floor hall, but the entire third floor lay engulfed in shadow.

I groped down another musty corridor. Every door stayed shut; every room remained quiet. At the far end faint starlight filtered through a small window nearly opaque with dust. By this meager light I made out a rickety ladder leading to an overhead trapdoor. For a moment I was impelled to climb up and push open the trapdoor, but I decided against it. The ladder rungs were probably brittle with age and perhaps termite damage. If one broke, I might be injured; I might lie for hours, crying out in the darkness. I might lie for days . . .

Cursing my overactive imagination, I returned along the corridor and carefully crept back down the stairs. I had seen no one, heard nothing.

I stood scowling, impatient and frustrated. On impulse, I pulled out my room key and tried it on the nearest door. The key turned in the lock. I opened the door, sensing at once that nobody was in the room. By the misty window light I saw the outline of a bed, a chair, and table.

Shrugging, I closed and locked the door. I stood hesitating, key in hand. Was it possible, I asked myself, that Mrs. Clendon, miser that she obviously was, issued the same key to all the roomers— because the locks were all the same? This would save money if a key were lost or stolen. And it had probably saved money for someone when the locks were first installed. No matter the chaos it must have created for unsuspecting roomers!

My suspicions were quickly confirmed. My key opened every room along the hall. Not a soul was in any one of them.

Ordinarily, fury would have excluded every other emotion. But my anger at this disconcerting discovery was now tempered by fear. If there were no other roomers in the house, what was the origin of those ghastly sounds which intruded in my dreams and ruined my sleep?

Apprehensive and restless, I descended the stairs to the first floor. Pools of darkness. Silence. Bulky furniture, some shrouded by dustcloths. Worn wooden floors and threadbare carpets. Ragged drapes, smelling of undisturbed dust.

For long minutes I stood outside Mrs. Clendon's barricaded private door, but at length I turned and padded back upstairs. I took off my shoes and lay down, but I made no effort to fall asleep.

What had I stumbled into? Were nightmares unhinging my brain or was Mrs. Clendon engaged in some weird and secretive operation?

I clung to the thought of the agitated roomer I had encountered in the corridor as he was hastening from the premises. It was a comforting thought. At least *one* other person had heard those unexplained night sounds.

Hours passed before I sank into a fitful sleep. Struggling out of nightmare and only half awake, I heard something slowly sliding down the corridor. As it drew close to my door, a sickening odor seeped into the room. I sat up, heart pounding.

Something ponderous and clumsy seemed to flop against the door. I could hear the hinges creak. I leaped out of bed, trembling.

A kind of snuffling sound, interspersed by groans, came from behind the door. Slowly, the sound grew fainter. I realized that whatever had paused outside was now moving off toward the stairwell.

I dressed and sat on the side of the bed, waiting for the prowler's return. Occasionally, I heard muffled thumps from below, as if an intruder was barging into furniture in the darkness.

I would leave the place, I vowed, as soon as I could locate another room in the vicinity—any kind of room.

As I pondered the matter, I became convinced that Mrs. Clendon was harboring some kind of human monster on the premises, probably a relative born hideously deformed and perhaps an idiot as well. It emerged from a hidden room only at night, to prowl the corridors. After one accidental glimpse of it, roomers fled—and undoubtedly talked. As a result, the house had acquired a sinister reputation. Unless she possessed other sources of income, Mrs. Clendon was probably on the brink of bankruptcy—or even starvation. Under these circumstances, her expression of abiding apprehension, as well as her abrupt manner, were understandable.

I must have fallen asleep for a few minutes, because I failed to hear the night roamer's return along the corridor.

Shivering and haggard, I dressed, left the now silent house and hurried down the cold sidewalks toward Mr. Karda and Eats. A light snow was drifting down before I reached my destination.

Karda took one look at me and shook his head. "You got to get out of that place. You look like death—not even warmed over!" I merely nodded in agreement. I was too tired to attempt talk.

I performed my duties mechanically, like a sleepwalker. I think Mr. Karda felt sorry for me. Later in the day he said he was giving me a two-dollar-a-day raise, adding that I could have the whole of Sunday off. He even presented me with a pair of sturdy secondhand shoes which he had picked up somewhere. They pinched a little, but the soles were thick and scarcely worn. Considerably cheered, I managed to hold out until quitting time.

It had snowed heavily all day. I labored back towards Mrs. Clendon's through formidable drifts built up by a driving wind. Under the circumstances, I was doubly grateful for Mr. Karda's gift of the shoes.

After I had shaken off most of the accumulation which adhered to my clothes and gained the scant shelter of Mrs. Clendon's porch, I went inside and knocked on her locked, near impenetrable private door. The bony hand shot out and drew back so quickly, once the bolts were drawn, I received only a momentary glimpse of my landlady's face. The glimpse shocked me. I saw a countenance distorted with terror.

It was good to have two dollars still left after the bolts banged shut, but my little advance now brought me small satisfaction. What had brought such an expression of overpowering, abject fear to the woman's face?

Wearily, I tramped upstairs, removed my tattered coat, shapeless hat, new secondhand shoes, and lay down. Mr. Karda had given me coffee and a couple of leftover salami sandwiches about four o'clock. I was still hungry, but not ravenous. Sleep was the important thing, I told myself.

Tomorrow, I decided, I would look for another room. I was reasonably sure that Karda would give me an hour or so to look around the neighborhood. Unless the storm turned into a blizzard, I vowed that the next evening would find me under a different roof.

Exhausted, I dropped off to sleep—and nightmare. I was fighting my way down darkened streets, nearly buried under huge drifts. Somewhere, miles off, a new room awaited me, a clean, quiet room. As I lurched along, groans, emanating apparently, from under the drifts, became audible. Frantically, I began digging into the nearest mound of snow. The faster I dug, the louder grew the groans.

I sat up in bed suddenly, trembling. The entire house echoed with groans, cries, muffled sobbing—and, at intervals, a high-pitched, half-stifled squeal of agonized rage.

Briefly, this storm of sound would subside. At these times I was grateful to hear wind rattling the windows. It was a sound I could comprehend, a comforting sound. But, inevitably, the frenzied outbursts began again.

I swung my legs over the side of the bed and groped for my shoes. As I did so, the wild cacophony seemed to merge into one continuous wailing shriek. I sat petrified as it grew ever louder.

All at once, this monstrous amalgam of tortured sound swept into the adjacent corridor. I experienced a sudden, terrifying conviction that the fearful concentration of sound had somehow contrived to take on substance and shape.

Something screaming and unnameable rushed down the hall. My door bent inward as it passed. An indescribable stench, almost like a physical blow, assailed my nostrils.

Stupefied and sickened, I sat unable to move as the repellent thing continued down the corridor. Whatever it was seemed to pause momentarily at the top of the stairwell. The next instant it apparently plunged down.

I heard the crash of falling furniture below, followed by the rending of wood and the screech of bolts and hinges as a door was exploded inward.

The screams which followed were not those which I had been hearing. They were the screams of a mortal human in ultimate throes of agony and terror. They rang through the whole house, on and on, distinct even above the renewed shrieking of the thing which caused them.

They stopped. I crouched by the bed, chill with fear, listening.

Silence ensued but lasted only seconds, though they seemed like long minutes. There were more breaking, crashing sounds; the wailing scream of the invader began again.

I waited, helpless. The volume of sound grew louder, closer. The unnameable was coming back up the stairs.

Cringing in panic, I considered a wild plunge through the door, down the corridor toward the rear of the house. I had never had occasion to use the back entrance, but I was sure one must exist.

Yet I hesitated. The rear door might be barred and bolted even as Mrs. Clendon's room. I might be trapped, still struggling to unbar it, even as the thing caught up with me.

I made some effort to move but my legs seemed paralyzed; by the time I rose to my feet and got them pointed toward the door, it was too late.

The shrieking grew louder, a burden of unbearable sound beating against my ears. The door bulged inward. A fetor of decay, foul and suffocating, flooded the room.

As I staggered backward and fell on the bed, the door crashed into the room with such force it ended up flat against the floor.

A nightmare shape reeled into the room. It was massive, with vaguely human contours, sheened over with the shining of corruption. Saturated rags clung to suppurating skin. Bones pushed outward against a misshapen sheath of discolored flesh and raveled bandages.

The face was indescribable—sacs of swollen skin cobbled over a mass of open sores, a blood-encrusted hole of a mouth shaped into a scream which never stopped.

The eyes were the worst. I stared into an inferno of agony, despair, and hate.

The frightful thing was not static and fixed in appearance. It remained huge in mere bulk but both its contours and its countenance underwent terrifying and incessant alterations. The face flowed in upon itself and switched identities as if a succession of monstrous masks were being swiftly interchanged. One second it was the distorted image of a diseased and dying old man; the next it became the oversized repellent caricature of an infant in the final stage of some fatal malady; then it shifted into the semblance of a haggard younger woman horribly disfigured with suffering, undergoing the last ravages of disease and neglect.

It was not amorphous; it did not fade or divide. But the swift, bewildering, kaleidoscopic metamorphoses never ceased. Some incarnations—for want of a better word—were repeated. Its appearance as it had first smashed into the room returned again and again.

And suddenly, even in the depths of my terror, I thought I understood the origin of the grisly thing. It was an amalgam of the forces and emotions of those who had suffered and died in this terrible house. No single one of them haunted the place, but the imprints of their agony, resentment, rage, and fear had remained in the house long after they were gone. Somehow, as these forces strengthened and multiplied over the years, they had merged into the hideous multiple-person entity which hovered before me.

It was, I felt, essentially mindless—but it was nevertheless motivated. The psychic remnants of pain, hate, and protest, unrelieved and perhaps even unexpressed in life, imbuing the house and steadily gaining power, had eventually grown strong enough to attain form and purpose.

But I had scant time for metaphysical speculation. I was convinced that what I saw before me existed, at least periodically, on my own earthly plane—that it was not merely an intermingled projection of thought forms.

I knew that it possessed explosive lethal force. I had heard the sounds of destruction coming from below—and I had seen my own door torn away.

All this raced through my mind in seconds.

As the ulcerous, squealing shape lurched toward me, I was finally galvanized into action.

My mind, in its excess of fright, seemed to go blank, but my body, as if automatically repelled by the approaching entity, sprang backward off the bed and literally catapulted itself through the glass panes of the window.

I was aware of stabbing pains in my back, the sensation of falling, sudden immersion into freezing darkness—followed by oblivion.

I awoke in a hospital bed with severe lacerations in my back and shoulders, a broken ankle, and a concussion. A drift of snow beneath my window, built up by the still-falling flakes and heavy winds, had saved me from a fractured spine or shattered skull. Luckily, a homeward-bound night watchman passing the house had spotted me and summoned help.

For a day or two I experienced nearly complete memory loss. And when memory returned, I wondered whether chronic amnesia might be preferable.

The local police, who had been anxiously awaiting the return of my memory, lost no time in questioning me. I learned that Mrs. Clendon had been discovered dead in the shambles of her room, with the door off its hinges and smashed furniture everywhere.

I told my story as well as I could, but the police remained skeptical and uneasy.

A detective lieutenant named Ralders hovered above me impatiently, shaking his head.

"You say you heard those screams from below just before you went out the window?"

I nodded. "Only minutes before."

He frowned. "Then how do you explain the fact that old Mrs. Clendon's body was found in a badly decomposed condition—like she'd been dead a long time? She was"—he groped for the word—"almost *liquescent!*"

I couldn't explain it—at least not to him. Privately, I was totally convinced that the thing that smashed down my door had killed Mrs. Clendon just before it came back up the stairs. When the invader caught and enveloped her, she was an immediate vessel for all its disease and putrefaction. As these foci of hoarded infection poured into her, her body underwent the changes which, ordinarily, would affect a corpse only after weeks or months of corruption.

I knew it would be useless to express this opinion to Ralders and his cohorts. Even after I was released from the hospital, they returned to interrogate me. They finally decided that, without question, Mrs. Clendon had been killed weeks before by a maniac prowler who had broken into the house. My version was shrugged away. They concluded I had been undergoing hallucinations or some kind of brain fever.

Later, after I had bid farewell to Mr. Karda and Eats, and my prospects had somewhat improved, I did a little research into the history of the area where Mrs. Clendon's place was located. Again and again, that part of the city had been plagued by waves of deadly diseases—typhoid, diphtheria, yellow fever, smallpox, lethal "Spanish" influenza, and a host of other ailments. The rest of the city had not been immune, but that particular section, whether from sewer stoppages and poor sanitation, or from prevalent malnutrition on the part of its occupants, seemed particularly vulnerable.

The old rooming house which Mrs. Clendon took over must have sheltered literally hundreds of suffering victims over the years. Thrust to the bottom rung of society's ladder, many had undergone agonizing deaths alone in their shabby rooms.

I believe the psychic residues of these poor souls had at last coalesced, as it were, into the deadly thing which prowled the halls as Mrs. Clendon sat chill with terror behind her bolted door.

The revengeful remnants of these hate-filled, disease-racked sufferers apparently remained quiescent during the day. At night, when pain and despair had been most intense during their lives, they combined into the horrifying entity which took on awful life.

For years after my nightmare adventure, the house stood boarded and vacant. When it was finally sold and demolished, the dirt cellar was dug up to put in the foundation of a new building. Beneath the sour, damp soil, workers found the skeletons of six persons—four children and two adults. They were rumored to have been murder victims, but my own belief is that they were the remains of occupants who died of fatal diseases and were interred in the cellar by relatives to avoid the expenses of formal funerals.

The projected new building was never constructed—whether because of the resultant publicity or because of other reasons, I never learned.

When, out of curiosity, I returned to the neighborhood for the last time, I found only a brush-and-weed-covered lot where Mrs. Clendon's place had stood. Some small boys were playing in the adjacent street.

As I stood watching, an elderly codger strolled up and pointed the stem of his pipe at the empty lot.

"They never plays in there," he volunteered. "Says the weeds or somethin' makes 'em feel sick. Kids get a lot of crazy ideas!"

I wonder.

Introduction

Nostalgia for the "good old days," for times when life was "more simple, less urban" does not always take into account the fact that "simple" doesn't mean "easy," and "good old days" doesn't mean people didn't have their shadows. They just didn't turn on the television to get rid of them.

Michael Cassutt is an executive for CBS-TV, has had numerous science fact and fiction pieces published in magazines and anthologies ranging from Omni *to* Universe, *and has just sold his first novel,* The Star Country.

STILLWATER, 1896

by Michael Cassutt

They are big families up here on the St. Croix. I myself am the second of eight, and ours was the smallest family of any on Chestnut Street. You might think we were all hard-breeding Papists passing as Lutherans, but I have since learned that it is due to the long winters. For fifty years I have been hearing that Science will take care of winters just like we took care of the river, with our steel high bridge and diesel-powered barges that go the size of a football field. But every damn November the snow falls again and in spring the river swells from bluff to bluff. The loggers can be heard cursing all the way from Superior. I alone know that this is because of what we done to John Jeremy.

I was just a boy then, short of twelve, that would be in 1896, and by mutual agreement of little use to anyone, not my father nor my brothers nor my departed mother. I knew my letters, to be sure, and could be trusted to appear at Church in a clean collar, but my primary achievement at that age was to be known as the best junior logroller in the county, a title I had won the previous Fourth of July, beating boys from as far away as Rice Lake and Taylors Falls. In truth, I tended to lollygag when sent to Kinnick's Store, never failing to take a detour down to the riverfront, where a Mississippi excursion boat like the *Verne Swain* or the *Kalitan,* up from St. Louis or New Orleans, would be pulled in. I had the habit of getting into snowball fights on my way to school, and was notorious for one whole winter as the boy who almost put out Oscar Tolz's eye with a missile into which I had embedded a small pebble. (Oscar Tolz was a God damned Swede and a bully to boot.) Often I would not get to school at all. This did not vex my father to any great degree, as he had only a year of schooling himself. It mightily vexed my elder brother, Dolph. I can still recall him appearing like an avenging angel wherever I went, it seemed, saying, "Peter, what in God's name are you doing there? Get away from there!" Dolph was all of fourteen at the time and ambitious, having been promised a job at the Hersey Bean Lumberyard when the Panic ended. He was also suspicious of my frivolous associates, particularly one named John Jeremy.

I now know that John Jeremy was the sort of man you meet on the river—bearded, unkempt, prone to sudden, mystifying exclamations and gestures. The better folk got no further with him, while curious boys found him somewhat more interesting, perhaps because of his profession. "I'm descended from the line of St. Peter himself," he told me once. "Do you know why?"

I drew the question because my given name is Peter. "Because you are a fisher of men," I told him.

Truth, in the form of hard liquor, was upon John Jeremy that day. He amended my phrase: "A fisher of dead men." John Jeremy fished for corpses.

He had been brought up from Chicago, they said, in 1885 by the Hersey family itself. Whether motivated by a series of personal losses or by some philanthropic spasm I do not know, having been otherwise occupied at the time. I found few who were able or willing to discuss the subject when at last I sprouted interest. I do know that a year did not pass then that the St. Croix did not take at least half a dozen people to its shallow bottom. This in a town of less than six hundred, though that figure was subject to constant change due to riverboats and loggers who, I think, made up a disproportionate amount of the tribute. You can not imagine the distress a drowning caused in those days. Now part of this was normal human grief (most of the victims were children), but much of it, I have come to believe, was a deep revulsion in the knowledge that the source of our drinking water, the heart of our livelihood—the river!—was fouled by the bloating, gassy corpse of someone we all knew. There was nothing rational about it, but the fear was real nonetheless: when the whistle at the courthouse blew, you ran for it, for either the town was on fire, or somebody was breathing river.

Out would go the rowboats, no matter what the weather or time of night, filled with farmers unused to water with their weights, poles, nets, and hopes. It was tedious, sad, and unrewarding work . . . except for a specialist like John Jeremy.

"You stay the hell away from that man," Dolph hissed at me one day. "I've seen you hanging around down there with him. He's the Devil himself."

Normally, a statement like this from Dolph would have served only to encourage further illicit association, but none was actually needed. I had come across John Jeremy for the first time that spring, idly fishing at a spot south of town near the lumberyard. It was not the best fishing hole, if you used worms or other unimaginative bait, for the St. Croix was low that year, as it had been for ten years, and the fish were fat with bugs easily caught in the shallows. I had picked up a marvelous invention known as the casting fly and had applied it that spring with great success. And I was only too happy to share the secret with a thin, pale, scruffy fellow who looked as if he had skipped meals of late. We introduced ourselves and proceeded to take a goodly number of crappies and sunfish during the afternoon. "That's quite a trick you got there," John Jeremy told me. "You make that up all by yourself?"

I confessed that I had read about it in a dime novel, though if Oscar Tolz had asked me, I would have lied. John Jeremy laughed, showing that his teeth were a match for the rest of his ragged appearance.

"Well, it works good enough. Almost makes me wish I'd learned how to read."

By this point, as I remember it, we had hiked up to the Afton Road and were headed back to Stillwater. As we walked, I was struck by John Jeremy's thinness and apparent ill health, and in a fit of Christian charity—I was just twelve—I offered him some of my catch, which was far larger than his.

John Jeremy regarded me for a moment. I think he was amused. "Aren't you a rascal, Peter Gollwitzer. Thank you, but no. In spite of the fact that it's been a long dry spell, I'm still able to feed myself, though it don't show, I'll grant you that. In fact, in exchange for your kindness"—his voice took on a conspiratorial tone

—"I shall reward you with this." And into my hand he pressed a five-dollar gold piece. "For the secret of the fly, eh? Now run along home."

My father was unamused by my sudden wealth, especially when he learned the source. "That man is worse than a grave robber. He profits through the misfortune of others." It was then that I learned John Jeremy's true profession, and that he had been known to charge as much as *five hundred dollars* for a single "recovery," as it was called. "One time, I swear by the Lord," my father continued, "he *refused* to turn over a body he had recovered because the payment wasn't immediately forthcoming! A man like that is unfit for human company." I reserved judgment, clutching the eagle in my sweaty palm, happier than I would have been with a chestful of pirate treasure.

June is a month to be remembered for tornados, with the wind screaming and trees falling and the river churning. In this instance there was a riverboat, the *Sidney*, taking a side trip from St. Paul—and regretting it—putting into town just as one of those big blowers hit. One of her deckhands, a Negro, was knocked into the water. Of course, none of those people can swim, and in truth I doubt Jonah himself could have got out of those waters that day. The courthouse whistle blew, though it was hard to hear over the roar of the wind, and Dolph (who had been sent home from the yard) grabbed my arm and tugged me toward the docks.

The crowd there was bigger than you'd expect, given the weather—not only townspeople, but many from the *Sidney*, who were quite vocal in their concern about the unfortunate blackamoor. Into our midst came John Jeremy, black gunnysack—he referred to it as his "bag of tricks"—over his shoulder. People stepped aside, the way they do for the sheriff, letting him pass. He sought out the *Sidney*'s captain. I took it that they were haggling over the price, since the captain's voice presently rose above the storm: "I've never heard such an outrage in my life!" But an agreement was reached and soon, in the middle of the storm, we saw John Jeremy put out in his skiff. It was almost dark by then and the corpse fisher, floating with the wind-whipped water with all the seeming determination of a falling leaf, disappeared from our sight.

The onlookers began to drift home then while the passengers

from the *Sidney* headed up the street in search of a warm, dry tavern. Dolph and I and the younger ones—including Oscar Tolz —stayed behind. Because of my familiarity with the corpse fisher I was thought to have intimate and detailed knowledge of his techniques, which, they say, he refused to discuss. "I bet he uses loafs of bread," one boy said. "Like in Mark Twain."

"Don't be a dope," Oscar Tolz said. "Books are not real. My old man says he's got animals in that sack. Some kind of trained rats— maybe muskrats."

"Like hell," said a third. "I saw that sack and there was nothing alive in it. Muskrats would be squirming to beat the band."

"Maybe they're *drowned* muskrats," I offered, earning a cuff from Dolph. Normally, that would have been my signal to shut my mouth, as Dolph's sense of humor—never notable—was not presently on duty. But that evening, for some reason, I felt immune. I asked him, "Okay, Dolph, what do *you* think he uses?"

One thing Dolph always liked was a technical question. He immediately forgot that he was annoyed with me. "I think," he said after a moment, "that John Jeremy's got some sort of compass." Before anyone could laugh, he raised his hand. "Now just you remember this: all the strange machines people got nowadays. If they got a machine that can make pictures move and another one can say words, how hard can it be to make a compass that instead of finding north finds dead people?"

This sounded so eminently reasonable to all of us that we promptly clasped the idea to us with a fervor of which our parents —having seen us bored in Church—thought us incapable. The boy who knew Mark Twain's stories suggested that this compass must have been invented by Thomas Edison, and who was to dispute that? Oscar Tolz announced that John Jeremy—who was known to have traveled a bit—might have busted Tom Edison in the noggin and stolen the compass away, which was why he had it and no one else did. "Especially since Edison's been suffering from amnesia ever since," I said. I confess that we grew so riotous that we did not notice how late it had gotten and that John Jeremy's laden skiff was putting in to the dock. We took one good look at the hulking and lifeless cargo coming toward us and scurried away like mice.

Later I felt ashamed, because of what John Jeremy must have wondered, and because there was no real reason for us to run. A body drowned, at most, three hours could not have been transformed into one of those horrors we had all heard about. It was merely the body of a poor dead black man.

I learned that John Jeremy had earned one hundred dollars for his work that afternoon, plus a free dinner with the captain of the *Sidney*. Feelings in Stillwater ran quite hot against this for some days, since one hundred dollars was the amount Reverend Bickell earned in a year for saving souls.

Over the Fourth I successfully defended my junior logrolling title; that, combined with other distractions, prevented me from seeing John Jeremy until one afternoon in early August. He was balancing unsteadily on the end of the dock, obviously drunk, occasionally cupping his hand to his ear as if listening to some far-off voice, flapping his arms to right himself.

He did not strike me as a mean or dangerous drunk (such a drinker was my father, rest his soul), just unhappy. "Florida!" he announced abruptly. "Florida, Alabama, Mississippi, Missouri, Illinois, Michigan, Wisconsin, here." He counted the states on his hand. "And never welcome anywhere for long, Peter. Except Stillwater. Why do you suppose that is?"

"Maybe it is better here."

John Jeremy laughed loudly. "I wouldn't have thought to say that, but maybe it is, by God." He coughed. "Maybe it's because I've kept the river quiet . . . and folks appreciate it." He saw none-too-fleeting disdain on my face. "True! By God, when was the last time the St. Croix went over its banks? Tell me when! Eighteen eighty-four is when! One year before the disreputable John Jeremy showed his ugly face in the quiet town of Stillwater. Not one flood in that time, sir! I stand on my record." He almost fell on it, as he was seized with another wheezing cough.

"Then the city should honor you," I said helpfully. "You should be the mayor."

"Huh! You're too innocent, Peter. A corpse fisher for mayor. No, sir, the Christian folk will not have *that*. Better a brewer, or a usurer—or the undertaker!"

He had gotten quite loud, and much as I secretly enjoyed my friendship with him, I recognized truth in what he said. "You wouldn't want to be mayor, anyway."

He shook his head, grinning. "No. After all, what mayor can do what *I* do, eh? Who speaks to the river like I do? No one." He paused and was quiet, then added, "No one else is strong enough to pay the price."

Though I was far from tired of this conversation, I knew, from extensive experience with my father, that John Jeremy would likely grow steadily less coherent. I tried to help him to his feet, quite an achievement given my stature at the time, and, as he lapsed into what seemed to be a sullen silence, guided him toward his shack.

I was rewarded with a look inside. In the dark, I confess, I expected a magic compass, or muskrat cages, but all that I beheld were the possessions of a drifter: a gunnysack, a pole, some weights and a net. I left John Jeremy among them, passed out on his well-worn cot.

Four days later, on a Saturday afternoon, in the thick, muggy heat of August, the courthouse whistle blew. I was on my way home from Kinnick's, having run an errand for my father, and made a quick detour downtown. Oscar Tolz was already there, shouting, "Someone's drowned at the lumberyard!" I was halfway there before I remembered that Dolph was working.

The sawmill at the Hersey Bean Lumberyard sat on pilings well into the St. Croix, the better to deal with the river of wood that floated its way every spring and summer. It was a God damned treacherous place, especially when huge timbers were being pulled in and swung to face the blades. Dolph had been knocked off because he had not ducked in time.

The water was churning that day beneath the mill in spite of the lack of wind and current. I suspect it had to do with the peculiar set of the pilings and the movements of the big logs. At any rate, Dolph, a strong swimmer, had been hurled into an obstruction, possibly striking his head, so observers said. He had gone under the water then, not to be seen again.

The shoreline just to the south of the yard was rugged and overgrown. It was possible that Dolph, knocked senseless for a moment, had been carried that way where, revived, he could swim to safety, unbeknownst to the rest of us. Some men went to search there.

I was told there was nothing I could do, and to tell the truth, I was glad. My father arrived and without saying a word to me went off with the searchers. He had lost a wife and child already.

John Jeremy arrived. He had his gunnysack over his shoulder and an oar in his hand. Behind him two men hauled his skiff. I stood up to meet him, I'm ashamed to say, wiping tears on my pantaloons. I had the presence of mind to know that there was business to be conducted.

"This is all I have," I told him, holding out the five-dollar gold piece I had carried for weeks.

I saw real pain in his eyes. The breath itself seemed to seep out of him. "This will be on the house," he said finally. He patted me on the shoulder with a hand that was glazed and hard, and went down to the river.

My father's friends took me away then and put some food in me, and made me look after the other children. I fell asleep early that warm evening and, not surprisingly, woke while it was still dark, frightened and confused. Had they found him? I wanted to know, and with my father still not home, I had no one to ask.

Dressing, I sneaked out and walked down to the lumberyard. The air was hot and heavy even though dawn was not far off . . . so hot that even the bugs were quiet. I made my way to the dock and sat there, listening to the lazy slap of the water.

There was a slice of moon in the sky, and by its light it seemed that I could see a skiff slowly crossing back and forth, back and forth, between two prominent coves to the south. A breeze came up all of a sudden, a breeze that chilled but did not cool, hissing in the reeds like a faraway voice. I fell forward on my hands and shouted into the darkness: "Who's there?"

No one answered. Perhaps it was all a dream. I do know that eventually the sky reddened on the Wisconsin side and I was able to clearly see John Jeremy's distant skiff.

Hungry now and deadly sure of my own uselessness in the affair, I drifted home and got something to eat. It was very quiet in the house. My father was home, but tired, and he offered nothing. I went out to Church voluntarily, and prayed for once, alone.

Almost hourly during that Sunday I went down to the St. Croix. Each time, I was able to spot John Jeremy, infinitely patient in his search.

It finally occurred to me about mid-afternoon that I had to do something to help, even if it came to naught. Leaving the house again, I walked past the lumberyard toward the brushy shallows where John Jeremy was, hoping that in some way my sorry pres-

ence would encourage a merciful God to end this. I was frankly
terrified of what I would see—a body drowned a goodly time and
in August heat at that—yet anxious to confront it, to move *past* it
and get on with other business.

Two hours of beating through the underbrush, occasionally
stepping into the green scum at water's edge, exhausted me. I
believe I sat down for a while and cried, and presently I felt better
—better enough to continue.

It was almost sunset. The sun had crossed to the Minnesota side
and dipped toward the trees on the higher western bluffs, casting
eerie shadows in the coves. Perhaps that is why I did not see them
until I was almost upon them.

There, in the shallow water, among the cattails and scum, was
John Jeremy's skiff. In it was a huge white thing that once was my
brother Dolph. The sight was every bit as horrific as I had imagined, and even across an expanse of water the smell rivaled the pits
of Hell . . . but that alone, I can honestly say, did not make me
scream. It was another thing that made me call out, an image I will
carry to my grave, of John Jeremy pressing his ear to the greenish
lips of my brother's corpse.

My scream startled him. "Peter!" he yelled. I was as incapable of
locomotion as the cattails that separated us. John Jeremy raised
himself and began to pole toward me. "Peter, wait for me."

I found my voice, weak though it was. "What are you doing to
my brother?"

He beached his nightmare cargo and stumbled out of the skiff.
He was frantic, pleading, out of breath. "Don't run, Peter, hear me
out."

I managed to back up, putting some distance between us. "Stay
away!"

"I told you, Peter, I talk to the river. I *listen* to it, too." He
nodded toward Dolph's body. "They tell me where the next one
will be found, Peter, so I can get them out, because the river
doesn't want them for long—"

I clapped my hands over my ears and screamed again, backing
away as fast as I could. The slope was against me, though, and I fell.

John Jeremy held out his hand. "I could teach you the secret,
Peter. You have the gift. You could learn it easy."

For a long second, perhaps a heartbeat and a half, I stared at his
grimy hand. But a gentle wave lapped at the skiff and the God-

awful creaking broke his spell. I turned and scurried up the hill. Reaching the top, I remembered the gold piece in my pocket. I took it out and threw it at him.

At twelve your secrets do not keep. Eventually, some version of what I'd seen and told got around town, and it went hard with John Jeremy. Stillwater's version of tar-and-feathering was to gang up on a man, kick the hell out of him and drag him as far south as he could be dragged, possessions be damned. I was not there. Sometimes, as I think back, I fool myself into believing that I was . . . that John Jeremy forgave me, like Christ forgave his tormentors. But that did not happen.

Eventually, we learned that John Jeremy's "secret" was actually a special three-pronged hook attached to a weight that could be trolled on a river bottom. Any fool could find a body, they said. Maybe so.

But the flood of '97 damned near killed Stillwater and things haven't improved since then. A day don't go by now that I don't think of John Jeremy's secret and wish I'd said yes. Especially when I go down to the river and hear the water rustling in the reeds, making that awful sound, the sound I keep telling myself is not the voices of the dead.

Introduction

The worst part about those who have died is the fact that they don't, always, go away. That's not very comforting if it's someone who was your enemy; and when it's someone who was close to you, it isn't always a blessing.

Susan Casper, a Philadelphian, has not been writing very long, but has already sold pieces to most of the major magazine and anthology markets.

THE HAUNTING

by Susan Casper

Victoria stood in the dark room, listening to the sibilant sounds of the people sleeping there. The rest of the house was closed to her now, but no matter. This room had always been her favorite. She loved the neatly spaced rows of violets that lined the night-darkened walls, the mahogany tallboy her father had placed in that corner himself on the day the house was first occupied. Slowly, the moon rose, peeking in and out between wispy, grey-handkerchief clouds, a pale lemon ghost of a woman combing her flaxen hair. It gave off enough light to show her the child sleeping soundly in his trundle bed, although he was getting quite old to still be here in his parents' room. She wanted to ruffle his bangs and kiss his unlined forehead. He stirred in his sleep. *Sleep well, my Jimmy.*

The scent of blooming lilacs caught Victoria's attention and called her to the window. A small red wagon sat forlornly on the lawn next to a rack of croquet mallets. Blooming azaleas hedged the property. A creaking dray wheeled sleepily down the street pulled by a large white horse that almost looked majestic in the dusky light. It was still dark enough to see the sparks struck by the horse's hooves on the cobbled street. For a lifetime she stood there, wishing that she could run her hands along the velvet drapes, the delicate chinese jars that lined the sill and the whatnot on the wall.

Outside, the sun was just beginning to rise. The morning glories twisted open and dew soaked the freshly cut grass. The sky was a rainbow in pink and purple. A shaggy, liver-colored dog bounded across the lawn. He was chasing a squirrel and barking loudly. Too loudly. The child crept out of bed and went to the window to quiet him. "Hush, Pomeroy," he called down, "people are sleeping." Victoria looked at the child. He was a beautiful boy, with golden curls and sparkling blue eyes. He was wearing a nightshirt she'd stitched for him on those long nights in the wooden rocker. She had even tatted the lace edging and embroidered his initial on the chest. Every stitch was done with love.

The dog was still barking and the child dressed swiftly, pulling on his sailor's shirt with the square starched collar that went so well with his navy blue shorts. She could hear the child's parents stirring in the master bed. The child looked up at them cautiously and ran out the door. Victoria tried to follow him, but she could go no farther than the door to the bedroom. She turned and crossed back to the window in time to see the child appear on the lawn.

The bedsprings creaked behind her and she turned to watch the first drowsy stirrings of the people in the master bed. Jimmy's father pulled himself slowly to a sitting position, shook his head and smiled down at the woman still sleeping beside him. He slid out of bed and stretched, and Victoria smiled to see what a fine man Jacob was, even in his floor-length bedgown, with that handsome walrus mustache and muttonchop sideburns, his face as yet young and strong. He went to the window and called something to the boy, waking the woman. Victoria watched her yawn and rub her eyes. It took the woman much longer to pull herself out of bed to begin her morning ritual. She washed her face in the basin and pulled an ivory screen from the corner and stood behind it to dress. Without shame, Victoria walked behind it to watch. It was so strange to think of herself that way. It had been such a long time. She reached out her hand in an attempt to touch the supple skin and the woman shivered, but Victoria felt nothing.

The room was empty now. Hers again for a little while only. She looked lovingly at the hard woods, the dainty enamels, the glass bottles on the vanity, wishing once again that she could hold them. Each detail, from the handmade quilt to the imported persian rug of her mother's, brought back a flood of memory. Soon, she would have to go, never to see it again.

Her reverie was short-lived. The boy was back in the room, tugging the dog behind him on a homemade hempen leash. She

remembered the day when she and Jimmy had made the leash out
of old pieces of rope; and though it was far from beautiful to her
eyes, Jimmy had thought it the best piece of craftsmanship ever
done. Now, dog-chewed as well, it could barely withstand the
pressure that Pomeroy was putting on it, for suddenly the dog *saw*
her, and began to lunge with all his might to get away from the
room.

"Hush, Pomeroy! Stop *keening* like that. Father will make me
give you up if I can't make you behave." Jimmy gave one final
yank, pulling the dog into the room and slamming the door behind
him just as the leash finally snapped. "Now look what you've done!
Listen, dog, you've *got* to be quiet." His voice was full of the
desperation of childhood, dreading the judgment of a court from
which he had no appeal. "There'll be an awful row if they find out
that I haven't left for my piano lesson yet, but you've got to settle
down before I go. Father told me last night that this was your last
chance."

The frightened dog gave one last eerie cry; a sound reminiscent
of fairy stories—the howling wolf, the banshee's wail. Then, as if it
were all too much for him, he curled himself into a tight little ball
and jammed himself under the tallboy.

"I don't know what's got into you today, but that's better. Now,
don't you start screeching again. I've got to get out of here, and
that won't be easy if I don't want Mother to see me." He ran to the
window and leaned out over the sill. Victoria peered out over his
shoulder. The woman had just come around from the rear of the
house, carrying a large wooden basket. "Mother!" she heard
Jimmy whisper. He pulled back at once, the look on his face becoming more and more anxious as he heard the front door slam,
the sound of footsteps on the stairs. He looked around. With the
trundle in place, there was no room under the bed, and the dog
had taken up the space under the tallboy. He couldn't slip under
the vanity, for that was where his mother always put the basket
when she came upstairs.

The footsteps were coming closer. He spotted the tiny closet
and slipped inside. *No, Jimmy!* She put out a hand to stop him, but
it did no good. Still, he had left the door open the tiniest crack.
Enough to let air in. Enough to hear when the woman left the
room and it was safe to come out. Enough to make sure that he
wasn't locked in. But the woman pushed it closed. She slammed

the main door against it when she pushed into the room with the basket. She placed the basket under the skirt of the vanity and quickly made up the beds. *The closet. My God, the closet.* The woman's hands were deft and sure. A tug here, a twist there. She pulled out the trundle, smoothed out the sheet and pushed it back underneath the main bed, then stood for a moment to admire her work.

The closet. Open the closet. Look in the closet. Don't leave! The child is in the closet! Victoria tried to block the doorway with her insubstantial body. The woman shivered and looked uneasily over her shoulder, but she walked out into the hallway where Victoria couldn't follow. Victoria knew where the woman was going. Downstairs to do her canning. Down to the basement kitchen two flights below, where the muffled cries and hammering of the boy would not be heard.

Victoria's father had made that closet. He had made it for her mother, with cedar-lined walls and a door that was strong and tight against vermin and the weather. There was no handle on the inside. Nor was there any reason for Jimmy's mother to be alarmed at the child's absence. She would not begin her frantic, desperate search until her husband came home at five-thirty, and even then it would not occur to her to search the house. But Victoria did not want the woman to open the closet door later that night and find the small crumpled form as it slid bonelessly to the floor, cold and lifeless, the blue face stained with tears, hands raw and bloody. She tried to open the door herself, but those hands, once able to make a bed in five minutes, were now unable to turn a knob. Jimmy was already screaming and hammering on the thick door, but even right outside, she could barely hear him. "Mother, Mommy, please!"

She looked around the room for some way to attract the woman's attention. "Someone please come help me," Jimmy shouted, and silently, she echoed his plea. If she could only knock some of the bottles from the windowsill, or knock the vanity mirror over. A loud noise would bring the woman. There had to be a way. She had been given an opportunity to try and so there *had* to be something she could do. To go through this again and to change nothing would be the worst sort of cruelty. "Mom-my!"

The dog. The dog could sense her presence, and the dog could make a lot of noise. She bent low and pushed her head under the tallboy. The dog inched backward, away from her, making a soft, high-pitched wail deep in his throat. *Bark, you fool! Bark for Jimmy!* She pressed forward, and the dog moved back until, free at last from the tallboy, he bounded across the room. He jumped on the bed and began to growl. *Don't growl. Bark! Jimmy's in the closet!* The dog jumped off the bed and backed himself against the wall. She followed, flailing at him with her fists. *Bark! Howl! Knock something over!* The dog began to bark and still she chased him. *Louder!* The dog barked. The dog howled as though all the demons of hell were after him. *Louder!!!*

The woman burst into the room. "Pomeroy, stop it this instant. This time you'll have to go," the woman shouted. *Stop now, dog. Let her hear the boy.* With the door open, the dog leapt the bed and ran out of the room. The woman turned to follow, still shouting after him. *Wait! Don't go again! You stupid fool! You've got to save Jimmy. Do you want the boy to die?* She tried to grab the woman's hair, to tear at her clothes, to tackle her. Again the woman shivered.

"Mother, Mother, please!" Victoria heard it faintly. The woman seemed to hear something too. She paused in the doorway and looked around. "Somebody, anybody, help me!" The woman cocked her head, listening, then crossed to the window. *Not there, you fool. The closet!* "Help me. Let me out!" The woman walked back to the closet and opened the door. Jimmy fell out into her arms. His face was red, his cheeks stained with tears, his hands bruised and sore. He was the most beautiful child that Victoria had ever seen. He clung tightly to his mother's waist, sobbing, frightened by his momentary imprisonment, but otherwise unaware of the dark wings that had brushed the back of his neck.

As Victoria watched, the woman and the child began to fade. Color went first, draining away until they looked like an old sepia-toned photograph. Then they faded away altogether, disappearing very slowly, an image retained on the eyelid, then they were gone. As she watched, the tallboy peeled and chipped and began to lean unsteadily to one side; a pane of glass suddenly cracked and fell away. Then it too had shimmered and vanished, replaced by a blond oak bureau on top of which sat a vase of artificial flowers. The walls behind it turned pink, then green, then blue, and finally white. And as she watched, the view from the window changed, the empty wooded lands across the road giving way to tracts of housing developments and tall factory smokestacks that puffed their wastes on the distant horizon. This room was plain and bare compared with the other, and yet they were the same.

Victoria looked at the old woman lying on the simple Hollywood bed. A paramedic worked feverishly, administering CPR, while another adjusted the dials on the defibrillator for another try. Finally, the first one sat up. "Forget it, Ed. Nothing's going to help this one." Ed wiped the jelly from the machine's paddles and put them away. "Not surprising," he said. "She must be a thousand years old. I'll call the hospital. You can go over and tell the neighbors. They'll probably want to call her son."

Her son! Victoria noticed that on the nightstand beside her bed —the same nightstand that had been bare when she called about her chest pains, a few moments or years ago—was a gilt-framed picture. A picture of Jimmy, grey and balding, surrounded by his own grown children. And as the room began to fade, Victoria smiled.

Introduction

Earl is Parke Godwin's brother and, like many a fine writer, didn't begin his career early on. Instead, he began writing when many of us will begin thinking that it's less than two decades until retirement. Earl currently lives in Texas, and this is his first published story.

DADDY

by Earl Godwin

I stay away from singles bars. I never was good at clever small talk, and I'm at my fumbling worst when the whole idea is to strike up a relationship with a woman. That's why I choose neighborhood haunts where the serious drinkers gather to pass the evening in comfortable ambience. However, the thought is always tucked away in the back of my mind that I just might meet a special lady who could laugh aside my clumsy, inarticulate style and find charming the rather eccentric limitations of my bachelor life.

I met her in spades.

It had been raining and there was a chill in the air, so I sat in the back of the crowded bar in my raincoat nursing a straight bourbon. There were a lot of women in the place, some very attractive, but not that special one with whom I'd consider dancing through a night's fantasy. In life I've settled for some very ordinary women. In my dreams I always go first-class.

She came in with a man, and they threaded their way back through the crowd until a waitress seated them in a booth right next to my table. The man hung up their raincoats and she stood next to me, shaking the water from her dark, shoulder-length hair. A drop landed on my upper lip; I slowly licked it off, staring at her.

They weren't happy: this I could see right away. Worry traced its path across her darkly beautiful features. This was a queen, not just worthy of my idle fantasy but one for whom I could work my whole life to wash the torment from that exquisite face and replace it with happiness. I don't say that easily, because I consider myself an accredited critic of beauty. I'm a photographer, and even if my sexual successes have been among the mediocre, I have a sharp eye for real beauty, and this creature with her eyes that leaped out and grabbed you would steal the heart out of a polar bear. The man? Who knows? I wouldn't remember him if he fell on me.

I tried not to stare. Her eyes flicked over me for a preoccupied instant and then away. I listened to the soft, tense tone of their conversation. He was saying things like, "Tired of it . . . had enough . . . impossible." I couldn't make out much. Most of it was in whispers and I don't hear well. They raised their voices slightly. The conversation was becoming more intense. The man leaned over the table, his face strained and angry, hers desperate and afraid. She hissed something that sounded like an ultimatum. He jumped up and shouldered his way through the crowd to the front door. I looked quickly at the woman. Her expression was one of weary defeat. It seemed to add years to her face.

Alone and nervous, she fumbled her way through several matches until she managed to light her cigarette. I caught her eye and raised my shot glass in a sympathetic toast. She started to raise hers, but the glass was empty. "I seem to be abandoned and the gentleman had all the money." She flashed a vulnerable smile.

I signaled the waitress. "May I join you?"

"By all means." Her confidence had returned, but there was still that air of vulnerability about her that excited me. I prayed I wouldn't overplay my hand.

I have a book at home called *How to Pick Up Women.* There are hundreds of opening lines for starting a conversation; I couldn't remember a single one of them. We looked at each other for an awkwardly long time until I blurted, "Was that your husband?"

"No."

"He sure ran off and left you like a lone duck."

"No, just a friend. It's not important now. Do you have the time? I have to go soon."

I felt my hopes plummet. "It's nine o'clock. Please—don't go. I love talking to pretty ladies."

She looked at me sharply, an appraising glance. "Aren't you the charmer." Then she fumbled with another match. I leaned over to steady her hand.

"Eres muy caballero."

"You're Spanish?"

"I've been a lot of things. Do you live around here?"

I hadn't expected that. My pulse started to hammer faster. "Yeah. I've got a studio apartment a couple of blocks from here. I'm a photographer," I added for no good reason.

"Oh?" Her fingers drummed lightly on the table.

"Yeah. Uh . . . I'd like to take some pictures of you." Oh Jesus! I winced inwardly to hear that tired old line come out of my mouth.

"I'll bet you would." She ground out her cigarette in the ashtray, stood up, and reached for her raincoat. My heart sank; she was leaving. She put her coat on and fluffed that wonderful hair out around her shoulders. I sat staring up, hypnotized by her. She was older than I thought at first, pushing forty but still an incredibly beautiful woman. I would have said younger when she first came in, perhaps a trick of the light. But now she was leaving, the kind of woman ministers leave home for, and I'd never see her again. Jesus.

She smiled at me. "Your place?"

I couldn't believe it.

I was all thumbs and stupid remarks as I tried to appear suave while attacking the suddenly impossible task of putting on my raincoat. She leaned against the booth with a tired patience and glanced up at the clock. She finally helped me with the coat before someone had to cut me out of the damned thing. We walked out of the bar with her in the lead, and I gave a few friends a debonair wave, as if leaving with the finest fox in the house was old stuff for me. Taking her hand, I couldn't help thinking how I'd almost let her get away from me.

My studio apartment was quite naturally a mess. I turned on a light and watched her as she picked her way through a maze of lightstands and reflectors. My furnishings were rather sparse, but I did have a studio couch and a couple of easy chairs. The kitchen area was in the rear corner of the big room, away from the window. The sink was full of vintage dishes and maybe some new life forms.

She moved around and studied the pictures on the walls as I fixed a couple of drinks and turned on the stereo. "Very pretty women. How many have you slept with?"

"All" would have been a great answer, "half" would have been half true. "None of them," I muttered.

"I love honesty," she laughed. Then in a husky whisper as she came to me: "It makes me feel so warm toward a man."

We were standing in the middle of my front-room studio with the stereo low and the dim light struggling against the chilled gloom of the big room. She took my hand and guided me to the bedroom in the back of the apartment.

I kissed her full lips. They felt soft and full of promise, parting under mine, searching with her tongue, bringing me to quick readiness. I didn't rush. I'd been waiting a lifetime for this and I was going to enjoy the hell out of it. We undressed each other, pausing to caress favorite parts. Her large breasts were straining to be touched. She stroked and teased me and I pushed her gently back onto the bed—not in a hurry. Hell, I could have foreplayed with her until the cows came home. She was the one in a rush. She cried out then, a sound of relief and hope and something like fear, wrapping her legs around me as we rocked together in abandon. She held me like a vise with her arms and legs, squeezing me tight.

"No, honey, stay. I want it all."

I came and felt a surge of relief flood through me. For her that was it: show's over. She rolled me off her and stood up. "Thank you."

Odd thing to say after an interlude like that. I rolled over and found myself staring up into the wickedest gun barrel I'd ever seen.

"I don't get it. We were having a good time. What gives?"

She stood naked before me, unsmiling, with the pistol leveled at my head. She looked stricken. "Please. I haven't much time and I'm going to need your help. Don't ask questions, I don't have the answers. You have to deliver my baby."

I must have looked classically stupid with my jaw down around my ankles. "You're not pregnant."

"I am now and you're the father."

I managed a laugh like a choking gargle. "Aren't we a little premature? I mean like this stuff usually takes nine months." I laughed again, feeling ridiculous, sitting on the edge of the bed naked as a baseball. But there was nothing funny about her rage or the fear it came out of.

"Stop laughing, goddamnit! I—" She gasped in pain. The pistol dropped from her hand and she fell face forward, curling into a fetal position, holding her stomach. I picked the gun up and dropped it into a drawer. Rolling her over onto her back, I couldn't help notice that she looked even older than I thought the last time. I couldn't explain any of it, the whole thing was beyond me, but I had the feeling that what was happening here was as unique as it was awful.

I showered and dressed. She was moaning and rubbing her stomach when I got back to her. I stood by the bed looking down at her. There was a grotesque aspect to the situation now. I watched in helpless horror as the woman's belly began to swell—a little at first, then faster, as if someone were blowing her up with an air pump. And all the while her hair was graying like flickers of light in the dark mass of it. Sagging, wrinkled skin and brittle bones, long past the ability to stretch against the obvious labor pains, punished themselves to do what they were made for. She looked— she *was* now—sixty years old, the sound of her breathing like a saw in wood.

"Help me, please! Oh God, it's almost too late!"

She gave a low animal growl and drew her knees up against her breasts, her hands clamped on the headboard. The gasps were coming every couple of seconds—and then I could see the first sign of a small head.

She'd asked me to help. Me? In a normal birth I would have been useless as pants on a bird. Here I was a blithering idiot. I could only stand frozen and helpless as the nightmare unfolded in front of me. The baby's head and shoulders protruded now; the woman writhed like a trapped fish. Unintelligible gibberish escaped from her withering lips. Then, somehow shaking out of the trance, I grasped the slippery little shoulders and began tugging, pulling life out of death. The woman was actually shrinking now, falling in on herself, seventy-five, eighty years old. She'd stopped moving by now, gone stiff, gone beyond that, *way* beyond it, and the smell emanating from the decaying mess of her was almost too much to bear. I had the baby almost all the way out. Only the feet were inside. By the time I cleared them, the thing on the bed had been dead a very long time. The smell was sickening. I fought the need to vomit, stumbling into the bathroom for a fresh razor blade to cut the umbilical cord binding the baby to something that didn't quite make it out of the body.

It was a girl. Remembering old movies, I held her up by the little feet and gave the tiny buttocks a sharp smack. Her gasp and yowl started her breathing.

My daughter.

I carried her into the bathroom and washed her down with lukewarm water. Then, messed with blood and other matter I'd rather not think about, I stared at my reflection in the mirror. He looked like I felt, every bit of it. And he was a father.

I wrapped the baby in a blanket and the now unrecognizable remains of my date in the sheets. What to do with the gruesome bundle was a problem. I couldn't take it to the police . . . Sure, they'd believe me. Sure they would . . .

The baby was crying. It was hungry. I collapsed by the picture window in the front-room studio with her in my arms as she nursed at the makeshift bottle I scrounged from my photo equipment, some milk from the icebox and—hell, why not?—an unused condom from a pack in the dresser.

What the hell was I going to do? The shock was wearing off, replaced by exhaustion. I wearily placed the bundle on the floor next to my chair, adjusted the bottle for her to work at it, and sat back with a very deep sigh. I'd had a hard night.

I watched the rain sifting past the streetlights as the drops splashed on the pavement. Cars plowed through puddles and sent sheets of dirty water up on the deserted sidewalks. The clock across the street said midnight. I yawned and looked down at the baby. She was happily pulling away on her bottle, watching me with clear blue eyes. A little while ago they were barely open and still milky, unfocused. God help me—she'd grown.

I fell asleep in the chair, lulled by the soft drumming of the rain against the window. I must have slept for over three hours when I snapped awake suddenly, more out of a sense of guard duty than from any particular noise. The rain had stopped but the streets were shining wet, and I caught the reflection of the stoplight on the corner in the damp sheen of the sidewalk. I remembered and sat up.

The blanket was empty and the bottle lay next to it. Behind me I heard faintly the soft tread of tiny feet. Turning, I could just make out the small form coming toward me out of the dark. My hair rose; I jumped up, knocking over the chair. She approached with careful child-precision. She was wrapped in a sheet that trailed

behind her, and her dark hair was tousled down around her bare
shoulders, and she pulled at my pants leg, urgent and trusting.

"I'm hungry, Daddy."

I went into the bedroom, picked up the bundle of bedding, and
carried it down to the dumpster in the back alley. And I disposed
of the remains of that thing I had made love to. The mother of that
thing in my apartment. I wasn't thinking; clear-cut thought was
impossible. I walked back into the apartment. The little girl was
standing by the window, peering out.

"Where'd you go, Daddy?"

"I just threw your mother in the garbage. From what I knew of
her, she ought to feel right at home."

Her eyes weren't that young anymore. She pulled her curls
away from her shoulders and shook her head. A beautiful child.
She didn't look anything like me. I made her a sandwich and a
glass of milk, watching her as she ate—six or seven years old, only I
knew better. She wasn't that many hours old. I retreated to my
chair by the window and stared hopelessly out into the wet streets.
Then she was at my side.

"What was my mother like?"

"I don't know. We didn't spend much time cultivating a relationship."

She giggled, pressing my hand in her two small ones. "I love you,
Daddy. You talk funny."

She leaned over and kissed me with a little hug. I felt myself go
soft but I couldn't let her know it. We held onto each other as a
fresh sheet of rain beat against the windows and made little wet
rainbows out of the blurry neon signs across the street. We talked
together about nothing much until finally, just before daylight, we
both drifted off to sleep.

The roar of a bus outside the front window woke me with a start.
I yawned and stretched; a glance at the clock across the street said
it was a little after 8 A.M.

"You want something to eat, Dad?"

A pretty adolescent girl carried a plate of eggs into the dining
area. "C'mon, Dad. I know you're hungry. The one without the
sausage is mine. I hate sausage."

I wasn't in shock anymore but still not ready to accept this thing
as it was. She sat down and scraped eggs off into her plate from the
skillet.

"What are you staring at, Dad? You act like you've never seen me before. C'mon—eat up before it gets cold."

While I ate, I studied her: seventeen or eighteen now, well formed, rapidly becoming the woman I had been with the night before. She devoured her food hungrily and downed a glass of milk in one pull, leaving a white mustache on her upper lip. I leaned over and wiped it off.

"Thanks, I'm always so messy. Okay if I do the dishes later? *All Quiet on the Western Front* is on TV, and I've never seen it. It's a classic."

Whoever, whatever, from wherever, these things were born with some memories. I waved my hand helplessly. She could do whatever she wanted as far as I was concerned. The only thing she couldn't do was leave this apartment. I'd have to see to that. Until whatever was going to happen . . . happened . . . I'd just sit tight.

The morning passed in front of the television as we watched Lew Ayres in a dated but vivid story of a doomed German infantryman in World War I. She sat with her eyes glued to the screen. I couldn't help admire the beauty budding, blooming in front of me. She was full-bodied now, the woman I'd loved and watched give birth to her about sixteen hours before. The same woman.

The movie ended. She stood up and stretched, her breasts straining against the sheet that fit her a lot better now. She caught my glance. "Like what you see?"

I felt the surge of heat. I must have blushed. "Sorry. You're very beautiful. But I shouldn't have been staring."

"Were you in the war?"

"I was in Korea," I mumbled, glad for the change of subject.

She sat down again, drawing the sheet up around her. "Men don't have much to look forward to, going off to war all the time. I'm glad I'm a woman."

I thought, *Honey, they've got a lot more to look forward to than you do, any way you slice it.*

In a moment she went over to the stereo, sifting through the records, smiling over her shoulder at me. "Got an idea." She put on a record and came to me, holding out her hands in invitation. "Let's dance, Daddy."

I moved with her to the music, feeling the same power begin to sap at me as the night before. She pressed against me and hummed in my ear. I wrapped my fingers in that lush head of hair and pressed my face to hers, completely lost to the moment. She tilted her head back and looked up dreamily through seductive half slits of eyes. Her lovely mouth was so close to mine.

"I love you, Daddy," she whispered.

Her mouth came up and I mashed mine down on it. That one second none of the sick, bizarre truth of this thing was going to rob me of the one moment a guy like me remembers all his life. Then, as she writhed her body against me, I felt something else, something cold. As if I were detached, across the room watching, I saw myself pressing back against her urgently thrusting body, sucking at her mouth, the mouth I remembered. A flash of her mother darted through my mind, the woman, the old woman, decaying before she was even dead. The same woman kissing me now. I saw the whole monstrous thing for what it was and pushed away from her so hard that she fell backward onto the floor, frightened.

"Get off of me!" I screamed. "Don't touch me. What are you? I don't think there's a *word* for you."

Tears of fear and rejection welled up in her eyes, a last piece of the fast-fading little girl in her. "I'm sorry," I said at last. "I shouldn't have done that. But . . . do you know what in hell you are?"

She sighed resignedly and got up, adjusting the sheet around her, slipped over to my liquor cabinet and fixed us both a drink. She handed me the glass, holding me with those eyes, the total woman now, cycle complete. "Yes. I know what I am. Does it matter? I know you want me."

"You're my own daughter."

She sipped at her drink. "I've been a lot of men's daughter. Does it bother you?"

"Damn right it bothers me. You can't possibly think I can treat this like your everyday affair."

I saw the lost look in her then, the same as the night before, only now I knew what it was: the sense of too little time already running out. "You'll just let me die."

"I don't know what I'm going to do."

I collapsed in the easy chair by the window. She moved to it and looked out at the rain. It was still blowing against the glass. The watery reflection did sad things to her face. She already looked much older. I felt I had to say something.

"How long has this been going on? How could it ever start?"

"Does it matter?"

"You've got to admit it's an awful lot for a man to accept."

"I don't remember how it started. A long time ago, hundreds of years. You wouldn't believe it." I heard the despair, saw it in her maturing face. She knew this was going to be her last night. I wasn't going to let her out of the apartment.

With a set of handcuffs sometimes used as a prop, I cuffed her to the radiator in the bedroom and made sure she was comfortable. She didn't fight it; maybe she figured it was time. I wasn't actually killing her, only allowing her to die. I guessed about six more hours would do it.

I'll say one thing for her, she never begged. While I cuffed her to the radiator, she just watched me with a weary resignation. When I started to leave the apartment, she was crying—softly, trying to hide it from me. Somehow I couldn't just close a door on her.

"Look . . . I'm sorry."

"I love you, Daddy."

"Don't say that."

"Why not? That's part of it. Can't there be that much beauty to it, and can't you believe that much?"

I closed the door between us.

Mostly, I just walked in the drizzling rain, stopping now and then for a drink in one of the bars I knew. I wanted to get drunk and blot out the whole impossible thing. I ended up in the bar where I'd picked her up the night before. I realized now that it wasn't a different woman at all; she was always the same. I sat nursing my drink, glancing at my watch now and then. Two hours . . . a long time yet. I couldn't even feel the drinks.

Just going to let her die, aren't you?

A friend came over to my booth. We talked for a while, how's business, that sort of thing.

How does it feel to be God?

I played the juke. All the songs sounded the same, but who listened? The hallway to the men's room was crowded with drunks. I fumbled my way through. Clear the way for The Lord Who Giveth and Taketh Away.

The mirror in the john was the sort that really tells you what you look like. I never should have looked. *Hey, you've seen it all before, a guy doing all the impossible things to keep a beautiful woman.*

I love you, Daddy.

What kind of guy would deliver a baby and dispose of a corpse every night for the rest of his life?

I love you. That's part of it. Can't there be that much beauty?

I walked out of the bar and headed up the street toward my apartment. It was raining harder now, and I pulled the collar of my raincoat up around my neck as I turned down my street, knowing when I got up in the morning I'd have to raise a little girl to womanhood. I climbed the stairs and walked down the hall to my door.

And then at night, make love to your own daughter so she can live one day to do it all over again. The full cycle of life a man goes through once, three hundred and sixty-five times a year. But the guys I knew, those guys back in the bar, how many of them ever found a woman like this?

You tell yourself: nobody is God. They can call it what they want —incest, Dracula's daughter, whatever. Me? I was going for it. I opened the door to my apartment and shed my raincoat, dropping it on the floor, and walked over to the stereo to put on something soft and dreamy. I walked into the bedroom; there she was, still wrapped in the sheet, the most beautiful woman in the world at the late end of her prime, still . . . the impossible best. Her head came up when I entered the room. She looked at me uncertainly a moment, reading me surely, reading me right, then a slow smile curled that seductive mouth. Hell, I'd need a decent nursing bottle and baby food.

"Hurry, Daddy, or we'll be too late."

Introduction

Vacations used to be a lot of fun; we remember them fondly, and the disasters that befell them often take on a comic overtone, almost as if they were planned. Sometimes they were.

Ramsey Campbell, winner of the British and World Fantasy awards, lives in England, and his latest works to appear in America are a novel, Incarnate, *and a superior collection of his short stories,* Dark Companions.

SEEING THE WORLD

by Ramsey Campbell

At first Angela thought it was a shadow. The car was through the gates before she wondered how a shadow could surround a house. She craned over the garden wall as Richard parked the car. It was a ditch, no doubt some trick the Hodges had picked up in Italy, something to do with their gardening. "They're back," she murmured when Richard had pulled down the door of the garage.

"Saints preserve us, another dead evening," he said, and she had to hush him, for the Hodges were sitting in their lounge and had grinned out at the clatter of the door.

All the same, the Hodges seemed to have even less regard than usual for other people's feelings. During the night she was wakened by Mozart's 40th, to which the conductor had added the rhythm section Mozart had forgotten to include. Richard mumbled and thrashed in slow motion as she went to the window. An August dawn glimmered on the Hodges' gnomes, and beyond them in the lounge the Hodges were sitting quite as stonily. She might have shouted but for waking Richard. Stiff with the dawn chill, she limped back to bed.

She listened to the silence between movements and wondered if this time they might give the rest of the symphony a chance. No, here came the first movement again, reminding her of the night the Hodges had come over, when she and Richard had performed a Haydn sonata. "I haven't gone into Haydn," Harry Hodge had declared, wriggling his eyebrows. "Get it? Gone into hidin'." She sighed and turned over and remembered the week she and Richard had just spent on the waterways, fields, and grassy banks flowing by like Delius, a landscape they had hardly boarded all week, preferring to let the villages remain untouched images of villages. Before the Mozart had played through a third time she was asleep.

Most of the next day was given over to violin lessons, her pupils making up for the lost week. By the time Richard came home from lecturing, she had dinner almost ready. Afterward they sat sipping the last of the wine as evening settled on the long gardens. Richard went to the piano and played *La Cathédrale Engloutie*, and the last tolling of the drowned cathedral was fading when someone knocked slowly at the front door.

It was Harry Hodge. He looked less bronzed by the Mediterranean sun than made up, rather patchily. "The slides are ready," he said through his fixed smile. "Can you come now?"

"Right now? It really is quite late." Richard wasn't hiding his resentment, whether at Hodge's assumption that he need only call for them to come—not so much an invitation anymore as a summons—or at the way Hodge must have waited outside until he thought the Debussy had gone on long enough. "Oh, very well," Richard said. "Provided there aren't too many."

He must have shared Angela's thought: best to get it over with, the sooner the better. None of their neighbors bothered with the Hodges. Harry Hodge looked stiff, and thinner than when he'd gone away. "Aren't you feeling well?" she asked, concerned.

"Just all that walking and pushing the mother-in-law."

He was wearing stained outdoor clothes. He must have been gardening; he always was. He looked ready to wait for them to join him, until Richard said firmly, "We won't be long."

They had another drink first, since the Hodges never offered. "Don't wake me unless I snore," Richard muttered as they ventured up the Hodges' path, past gnomes of several nations, souvenirs of previous holidays. It must be the gathering night that made the ditch appear deeper and wider. The ditch reminded her of the basement where Harry developed his slides. She was glad their house had no basement: she didn't like dark places.

When Harry opened the door, he looked as if he hadn't stopped smiling. "Glad you could come," he said, so tonelessly that at first Angela heard it as a question she was tempted to answer truthfully. If he was exhausted, he shouldn't have been so eager to have them round. They followed him down the dark hall into the lounge.

Only the wall lights were on. Most of the light surrounded souvenirs—a pink Notre Dame with a clock in place of a rose window on the mantelpiece, a plaster bull on top of the gas fire, matches stuck in its back like picadors' lances—and Deirdre Hodge and her mother. The women sat facing the screen on the wall, and Angela faltered in the doorway, wondering what was wrong. Of course, they must have been gardening too; they were still wearing outdoor clothes, and she could smell earth. Deirdre's mother must rather have been supervising, since much of the time she had to be pushed in a wheelchair.

"There you are," Deirdre said in greeting, and after some thought her mother said, "Aye, there they are all right." Their smiles looked even more determined than Harry's. Richard and Angela took their places on the settee, smiling; Angela for one felt as if she was expected to smile rather than talk. Eventually, Richard said, "How was Italy?"

By now that form of question was a private joke, a way of making their visits to the Hodges less burdensome: half the joke consisted of anticipating the answer. Germany had been "like dolls' houses"; Spain was summed up by "good fish and chips"; France had prompted only "They'll eat anything." Now Deirdre smiled and smiled and eventually said, "Nice ice creams."

"And how did you like it, Mrs. . . . Mrs. . . ." They had never learned the mother's name, and she was too busy smiling and nodding to tell them now. Smiling must be less exhausting than speaking. Perhaps at least that meant the visitors wouldn't be expected to reply to every remark—they always were, everything would stop until they had—but Angela was wondering what else besides exhaustion was wrong with the two women, what else she'd noticed and couldn't now recall, when Harry switched off the lights.

A sound distracted her from trying to recall, in the silence that seemed part of the dark. A crowd or a choir on television, she decided quickly—it sounded unreal enough—and went back to straining her memory. Harry limped behind the women and started the slide projector.

Its humming blotted out the other sound. She didn't think that was on television after all; the nearest houses were too distant for their sets to be heard. Perhaps a whim of the wind was carrying sounds of a football match or a fair, except that there was no wind, but in any case what did it matter? "Here we are in Italy," Harry said.

He pronounced it "Eyetally," lingeringly. They could just about deduce that it was, from one random word of a notice in the airport terminal where the Hodges were posing stiffly, smiling, out of focus, while a porter with a baggage trolley tried to gesticulate them out of the way. Presumably his Italian had failed, since they understood hardly a word of the language. After a few minutes Richard sighed, realizing that nothing but a comment would get rid of the slide. "One day we'd like to go. We're very fond of Italian opera."

"You'd like it," Deirdre said, and the visitors steeled themselves for Harry's automatic rejoinder: "It you'd like." "Ooh, he's a one," Deirdre's mother squealed, as she always did, and began to sing "Funiculì Funiculà." She seemed to know only the title, to which she applied various melodies for several minutes. "You never go anywhere much, do you?" Deirdre said.

"I'd hardly say that," Richard retorted, so sharply that Angela squeezed his hand.

"You couldn't say you've seen the world. Nowhere outside England. It's a good thing you came tonight," Deirdre said.

Angela wouldn't have called the slides seeing the world, nor seeing much of anything. A pale blob which she assumed to be a scoopful of the nice ice cream proved to be St. Peter's at night; Venice was light glaring from a canal and blinding the lens. "That's impressionistic," she had to say to move St. Peter's, and "Was it very sunny?" to shift Venice. She felt as if she were sinking under the weight of so much banality, the Hodges' and now hers. Here were the Hodges posing against a flaking life-size fresco, Deirdre couldn't remember where, and here was the Tower of Pisa, righted at last by the camera angle. Angela thought that joke was intentional until Deirdre said, "Oh, it hasn't come out. Get on to the proper ones."

If she called the next slide proper, Angela couldn't see why. It was so dark that at first she thought there was no slide at all. Gradually, she made out Deirdre, wheeling her mother down what appeared to be a tunnel. "That's us in the catacombs," Deirdre said with what sounded like pride.

For some reason the darkness emphasized the smell of earth. In the projector's glow, most of which nestled under Harry's chin, Angela could just make out the women in front of the screen. Something about the way they were sitting: that was what she'd noticed subconsciously, but again the sound beneath the projector's hum distracted her, now that it was audible once more. "Now we go down," Deirdre said.

Harry changed the slide at once. At least they were no longer waiting for responses. The next slide was even darker, and both Angela and Richard were leaning forward, trying to distinguish who the figure with the outstretched arms was and whether it was shouting or grimacing, when Harry said, "What do you do when the cat starts molting?"

They sat back, for he'd removed the slide. "I've no idea," Richard said.

"Give the cat a comb."

"Ooh, he's a one, isn't he," Deirdre's mother shrieked, then made a sound to greet the next slide. "This is where we thought we were lost," Deirdre said.

This time Angela could have wished the slide were darker. There was no mistaking the fear on Deirdre's face and her mother's as they turned to stare back beyond Harry and the camera. Was somebody behind him, holding the torch which cast Harry's malformed shadow over them? "Get it?" he said. "Cat a comb."

Angela wondered if there was any experience they wouldn't reduce to banality. At least there weren't many more slides in the magazine. She glanced at the floor to rest her eyes, and thought she knew where the sound of many voices was coming from. "Did you leave a radio on in the basement?"

"No." All the same, Harry seemed suddenly distracted. "Quick," Deirdre said, "or we won't have time."

Time before what? If they were ready for bed, they had only to say. The next slide jerked into view, so shakily that for a moment Angela thought the street beyond the gap in the curtains had jerked. All three Hodges were on this slide, between two ranks of figures. "They're just like us really," Deirdre said, "when you get to know them."

She must mean Italians, Angela thought, not the ranks of leathery figures baring their teeth and their ribs. Their guide must have taken the photograph, of course. "You managed to make yourself understood enough to be shown the way out then," she said.

"Once you go deep enough," Harry said, "it comes out wherever you want it to."

It was his manner—offhand, unimpressed—as much as his words that made her feel she'd misheard him. "When you've been down there long enough," Deirdre corrected him as if that helped.

Before Angela could demand to know what they were talking about, the last slide clicked into place. She sucked in her breath but managed not to cry out, for the figure could scarcely be posing for the camera, reaching out the stumps of its fingers; it could hardly do anything other than grin with what remained of its face. "There he is. We didn't take as long as him," Deirdre said with an embarrassed giggle. "You don't need to. Just long enough to make your exit," she explained, and the slide left the screen a moment before Harry switched off the projector.

In the dark Angela could still see the fixed grin breaking through the face. She knew without being able to see that the Hodges hadn't stopped smiling since Harry had opened the door. At last she realized what she'd seen: Deirdre and her mother, she was certain, were sitting exactly as they had been when their record had wakened her—as they had been when she and Richard had come home. "We thought of you," Harry said. "We knew you couldn't afford to go places. That's why we came back."

She found Richard's hand in the dark and tugged at it, trying to tell him both to leave quickly and to say nothing. "You'll like it," Deirdre said.

"It you'll like," Harry agreed, and as Angela pulled Richard to his feet and put her free hand over his mouth to stifle his protests, Deirdre's mother said, "Takes a bit of getting used to, that's all."

For a moment Angela thought, in the midst of her struggle with panic, that Harry had put on another slide, then that the street had jerked. It was neither: of course the street hadn't moved. "I hope you'll excuse us if we go now," Richard said, pulling her hand away from his mouth, but it didn't matter, the Hodges couldn't move fast, she was sure of that much. She'd dragged him as far as the hall when the chanting under the house swelled up triumphantly, and so did the smell of earth from the ditch that was more than a ditch. Without further ado, the house began to sink.

Introduction

Love in the present tense isn't as much fun as love in the past—then, as you recall, it was a whirlwind of marvels and miracles. A marvel, however, isn't always marvelous, and a miracle in the literal sense doesn't always gasp with wonderment.

Tanith Lee, currently finishing a long historical novel on the French Revolution, is known for her exquisite imagery and finely drawn characters. Her favorite color, it seems, is black.

THREE DAYS

by Tanith Lee

The house was tall, impressive, peeling, and seemed old before its time. The only attractive thing about it, to my eyes, was the dark-lidded glance of an attic, looking out of the slope of the roof, which such houses sometimes have. The attic eye seemed to say: "There is something beautiful here, after all. Or, there *could* be something beautiful, if such a thing were allowed."

Below and before, a green haze of young chestnut trees lined the street, which gave on the Bois Palais. Behind, rising above the walled gardens, were the stepped roads and blue slate caps of distant Montmoulin over the river, with, as their apparent apex, the white dome of the Sacré. All this was of course very pleasant. Yet I never come into the area now without a sense of misgiving. That is due to the house, and to what took place there.

One felt nothing extravagant could ever have issued from such a proper dwelling. And one would have been wrong. My friend (I use the term indiscriminately) Charles Laurent had issued from it. He was at that season making something of a star of himself in the legal profession, and also by way of a series of books—fictionalized, witty, rather brilliant studies of past trials and case histories. It was in the latter capacity, the literary side, that our paths crossed. I took to him, it was difficult not to. Handsome and informed was Laurent, an easy companion, and a very entertaining one. I suppose too the best of us may agree it is no bad thing to be on good terms with a clever lawyer. I was at this time also attempting to become engaged, and the girl's father had suddenly begun to make my way stony. After a stormy, possibly hysterical scene, worthy of the opera, my love and I had agreed we should put some physical distance between us for a while, allowing Papa's temper to cool, and relying on letters and the connivance of the mother—who liked me, and was no less than an angel—to save our hopes and prevent our mutually going mad. It is a shabby thing for a young man to be in love with one he may not have. It puts an end to a number of solaces, without replacing them. In short, life was not at its nicest. To take up with a Charles Laurent was the ideal solution.

To say our relationship was superficial would be a perfect description; its superficiality was the shining crown of it. We knew just enough of each other as might be helpful. For the rest—food, drink, music, the arts—such as these were ably sufficient to carry us across whole continents of hours into the small ones before dawn. So it was with slight surprise that I found one day he had invited me to dine at his home.

"And well your face may fall," he said. "Believe me, it will be a hideous evening, I can promise you that. I'm asking you selfishly, to relieve the tedium and horror. Not that anyone conceivably could."

Not unnaturally, I inquired after details. He told me with swift disdain that his father observed yearly the anniversary of his mother's death.

"I'm a stranger," I said. "At such a function I could hardly be welcome."

"We are *all* strangers. He hates everyone of us. My brother, my sister. He hated my mother, too." He spoke frivolously. That did not stop a slight frisson of interest from going over me. "Now I have you, I see," said Charles. "The writer has been woken up and is scenting the air."

"Not at all. But you never mentioned a brother, or a sister."

"Semery won't be there. He never comes near the house on such occasions. Honorine lives there, as I do, and has no choice."

"Honorine, your sister?"

"My sister. Poor plain pitiful creation of an unjust God."

I confess I did not like his way of referring to her. If it were true, I felt he should have protected, not slandered her, with that able tongue of his, to loose acquaintances such as I. He saw me frowning and said, "Don't be afraid, my friend. We shan't try to marry her off to you. I recall too well la bonne Anette."

I frankly thought the entire dialogue would be forgotten, but not so. The next morning an embossed invitation was delivered. A couple of nights later I found myself under the chestnut trees before that tall, unprepossessing house, and presently inside, for good or ill.

I was uneasy—that was the least of it—but also, I confess, extremely curious. Charles had hit home with that remark about the writer in me waking up. What was I about to see at this annual wake? Images of the American writer Mr. Poe trooped across my mind: an embalmed corpse, black wreaths, a vault, a creaking black-clad aristo with long tapering hands. . . . Even the daughter had assumed some importance. I think I toyed with the picture of her playing an eastern harp.

Naturally, I was far out. The family, what there was of it, seemed familiarly normal. Monsieur Laurent was a wine-faced, portly *maître d'affaires*. He looked me up and down, found me wanting (of course), greeted me, and let me pass. He reminded me but too well of that other father I had to do with, Anette's, four miles to the west, and I felt an instant depression. There was also an uncle on the premises, who stammered and was not well dressed, two deaf and shortsighted old ladies whose connection I did not quite resolve, and a florid, limping servant. I began to feel I had come among a collection of the deaf, the dumb, the halt, and the lame. Charles, obviously, was not to be numbered among these. Like a firework, he had exploded from the dull genetic sink, as sometimes happens. The younger brother, Semery, who after all attended, was also an exception. Good-looking, he had a makeshift air; Charles and he hailed each other heartily, as rival bandits meeting unarmed in the hills. Semery was the ne'er-do-well with which so many families attempt to equip themselves. Some twist of fortune, some strain of energy, had denied the role to Charles who, I felt, might have handled it better.

The sister came down late. She did not have a harp about her, but alas, everything Charles had said seemed a fact.

The sons perhaps had taken their looks from the dead mother we were supposed to be celebrating. Poor Honorine did not even favor her father. She was that sad combination of small bones and heavy flesh that seems to indicate some mistake has been made in assembly. She ate very little, and one knew instinctively that her dumpy form and puffy features were not the results of gluttony, or even appetite. She was not ugly, but that is all that can be said. Indeed, had she been ugly, she would have possessed a greater advantage than she did. For she was unmemorable. Her small eyes, whose color I truly do, God forgive me, forget, were downcast. Her thin hair, drawn back into a false chignon that did not exactly match, made me actually miserable. We writers sometimes postulate future states of freedom for both sexes, regardless of physical advantage. Never had one seemed so necessary. Poor wretched girl.

That her father detested her was obvious, but—as Charles had told me—Monsieur Laurent cared little for any of them. The dire lucklessness of it was that, while his sons escaped or absconded, the daughter was trapped. She had no option but to wait out, as how many do, the death of the tyrant. He was hale and hearty. It would be a long wait. How did she propose to spend it? How did she spend her days as it was?

No doubt my remarks on Monsieur Laurent sound unduly callous. Patently, they are colored by hindsight, but I took against him immediately, and he against me, I am sure. Yes, he resembled my own reluctant intended father-in-law, but there was more to it than that. Lest I do myself greater injustice than I must, I will hastily reproduce some of the conversation and the events of that first, really most unglittering, dinner party.

To begin with there was some sherry, or something rather like it, but very little talk. Monsieur Laurent maintained guard across the fireplace. Aside from snapping rudely a couple of times at the old ladies and the limping servant, he only stood eyeing us all, as if we were a squadron of raw troops foisted on him at the very eve of important hostilities. Annoyance, contempt, and actual exasperation were mingled in that glance, which generously included us all. I found it irritating. He knew nothing of me, as yet, to warrant such an opinion. In the case of Charles, most fathers would have been proud. We were meanwhile talking sotto voce and Charles said, as if reading my thoughts, "You can see what he thinks of me, go on, can't you?" "I assume," I said, "that his expression is misleading." "Not at all. When I won my first case, he looked at me just that way. When I foolishly spoke of it, the old wretch said to

me, 'The stupidity of other men doesn't make *you* clever.' As for
the first book—well, it was a success, and I recall we met on the
stairs and he had a copy. I was stunned he'd even looked at it, and
said so. At which he put the book in my hand as if I'd demanded it
and replied, 'I suppose you'll sell this rubbish, since the majority of
the populace is dustbin-brained.' "

Just then the food was ready and our host marched before us
into the dining salon. No pretense was made of escort or invitation.
Charles conducted the two elderly ladies. Semery idled through. I
looked round to offer my arm to Mademoiselle Honorine, but she
was making a great fuss over the discarded sherry goblets. I sensed
too exactly the dreadful embarrassment of the unlovely, and left
well alone.

Needless to say, I wondered how on earth, and why on earth,
Charles had procured me a place at this specter's feast. I could
only conclude that Monsieur Laurent's utter disgust with human-
ity en masse did not deign to distinguish between absence and
arrival. Come or go as we would, we were a source of displeasure.
Perhaps even, new specimens of the loathsome breed momentarily satisfied him, bringing him as they must the unassailable
proof that nothing had altered, he was still quite right about us all.

"*Sit,*" rapped Monsieur Laurent, glaring around him.

Obedient as dogs, we sat.

Some kind of entrée was served and a vintage inspected. Monsieur Laurent then looked directly at me. "The wine isn't so good,
but I expect you'll put up with it." This, as if I were some destitute
who had scrounged a place at the board. A number of retorts
bolted into my mind, but I curbed them, smiled politely, and had
thereafter a schoolboy urge to kick Charles' shins under the table.

Whether the wine was good or not good, after a glass or two, the
demon father began noticeably to brighten. I was struck by the
flash of his eye, and realized that generalized contempt was about
to flower into malice. I am afraid only two thoughts occurred to me
at that moment. One was, I regret, that this was very intriguing.
The other was concerned with wondering what *I* would do if he
grossly insulted me. For I could sense, the way animals scent a
coming storm, how the thunder was getting up. I reasoned though
I was safe, being not such fun to attack as his own. He had not had
time to learn my weaknesses and wants. While the rest of them—
they had been his playground from birth.

Honorine—there was no attempt at fashionable order—sat three seats away from me, with Semery and an empty chair between. Behind Honorine, above the mahogany sideboard, a large framed photograph with black ribbon on it seemed to depict the dead wife and mother. My current angle prevented any perusal of this, but to it Monsieur Laurent now ordered our attention.

"That woman," he said, "was a very great nuisance while she lived. I drink, as you see, to her departure. Ah, what a nasty, wicked sentiment. Correction, an honest one. Besides, she has taken her revenge. Look what she saddled me with. All of you." There was a concerted dismal rustle round the table. One of the old ladies dabbed her face with a handkerchief, but one saw it was a sort of reflex. It was plainly not the only occasion all this had been voiced. I looked surreptitiously at Charles. He was a perfect blank, composed and cool. Small wonder he could keep his head in a courtroom after being raised to the tune of this!

Beside me, however, Semery either deliberately, or uncontrollably, acted out the role of foil by snarling: "Cher Papa. Can't you leave anything in decent peace?"

"Ah, my little Semery," said Cher Papa, smiling at him now. "You have toiled up from the slime of your slum to say this? And how is the painting going? Sell well, do you, my boy? You came to ask . . . now what was it for? Ah, yes. For money. And I told you I would think about it, but after all, what use is it to give you cash?" (Semery had gone white. I could hardly believe what I was hearing or that Semery could have given such a faultless cue for his own public castigation. It was as if he had *had* to do it.) "You squander everything. And have such slender talent. No, I really think after all you must do without. Tighten your belt. Or, you could return and live here. My doors are always open to you."

"I'd rather die in the gutter," shouted Semery.

"No you wouldn't. Or why are you here?"

"Not to ask anything from *you*, as you well know."

"Begging from your brother Charles then. This afternoon's most touching scene. Such a pity I disturbed you. But Charles isn't a fool with his money if he's a fool with everything else. You won't get it from him. And I promise you, you won't get it from me."

Semery rose. An amazing change reshaped the monster's face. It grew rock-hard, petrified. But the eyes were filled by potent electricity. "Down," rasped the father. The room seemed to shake at the command. Semery sank back into his chair and his trembling hands knocked over his wineglass. Seldom have I witnessed such a display of the casual, absolute power one mortal thing may obtain over another. I felt myself as if I had received a blow in the stomach, and yet what had actually happened? To set it out here does not convey anything.

"Yes, Semery," Monsieur Laurent now said, "you should return under my roof, and make your name painting portraits of this beautiful sister of yours."

Having leveled one gun emplacement with his unerring cannon, the warmonger had turned his fire from the rout of the wounded to the demolition of the totally helpless. I could not prevent myself glancing at her, in horrid fascination, to see how she took it. Of course, she too was well used to such treatment. She cowered, her eyes down, her terrible, unmatched chignon shuddering. Yet the pose was native to her. It seemed almost comfortable. Her body sagged in the lines of abjection so readily, easily.

"Compliment your coiffeur, Honorine," said Monsieur Laurent. "These enemies of yours have succeeded in making of you, yet again, a fright. Heaven hurry the day," he added, drinking his wine in greedy little sips, "when this pretense at having hair is done. A daughter who is completely bald will be a novelty. All this scraping and combing and messing. Fate intended you as a catastrophe, my child. You should accept the part. Look at you, my dear, graceless lump—" At this point I put out my hand and picked up my own glass. I believe I had every intention of throwing it at his head, anything to make him stop. But thank God Charles interrupted with a (perhaps faked) gargantuan sneeze. The father turned slowly, fire duly drawn. "And you," he said to the recovering Charles, "our own moneylender, the wealthy gigolo of the bookstalls. What have you to say for yourself?"

Charles shrugged. "What I always say for myself. And what you also have just said. I've a private income and you don't frighten me. You could put me out on the street tomorrow—"

"I put none of my own tribe onto the street. They put themselves there. As for your books—what are they? You plagiarize and you steal, you botch and bungle—"

"And *livres* pour into my hands," said Charles.

My God, I thought, at last the razor of the father's tongue was going into a block of cork. Naturally, the confounded devil knew it.

This means of hurting pride no longer worked, it seemed, or at least without evidence. Talented, loved, an egoist, and lucky, Charles was not a happy target. Unerringly, the father retraced his aim.

"A pity," he said, "your sister has taken to reading your works. Filling her hairless skull with more predigested idiocy than is already in there. She puts her hat on her bald head and goes puttering off to the bookshop to discuss your successes. And so has fallen into the clutches of madwomen."

Strangely, Honorine was moved by this to murmur quickly, "No, Father, no, you mustn't say they are—"

"*Mustn't?* Mustn't I? You keep your mouth closed, my fat, balding daughter. I say what I know. Your great friends are lunatics, and I'm considering whether or not I shall approach the police—"

"Father!" The cry now was anguished.

"What? You think they're friends of yours, hah? You, with a friend? How should you have friends, you overweighted slug? Do you think they're captivated by your prettiness and charm? Eh? It's my money they like the idea of, and your insane acquaintances from the bookshop are a fine example of a certain animal known as a charlatan."

"I won't go there ever again," said Honorine.

This startled me. Her voice was altered when she spoke. It had grown deeper, it was definite. By agreeing with him she had, albeit temporarily, removed the bludgeon from his grasp.

At the time, the business of the "charlatan madwomen" and the bookshop were only a facet of an astonishing whole. I paid no particular attention. Nor do I think much more needs to be said of the dinner. Dishes came in and were taken away, and those with the heart to eat (they were few) did so. There were many and various further sallies from the indefatigable Monsieur Laurent. None were aimed at me, though I was now primed and eager for them and, I imagine, slightly drunk. In my confusion, even as I sat there, I was already mentally composing a letter to Anette, telling her everything, word for word, of this unspeakable affair. (It is from the same letter, penned fresh and with the vivid recall of insomniac indignation at two that morning, that I am able to quote fairly accurately what I have just set down.) I also wished him dead at least twenty times. I backed the big heavy body and the thick red face for an apoplexy, yet they looked more like ebullient good health.

As soon as I could, without augmenting the casualties of that war zone of a table by slamming out halfway through the meal, I left. I bade Charles a brisk adieu and walked by myself beside the river until well past midnight, powerlessly on the boil. As I told Anette, my entertaining friend was out of favor now completely. I reckoned never to see him again, for it was not simple, after the fact, to forgive him this exposure to alien filial strife. I even in a wild moment suspected some joke at my expense.

However, my having ignored two notes and a subsequent attempted visit, he finally caught me up in the gardens of the Palais. There was an argument, at least on my side, but Charles was not to be fought with if he had no mind for it.

"I can only apologize," he said, in broken accents. "What more can I say?"

"Why in God's name did you make me a party to the bloody affair?"

"Well, frankly, my friend, because—though you'll find it hard to credit—he is kinder to us when there is some stranger present."

I fell silent at that, moodily staring away between the green groves of trees. Now and then, Anette and I had contrived a meeting here, and the gardens filled me always with a piercing sweet sadness that tended to override other emotions. I looked at Charles, who seemed genuinely contrite, and acknowledged there might be some logic in his statement. Although the idea of Monsieur Laurent *un*kind, if such was a version of his restraint, filled one with laughing horror.

So, if you will, ends the first act.

The second act commences with a scene or two going on off-stage. There had been an improvement in my own fortunes, to wit, Anette's father deeming it necessary, in the way of business, to travel to England. This brought an unexpected luster to the summer. It also meant that I saw very little of Charles Laurent.

Then one morning, strolling through the covered market near the cathedral, I literally bumped into Semery and, after the usual exchanges, was invited to an apartment above a chandler's, on the left bank of the river.

Here is the area of the Montmoulin, the medieval hill of the windmill, the namesake of which is long since gone. One hears the place referred to frequently as being of a "picturesque, quaint squalor." Certainly, the poor do live here, and the fallen angels of the bourgeoisie perch in the garrets and studios above the twisting cobbled lanes. The smell of cabbage soup and the good coffee even the poverty-stricken sometimes manage to get hold of, hang in the air, along with the marvelous inexpressible smell of the scarlet geraniums that explode over balconies and on walls above narrow stairways, and against a sky tangled with washing and pigeons.

We got up into a suitable attic studio and found a table already laid with cheese and bread and fruit and wine, and a fawn cat at play with an apple. A very pretty girl came from behind a curtain. She ran to kiss Semery and, her arms still around him, turned to beam at me in just the way women in love so often do when another man comes on the scene. Even in her loose blouse, I could tell she was carrying a child. Little doubt of the father, though her hand was ringless. I remembered, with a fleeting embarrassment, Semery's supposed request for money from his brother, or Monsieur Laurent. Here might be the excuse.

There were pictures, naturally, everywhere—on the walls, on easels, stacked up, or even horizontal on the floor for the cat to sit on.

"Courage," said Semery, seeing me glance around, "I won't try to sell anything to you. Not at all." This in turn reflected Charles' avowal, on first inviting me to the gruesome dinner party, that they would not try to marry Honorine off to me. It was a little thing, but it made me conscious of some strange defensiveness inherent, and probably engendered in them by their disgusting father. "But," added Semery, "look, if you like." "Of course he will like," said the girl mischievously. "How nice the table is, Miou," said Semery. "Let's have some wine."

A very pleasant couple of hours ensued. Semery was acting at least as fine a companion as Charles; I was charmed by Miou, and by the cat, and the simple luncheon was appetizing. As for the art —I am no critic, but suppose I have some slight knowledge. While not being in that first startling rank of original genius, Semery's work seemed bright with talent. It had enormous energy, was attractive, sometimes lush, yet never too easy. Particularly, I liked two or three unusual night scenes of the city, one astonishingly lit by a flight of birds escaping from some baskets and streaming over a lamp-strung bridge.

"Yes," he said, coming to my side, "I call that one *Honorine.*" I was at a loss to reply. "I don't mean to make you uncomfortable," he said. "But you've been blooded, after all. You were there just the last time I was."

"Hush, Semery," said Miou, who was rocking the cat in an armchair, practicing for her baby. "Talking of *him* makes you sick and gives you migraine."

"True," said Semery. He refilled our glasses with wine. "But I can talk of Honorine? Yes? No? But I must. That poor little sack of sadness. If there were any money, I'd take her in with me, though God knows she bores me to despair. Our dear father, you understand, has stamped and trampled all the life from her. She can no longer talk. She only answers questions. So you say to her, 'Would you care to do this?' And you get in return, 'Oh yes, if *you* wish.' And she drops things. And she stumbles when she walks even when there's nothing to stumble over. However," he said, with a boy's fierceness, "there was one service I think I did her. I first took her to the bookshop on the Rue Danton. And so introduced her to the three witches."

Miou began to sing a street song, quietly but firmly disowning us.

"That's the bookshop your father objected to? And the witches?"

"Well, three old ladies, in particular one, very gray and thin, read the tarot there in the backroom. And sometimes, when the moon is full, work the planchette of a Ouija board."

"And Honorine . . ."

"Honorine attended a session or two. She wouldn't reveal the results, but you could tell she enjoyed every moment. When you saw her after, her cheeks would be flushed, her eyes had a light in them. Unfortunately, that limping gargoyle who serves *mon père* found out about it all and duly informed. Now Honorine's one poor, pitiful pleasure is ended. Unless she can somehow evade the spies, and our confounded father—"

"*Sur la chatte, le chat,/Et sur la reine le roi . . .*" naughtily sang Miou to the cat-baby.

"On the other hand," Semery added, now with great nonchalance, "I did visit the shop today, and one of the eldritch sisters—

good lord, I must paint them—no rush, they're each about three hundred years old and will outlive us all—well, Miou-who-has-stopped-singing-and-is-all-ears-and-eyes, well, one of them gave me a note to give to Honorine. Something the spirit guides had revealed that my sister apparently desired to know." And from his jacket Semery produced a piece of paper, unsealed, merely folded in the middle, which he held aloft quizzically. "I wonder what it can be?"

"You shouldn't have brought it here," said Miou. She crossed herself between fawn paws. "Magic. Ghosts."

"Where else then? Papa is out tomorrow afternoon and I can take it to the house. But I could hardly do so today, could I now? One foot on the threshold, and he'd have seized me in his jaws."

"Well," said Miou. "Put it away somewhere."

"Don't you think I should read it? Secret communications to my little sister . . ." He looked back at me. "Actually, I did. Here, what do you make of this?"

And he opened the paper and put it in my hand.

I admit I was curious. There seemed no harm in it, and I have always had a quiet disrespect for "supernatural" things.

On the paper from the mysterious bookshop were these words as follows:

As we have told you, she is to be found as a minor character in some of the history books, and there has also been at least one novel written about her. The name is correct, Lucie Belmains. She did indeed die as a result of hanging herself. The date of her death is the morning of the eighth April, 1760.

"Fascinating, isn't it," said Semery. "What does it mean? Who is Lucie Belmains?"

Miou and the cat were already peering between our shoulders at the paper.

"Lucie Belmains," said Miou, "was a minor aristocrat, very beautiful and very wicked. She would drink and ride a horse and swear better—or worse—than a man. She was the mistress of several princes and dukes. She once dressed as a bandit and waylaid the king on some road, and was his mistress too perhaps, till she became bored with all the riches he lavished on her. Then she fell in love with a man five years her junior. He loved her too, to distraction, and when he was killed in a duel over her, Lucie gave a great party, like a Roman empress, and in the morning she hanged herself like Antigone from a crimson cord."

Semery and I stood amazed until Miou stopped, breathless and in triumph.

"It seems," said Semery then, "there is indeed one novel, and you have read it."

"Yes. When I was a little girl," said Miou, all of seventeen now. "I remember my sister and I read the book aloud to each other when we were supposed to be asleep. And how we giggled. And we dressed up in lace curtains and our mother's hats and raised glasses of water pretending they were champagne and said, 'I am Lucie and you are my slave!' And fought like cats because neither of us would *be* the slave. And then one day Adèle hung her doll up by the neck from a red ribbon and we had a funeral party. Maman found us and we were both beaten."

"Quite right. These are most corrupting activities for a future wife of France's leading painter, and the mother of his heir." At which Miou smiled and laid her head on his shoulder. "But even so," said Semery, stroking her hair, "what has all this got to do with Honorine?"

I said, "She's making a study of this woman, or the period?"

"No. She has no interests anymore."

Later, toward evening, we strolled along the riverbank. The leveling rays of the sun flashed over the water. I had arranged to buy the picture of the escaping birds for Anette. I knew she would like it, as indeed she did—we have it still, and since Semery's name is now not unknown, it is worth rather a deal more than I paid for it. But there was some argument with Semery at the time, who thought I was patronizing him, or trying to pay for my luncheon. Thank God, all that had been settled, however, by the hour we emerged on the street, Miou in her light shawl and straw bonnet with cherries. When we reached the Pont Nouveau and I was about to cross over, Semery said to me, "You see, that business with the paper—belle Lucie Belmains. Something about it worries me. Perhaps I shouldn't let Honorine have it. Would that be dishonorable?"

"Yes."

"Or prudent?"

"Maybe that too. But as you don't know—"

"I think perhaps I do. The purpose of the witches' Ouija has often to do with reincarnation—the passage of the soul through many lives and many bodies."

We had all paused in mutual revelation.

"Do you mean your sister is being told she lived a previous life in which—"

"In which she was beautiful and notorious, kings slobbered at her feet, and duels were organized for her favors."

We looked at the river, the womb and fount of the city, glittering with sun, all sequins, which on the dark days of winter seems like lead.

"Well," Semery said at last, "why not? If it makes her happy for a moment. If it gives her something nice to think about. There's nothing now. What has she got? What can she hope to have? If she can say to herself, just one time in every day, *once* I was beautiful, *once* I was free, and crazy and lavish and adored, and loved."

I looked at him. His eyes were wet, and he was pale, as if at the onset of a headache. Impulsively, I clasped his hand.

"Why not?" I said. "Yes, Semery, why *not?*"

Miou let me kiss her blossomy cheek as a reward.

I went over the bridge with the strangest feeling imaginable. I find no name for it even now. It seemed for a moment I had glimpsed the rickety facade of all things and the boundless, restless, terrible truth beyond. But it faded, and I was glad of it.

As the glorious summer drew to its close, intimations of winter and discontent appeared. The birds and golden leaves began to be displaced by emptiness in the trees of the Bois; Anette's father returned, foul-tempered, and shut his house like a castle under siege against all comers, particularly one.

It was nearly three months since my chance meeting with Semery. We had met deliberately a couple of times since; I had even been invited to his wedding, the thought of which now made me rather melancholy. As for Charles Laurent, I was sitting at a café table one morning, curiously enough reading a review of his latest book—as usual a success—when I happened to look up and saw two women seating themselves a few tables away. I was struck at once by a sense of confusion, such as comes when one is accosted by an old acquaintance whose name one forgets. But it was not that a name had been forgotten, for frankly I was not familiar with either of these women. It must be, then, that they put me in mind of others with whom I was. Because of this I studied them surreptitiously over my newspaper.

The nearer woman, with her back to me now, was apparently a maid or companion, and a withered specimen at that. She seemed ill at ease, full of humble, insistent protestation. No, I did not know her at all. The other, who sat facing me, was not particularly remarkable. Not tall, quite slim, and plainly dressed, her fine brown hair had been cut daringly short and she was hatless. Two little silver earrings flickered attractively in her earlobes. That was all. Her skin was sallow, her features ordinary. Then the waiter came and I was struck again, this time by a quality of fearlessness, *boldness,* out of all proportion to what she did, which was merely to order a pot of chocolate. There was something gallant in this minor action, such as you sometimes find in invalids taking their first convalescent stroll, or the blind listening to music.

Quite suddenly, I realized who she was. It was the graceful bravery, though I had never seen her exhibit it previously, that gave her away. Honorine, of course.

I resolved immediately I would not go over. I had no real wish to, heaven knows. Memories of her wounded social clumsiness did not inspire me. I could only be a ghastly reminder of a hideous event. Let her enjoy her chocolate in peace, while I stayed here, keeping stealthy watch from my covert of newspaper.

So I kept watch, true to my profession, taking rapid mental notes the while. Surely, she was not as I recalled. It was small wonder I had not recognized her at once. She had lost a great deal of weight, yet here she sat eating gateau, drinking chocolate, with the accustomed appetite of a famished child. And there truly was about her a gracefulness—of gesture, of attitude. And a strange air of laughter, mischievous and essentially womanly, that despite myself began to entice me to her vicinity. In the end I gave in, rose, walked across and stood before her.

"Mademoiselle Laurent. Can I hope you remember me?"

Her eyes came up. Those eyes not large nor bright—but they were altered. They shone, they were alive. The oddest thing happened now. The loud blush of shyness, which one might have expected, rushed over her face. It was the order of blush well known to the adolescent, which makes physically uncomfortable with its heat, the drumming in the ears, the feeling the brain may explode under its pressure. All is instant panic and surrender to panic. What is there to be said or done when such a mark of shame is branded on one's forehead? But the eyes of Honorine Laurent did not fall. She drew in a long breath and said, calmly, as if blood and body did not belong to each other, "Why, monsieur, of course I remember you. My brother's friend. Please, will you sit down? We have greedily eaten all the cake, but there's some chocolate left." And she smiled. As she did so, the red blush went out, defeated. Her smile was open, friendly, not afraid—nor false. And her eyes sparkled so they were pretty, just as the smile was pretty. One writes of auras. Honorine had just such an aura. I knew in that moment that I was in the presence of a woman who found her own lack of beauty no disadvantage, who therefore would not use pain or sullenness as a weapon, who believed that in the end she herself was all that she required, although others were quietly welcomed should they come close to warm themselves in the light. In short, the look of a confident woman, a woman who has known great love, and awaits, without impatience or aggression, some future, unhurried, certain joy.

As if I had been hypnotized, I drew out a chair and sat down. I had only just breakfasted, but I drank the chocolate that was poured for me in a daze. Presently, the withered lady companion, fretting like a horse for hay, was thankfully dispatched to collect some cotton, and arm in arm, Mademoiselle Honorine and I turned toward the graveled paths of the Bois Palais. I had offered to see her to her door, and she had said, "Yes, do. Charles is home in a filthy temper—one bad review, I think, of his excellent book. He'll be delighted to see you. And my father is . . . out." And there was that mischief again. She did not then hate Monsieur Laurent, this elfin woman with her slim hand so lightly through my arm. She did not hate me for being witness to his humiliation of her. And she was used to escorts, she was used to friends.

I recall she asked me about Anette, very graciously and tactfully, and abruptly all my cares came flooding out in a torrent of words that astonished me, so in the end we sat down by the fountain with the nymphs as I made my complaints to life and heaven. Sometimes Honorine patted my arm gently. "Oh, yes," she said, "ah, no?" with such unflurried kindness and sympathy—*she* with all her woes, so tender toward mine—and at the finish I remember too she said, "You have a sound literary reputation and I would say your prospects are fine. Besides, you and she love each other.

Could you perhaps," and those eyes of hers flashed like her ear-rings, like the summer river, "run away together?" I realized, even at the time, that this last piece of advice came straight from the idiomatic guide book of Lucie Belmains.

For that, naturally, was who I had beside me, there on that bench: Lucie Belmains, who had died on the eighth of April, 1760. Lucie Belmains, but at her softest, sweetest—who knew love, and love's fulfillment, and touched my hand from her greater knowl-edge, ready to listen, and to reassure me. Even to suggest a mad-cap means of how to win the age-old game. The means *she*, more daring than I, might have taken.

Why not? Semery had said. Why not let that poor little dumpy bundle of a sister, that sack of sadness, creation of an unjust God, think of some better chance she had been given, once, if it could make her glad? And, *Why not?* I had magnanimously echoed. My God, why not indeed, if this exquisite person was to be the result . . . No, I did not believe in her reincarnation. But her *alteration* —*this* I believed. How could I avoid belief? The living proof sat with limpid laughing eyes beside me. As tyrants are changed by faith to flawless saints, so faith of her own kind had changed this human failure to a glowing being. There was a loveliness about her —yes, loveliness. Some latent charm, extant in her brothers, for-merly lost in her, had evolved and possessed her perfectly. And that smile, those eyes. And her walk. Her carriage. Years have gone by since that day, to dim the vista. I loved Anette then, I love her still, and no woman in the world, in my eyes, can equal Anette. And yet I look back to this Honorine I had the happiness to find that far-off morning, and I must set down the truth as it seemed to me then, and seems to me now, older, wiser, and less innocent as I am. I have never, save for my wife, met any woman who en-chanted me so thoroughly. For she was beautiful. Her beauty lay all around us on the air. And even if I did not credit the transfer-ence of the soul, yet the soul I did credit. And it was the soul of Honorine that brought the loveliness and the beauty and the en-chantment. For you see, she was then completely those things so few of us ever are, and if we are, so briefly: at peace, joyful, *sure.*

We reached the house, that dire house, and even this seemed less awful by her light. She was no longer afraid of it. She went up the steps and beckoned me in as if I might be comfortable there, and so I, too, felt no foreboding.

Charles was in the drawing room and jumped up when he saw me out of a snowfall of papers. Having brought us together, she was gone. I stared after her and then at the closed door. Presently, Charles left off talking of his book and said, "Well, what do you think of *her?*"

She had made me skittish too. I said, no doubt rudely, "This is not the same sister."

Charles nodded vigorously. "It can't be, can it? Isn't she a jewel?" He was proud of her. "If she keeps this up, we'll get her married to a rich potentate in half a year. You've seen Semery and know the cause, I understand?"

"Yes."

He gazed at me and said mock-seriously, "Of course, it's a form of madness. If she killed someone, I could get her off on a plea of this. My client reckons she is actually a lady who is dead."

"Surely she reckons she has *been*, not is, Lucie Belmains."

"Hairsplitting worthy of the bar. But it's a miracle. If she's gone a little mad, so nicely, why not?"

And thus the third culpable party added his careless *why not?* to Semery's and mine.

"But does she," I said, "know that you—"

"She knows Semery and I—though not you, *cher ami*—are in on it. But she doesn't review the matter with us, nor we with her. Then again, considering the extravagance of the idea, not to mention results, she's very serene about it all. I don't think she's even read anything, no history of this woman. Save the smallest outline in some encyclopedia. On the other hand, I suspect her of writing about her feelings. I gather a diary has been started. But she only revealed that to me because I caught sight of the article on her vanité. She's said nothing else. After all, she knows we're a bunch of vile skeptics. As for father—well, no whisper must reach *his* ears. And you can guess, all this of hers has thrown him off balance. She eats more and grows more slight, she cuts off her hair and buys earrings. But you should see her with him. Stay and lunch with us and you will."

The prospect of encountering Monsieur Laurent again brought me to with a jolt.

"Unfortunately, I must be elsewhere."

"And anywhere but here? Well, you'll be missing a treat. And by the way, have you seen what this devil in the *Journal* has the wretched audacity to say about my book . . . ?"

Half an hour later, just as I got out into the hall, the limping servant hobbled by me and flung open the street door. And there stood Monsieur Laurent, his horrible puce face thrust forward, seeing me at once, before Charles and all things else. I felt like a seven-year-old boy caught stealing fruit in someone's orchard. I had been so determined to avoid the monster. Nor had I heard any summons to warn me of this collision; the sinister limper seemed to have known of his master's arrival by telepathic means alone.

"Good day," said the *maître* to me, advancing into his domain. "Hoping for lunch?"

I writhed to utter as I wanted, but did not.

"No, monsieur. I am lunching with friends."

"I thought my plagiarist son was your friend. Or have you grown wise to him, seen through him? I note," he added, directing his attention now to Charles, "one critic at least has had the wit to penetrate your sham nonsense. I must send him my congratulations."

Charles, touchy over the review (for which his father must truly have scoured the journals) was plainly for once caught on the raw spot. Without looking at him, I saw his anger reflected in the momentary pleasure of Monsieur Laurent's little eyes.

"And where's your beauteous sister? I've some news for her."

"Here I am," said a voice from the stairs.

Monsieur Laurent gave vent to that toneless, noisy amusement generally called a guffaw. "Yes, there you are. What plenteous abundance of hair! Where is it? Have I gone blind? Do you still go out on the street like that and make yourself a laughingstock?"

Turned to stone, my eyes only on the shut front door, I waited. And I heard her gentle voice say casually, light as down, "Yes, Papa, I'm afraid I do."

"You silly sheep. Look at you. Well, I suppose it's generous of you to give everyone, complete strangers, such a good laugh. But do I permit you to draw money to buy earrings and make yourself resemble a circus monkey?"

"No, Papa, the earrings were purchased from the small allowance Mother left me. But if they worry you, I'll take them off."

"Worry me? *You* worry me. You brainless thing, flapping about the house, scribbling, mooning. What's wrong with you?"

"I am very well, thank you, Papa."

"That damnable fool, your female parent, what a curse she left me. A sniveling, profligate dunce and a literary jackal for sons. An idiot daughter."

She was down the stairs now; I heard the rustle of her gown. She seemed to bring a coolness with her, a freshness, like open air, escape from the trap.

She said, "Come and see the new sherry, Papa. I took your advice on the business of wines and have been trying to improve my knowledge. I'd like you to taste this latest bottle and see what you think."

"If you chose the stuff, it must be worthless muck," said this charming father.

"Not necessarily," replied Honorine, for all the world as if she were talking to a sane and rational human being instead of to a thing from the Pit. "I've tried, in my choice, to apply all you told me the other day. But if you think the sherry is poor and I'm mistaken again, of course I shall want you to correct me. How can I benefit from your superior understanding in these matters if you're lenient?"

What could he say, the beast? She had him, as seldom have I heard any so had. What had gone on? I can only conclude she had begun to take an interest in the ordering of the cellar, as la Belmains would certainly have done, and Monsieur, true to himself as always, had insulted her and attempted to belittle her over it, as over all else. Whereupon she must have assumed the attitude that she was being given an altruistic lesson for her own benefit, which notion she here continued. I have done just as you said, she informed him now. But if I am wrong—for naturally, I do not for a moment deny you are more clever than I am—you must let me know. And *do* be as harsh, as discourteous as you can be. I shall regard it as a mark of your concern and patronage. My God! I nearly laughed aloud. Whatever revolting abuse he threw at her now came with her awarded license. She would sit meekly before him, nodding as he ranted, presently thanking him for the tutorial. I was, despite everything, after all tempted to stay for lunch.

I compromised then, and indicated to Charles I would remain long enough to try the new sherry. And when the monster eyed me and made some remark about there being no luckier club for a minor writer than the free one of somebody else's house, I snatched a leaf from her book, grinned wildly at him, and cried, "And such an entertaining club, too."

It goes without saying he hated the sherry, which was a discerning one. But he said not much about it, save it was ditchwater. Honorine promised to bear this in mind. It was at this point that he recollected the news he wanted to tell her.

"Your hags of the tarot have gone," he said. "Did you know? An end to clandestine sorties to the bookshop and table tappings at my expense. Perhaps an end to the silliness you've been parading these last months, eh?"

"Ever since you showed such displeasure," said Honorine placidly, "I've not visited the shop."

"No. But things have come here from there. From your faker parasites. Bits of paper brought by your ugly maid. Or by dear Semery when I'm out—you thought I wasn't aware? There's not much I miss. I've read some of these secret notes, *billets doux*. Let me see. What did they say?"

We had all turned very silent. Honorine was pale and she put down her glass. From the erratic glitter of those delightful earrings of hers I could learn the quick, erratic motion of her pulse.

Monsieur Laurent made a great drama over recalling. He, like the soulless evil he was, had sound instincts for a victim's shrinking and fear. Yet, if he had got hold of any communications from Honorine's three witches, it seemed to me they would probably mean nothing to him. His was a sly mind, but not an intellectual slyness. He pulled the wings from insects to agonize them and prevent their flight, not to study the complexity of their pain and flightlessness. But the information of the Ouija board, ridiculous as it might be, was also intensely personal. He had, no doubt, always been in the habit of opening his children's private correspondence and taunting them with its closest passages.

Eventually, his head tilted back in a sort of cold, dry ecstasy, he announced: " 'Lucie Belmains. Born at Troy-la-Dianne in April 1729. Hanged dead on April 8, 1760.' Now do I quote that as it should be? Hah? And do I have *this* right—that you, my dollop of dough, unlovely, loveless, hopeless wreck that you are, are the reborn Lucie, so beautiful, kings paid ransoms for her company, and duels were fought to the death?"

There was a long terrible pause, with no noises in it save a patter of leafy rain on the road outside.

I did not look at her. I do not know how she seemed, but I can conjure it. Who needs to be told? This was her sacrament, holy, and hidden. And now he had it in his fangs, mauling and maiming it before us all. He had only been waiting, only *seeming* muzzled. But how could he be? All the servants were in his thrall. And her diary, maybe he had even got a grip on that, this savage, rabid dog. Yes, so he must have done, to come at the roots of her dream, the beautiful, abnormal structure that had made bearable her life. But it was not to be bearable. *He* could not bear that. She should not spring up from the crushing. He would pile on another weight.

I suppose seconds went by, no more, while I thought this, and suffered for her, and yearned again to kill him.

Then she spoke, and my head cleared of the black cloud, because her voice was steady, self-possessed. She had made a virtue of passivity. She gave no resistance now, since it would only lead the torturer on. She said, "Yes, Papa. Isn't it absurd? For me to imagine, even for an instant, I might have been such a person. But you seem to have discovered that I do imagine it. And I do. While, truly, thinking it every bit as unlikely and preposterous as you do yourself."

The cold ecstasy left him at that. Temper came instead. For a moment I thought he would strike her, but physical blows were not what he enjoyed.

"And what gives you to think such errant twaddle? This salivatory drivel from what? A *Ouija board?* Fakers and schemers —they take your money—*my* money—and tell you anything you like to hear."

"No, Father. They never asked a sou from me."

"So you say. You *say.* But no doubt you make donations? Eh? And you've done their dubious reputation good, I expect, babbling to those you know of the *accomplishments* of this hocus-pocus. Lucie Belmains. *Lucie Belmains.* Does she even exist? Tell me that, you dunce. You'd swallow anything to make you out not the clod you are."

I could hold myself no longer. I regret it, but I think in the long term it made no difference. He was on the trail, this bloody dog. He would have found it all at length, whatever was done or said or omitted.

"Monsieur. Lucie Belmains most decidedly did exist. I'm surprised, sir, with your exceptional bent for knowing everything and missing nothing, that you've never heard of her."

"*Ah,*" he said, turning his gaze on me. "So we're to be paid for our sherry with information. This is not," he said, "your concern. You may leave my house." And he smiled.

"I can think of nowhere, offhand, I could leave with greater pleasure."

"Brave words for a sponger," he said. "Or did you steal something while my back was turned?"

"In the sight of God!" shouted Charles.

But I, at the reckless, heedless spur of immaturity, answered, "Steal from you, monsieur? I'd be more fastidious."

"Would you?" he said. "From Anette Dupleys then, that fine, plump dowry of hers and her property in the south that goes with it. Indeed, a much juicier theft than anything the poor Laurents could offer you."

It seems he had done me the honor of finding out something about my circumstances also. And what he had found out, of course, was the thing set to cut me to the bone. I forget what I said or anything at all, until I got out, burning as if in flames and in an icy sweat, onto the street. Unfortunately, whatever I did in my passion, I did not seize a fire iron and murder him.

Charles came flying after me and grabbed my shoulder as I reached the Bois.

"In God's name—what can I say? Oh my God—forgive me."

I had chilled in the fire-following ice by then and said stiffly, "There's nothing to forgive you. I stayed when I was aware I should not. As for Anette's money, who doesn't know? That is all the argument between her father and myself. I am a fortune hunter. Naturally."

We quarreled about all this for a while, aimless and appalled. Finally, I accused him of leaving Honorine to face horror alone. "No, no," he said, "it was she sent me after you. She was quite calm still. He hasn't broken her. I thought he had. But she's talking to him so delicately, saying yes, she agrees with everything he says, but there it is."

I thought of her grey face. I said, "Now he has the name of her hopes in front of him, he'll go on until he has destroyed them all."

"How? She believes exactly what her witch ladies told her. He can't touch that."

"He'll find some way," I said.

As I walked alone back along the leaf-lit paths I had traveled with Honorine, through the somber dusk of a coming storm, I knew my premonition was a true one.

The week before Semery's wedding to Miou, the two brothers and I dined in a good restaurant on the Boulevard du Pays. Charles seemed vaguely troubled at the outset, but he neither explained nor made a burden of it, the wine flowed, and soon enough there were no troubles in the world.

I judge it was about midnight when a written message was brought to Charles at the table. He read it and went very white.

"What?" said Semery. But a sense of dread and dismay had passed unsounded between them, not by any mystical means, but from old habit, a boyhood terror that came back whenever some dark shadow proceeded from their father.

I put down my glass and sat in silence.

Presently, Charles covered his eyes with his hand.

"We must go to the house," he said.

"Very well," said Semery, his bright tipsiness all gone. "But why?"

Charles took his hand from his eyes. He looked at me.

"This isn't your affair. There's no need for you to be caught up in it."

"If you prefer," I said. It had had echoes of his father's words in showing me the door.

"No, no, I don't mean to offend you. Oh my God, my God." He stumbled to his feet and the chair clattered over. He did not even seem to see the obstacle as he avoided it.

In a few minutes we were out in the autumn night, still without an answer. Only a pall of black disaster hung about us, sure as the smell of death. It needed no name. In some degree, each of us knew.

I think he told us on the way to the house. I am not positive. It may have been on the very threshold. Or perhaps he did not tell us at all, was not required to. It seems to me now he never did say, in words. Yet I remember later, when we were in a room downstairs, lighted only by a lamp, and cold, he took up the open book left lying on a table and directed me to the place. I remember I read it and for a moment it made no sense, and then I fathomed the sense and my heart sank through me, leaden and afraid, for her sake.

To piece it together now will, perhaps, be better. What use is there, after all, to hesitate? As I had known, Monsieur Laurent must destroy her dream, and so he had, by the very simple expedient of doing what she had not. Honorine had taken her enlightenment almost solely from her ladies of the bookshop. What she had already read of Lucie Belmains had not been, presumably, specific in the matter of dates.

Honorine had trusted her mediums implicitly. She had believed what she had been told. Every fragment of it. But every fragment rested on every other. It was not a house of stone, not even of cards, but of glass, that whole, harmless, shining, starry edifice, and it shattered at a tiny mortal blow. How gratified he must have been, that demon, the weapon so easily come by, and so sharp.

They had told her—I had myself witnessed it—that Honorine's former self, her belle Lucie, had hanged herself, and died on the eighth of April, 1760. But if they were wrong in this, then the entire codex must be mistaken, a lie. And so it was proved. For this date was in error. Lucie Belmains, as history has recorded, as that very book Charles handed to me had recorded, had hanged herself on the morning of the fifth of April and, being cut down, was buried on the evening of the seventh, for the summer was forward that year. Of the eighth of April there was, and needed to be, no mention.

Three days out. Only that. Three days.

Monsieur Laurent had been at pains to tell her, and to show her, no doubt. I can envisage the scene that passed between them, father and daughter, there in that dank, fireless room, as *we* dined on the Boulevard du Pays. I have seen it often in my mind's eye, and listened to it over and over in those half dreams that come between sleep and waking when one is unhappy or very tired.

So she was rid of her fantasy and her madness. So he gave her back the single and only life she had, that dreary, pointless, loathing life, and her own former self, he gave her that, too. He widowed her of beauty and of love, love which had been, love which might yet come, if not as Honorine then in some future when she might be born once more another Lucie. And worse than all that, he throttled the sweet dignity and charm of what she was becoming, had become. God damn him. I do not ask for lives, but for a hell of fire and shrieking where he may burn and scream for all eternity.

After he had instructed her, Monsieur Laurent went out to his own gentleman's club. And Honorine, climbing up to that attic room whose window I had first admired, swallowed a dose of some poison kept for rats. She died in convulsions about an hour after we arrived.

She had written none of those parting notes so common in such cases. I do not think her wish was to instill in anyone feelings of guilt. In her father, the prime offender, it would have been impossible. I gather, though I never met him again, that his attitude remained consistent toward her, even after her death. She was a fool who had always displeased him, and displeased him only a fraction more by dying so violently under his roof. He used to say, I believe, that if she had desired an end so greatly, she should have drowned herself in the river and thereby saved them all the fuss and the expense her domestic suicide entailed. And of course, there was fuss and expense. The newspapers carried the story in a riot. This did Charles no good, but it was the shocking death itself, I am sure, which wore him down and eventually changed the pattern of his life, as is generally reckoned to its detriment. He left the bar less than a year after. His elegant and carefree wit, which had long deserted him, began to return in a strange little lay community attached to a monastery of the Languedoc. Occasionally, we correspond; I do not presume to understand his present existence, or to approve or disapprove of it, but he apparently does some good for himself and for those around him. Other than these messages to me or to Semery, he writes nothing now.

Semery himself, who in his way had already broken off the chains of a false life, was not fundamentally altered, but his grief and his remorse were awesome. Though the marriage went forward on the day assigned, he faltered through it all barely coherent and blind with tears. Later, I gather, he made some attempt to destroy his canvases, but fortunately, friends arrived and prevented it. Miou helped as only she could, by her persevering tenderness, until in the end some care of her and of their approaching child brought him to his senses.

But none of us was untouched.

Honorine, as I said, surely did not intend this torrent of guilt.

That guilt should be experienced was unavoidable. Yet she, she was in that last hour so isolate, I would say she thought of no other, either to long for their comfort or to wish them ill. She must have climbed those stairs up through the house in an utter darkness of heart and mind, and soulless too, for her soul had been wrenched from her, as in the myths it is, by the devil. Her imaginings, or rather the black void within her—one shrinks from its contemplation.

However, though she left no concrete parting gift of bitterness in the form of a letter, there is that journal of hers, which Semery now possesses, and which he has allowed me to see. She wrote nothing in it of despair. It was all joy from start to finish. The finish being where she had left it off in the midst of a sentence, probably because she had been told her father required her downstairs. It is the joy, of course, which is unbearable. It is the unfinished sentence that fills one with terror, as if reading the order for an execution. What breaks the heart is the motto she has written just inside the cover: *Je suis parce que j'ai été.* *

For none of us were untouched.

At six o'clock on the morning after her death, not having slept or shaved, nor completely in my right mind, I hurried westward across the city. The dawn was beginning to wash stealthily in along the dry riverbeds of the streets, and I remember I met a flock of sheep being ushered into the Faubourg St. Marie. When I reached the house of the Dupleys, I woke it, and its neighbors, by hammering on the door.

What was said and performed was madness, and I can recollect only fragments of it now, that to this day have the power to embarrass me, or sometimes to make me laugh. Suffice it to relate, I fought my way by means of shouted threats through several servants and eventually through Anette's father himself (who thought me dangerously insane), all the way to Anette's mother (who thought much as he did, but with more compassion). And so to Anette herself, who, whatever she thought, did not love me less. There in a corner of a room, her good, kind mother outside the door as our protector, the father in the hall roaring that the police should be called, I said nothing of what had happened, only perpetrated yet one more scene worthy of the opera, crying in Anette's

* I am because I was.

arms and then seizing her hands and asking her to get dressed and come away with me at once. There was the briefest addendum to this plea. It concerned her trusting me, it concerned our being married by the quickest means the law allowed, it concerned my ability to support her, that she was of age but would lose all her money and inheritance. That maybe we should live without pecuniary margin forever. That she should bring warm clothing and whatever else she might need, and her pet kitten. And that I could not swear not to attack her father if he interfered any further. To all of which she listened gravely, then said that I must go away at once, and that she would then meet me, with her mother's help, complete with one small valise and the kitten, in an hour's time in the Bois Palais. At first I argued. Not because I thought she was putting me off—wretch that I was I had every right to think that she might be—but simply because I was so shaken and wild I could not bear to leave her. Nevertheless, in the end she persuaded me. I went, while Monsieur Dupleys, standing on his steps in his dressing gown, with the manservant, waved a purportedly loaded pistol at my back. And in just over an hour mother, daughter, and kitten appeared in the Bois, and we and the fountains wept, and the little cat wailed in astonishment, and God alone knows what the early strollers made of it all.

As it turned out, there was a later reconciliation, and Anette lost nothing by her elopement. We were, though, a year married by then, and my own financial prospects had taken a soaring turn toward fortune. I like to suppose that even if they had not, we could still have possessed the great happiness we had from the commencement, and still share together. I am now received by Monsieur Dupleys, who pompously and placatingly, and also out of a need to make me uncomfortable, sometimes refers to that tempestuous morning, as if it were some game we all played. But it was nothing of the sort. Or, if so, it was Honorine's—Lucie's.

For it was because of Honorine that I risked, as I did, our chances. This I have since explained to my wife. Not only through the upheaval of that ghastly suicide. No, more because of those ephemeral moments of a woman's *life*, in which I had participated. I had been trying, desperately, to make at least one iota of the dream be true. *Could you perhaps run away together?* she had said to me. Lucie's scheme—brave, beautiful, reckless Lucie. Lucie gracious enough to assume Anette's money meant nothing to me, in which assumption she and Anette have been, probably, quite alone. And so I honored Lucie. I went to my love and asked her to run away with me, and she consented. I shall be grateful for that, to Honorine, until the day of my death.

The last act is now concluded, and yet there remains something in the way of an epilogue. I have said I have no leanings to superstition, or to esoteric occult ideas, and part of me clamors here to leave well alone. After all, if, as I believe, it proves nothing, then the circumstances I have outlined turn only darker, and they are surely dark enough. On the other hand, the inveterate storyteller finds it hard to reject such a gem. For gem it is, of a sort.

Some years had passed; the great-grandchildren of Anette's first cat were playing with two children of our own across the floors of our house. Researching in an area that had nothing whatever to do with Lucie Belmains, I suddenly came across a strange reference to her. It dealt, as did the rest of the rather obscure material I was examining, with the negligence, connivance, and ineptitude of some doctors when presented with various classic but misleading symptoms. There was, for instance, a case of hysteria amusingly and dreadfully diagnosed as *la rage,* and a nastier affair of the same rabid condition, genuine, thought to be lycanthropy. Then came an interim paragraph, and next a name (Lucie's) that caught me unawares and made me start. Some wounds, though they heal, retain a lifelong capacity for hurt.

"Lucie Belmains," my material went on after a token biography, "having slain herself on the morning of the fifth of April, was medically certified as mortal, and buried swiftly, due to the extreme and unusual heat of the season. Readers who have scanned the novel *La Prise En Geste* will be familiar with the following quotation from it." The quotation does indeed follow, but I will omit it here. It was from a flowery work, the very one I am sure Miou and her sister had giggled over under the covers, and as a result of which their poor doll was hanged on a ribbon. The substance of the quotation was this: That on the sixth of April, one of Lucie's living admirers, having entered the bedroom where the body was laid out, and kneeling by the bed in a transport of grief, was abruptly terrified to see the dead woman's left hand flutter as if beckoning to him. Hastening to uncover her face, however, he found only the discoloration and popping eyes such a corpse would exhibit and, running out of the room, he fainted.

"What is not widely known," the material went on, "is that this incident is a fact, and not merely a flight of fancy on the part of a romantic author. There are two other facts, even more slenderly recorded, and not utilized by the writer of *La Prise En Geste*. Firstly, that Belmains' maid, on the evening of the seventh, the actual night of burial, found disturbed the veil which covered the cadaver's face, it being partly pushed or drawn in between the lips. Secondly, that several comments were made on the suppleness of the limbs. This was put down to the hot weather. While the whole affair was meanwhile thought so scandalous, its sequels were largely rushed and overall camouflaged, to the point that for several years even the Duc de M——, who had been for so long the lady's intimate protector, thought she had died from accidental choking."

The conclusion my material evolved from all this is a fairly obvious one. That though Lucie had sufficiently strangled herself as to induce a kind of catalepsy, she was not dead, and did not die until the injury of a mainly collapsed windpipe was augmented by the disadvantages of the grave. Not the material but I myself venture to suggest she could not, in this state, have lingered very much longer. No doubt only until the morning of the eighth of April.

Introduction

Remember how rough it was when you were starting your career? All the prejudices to overcome, the learning to do, the constant display of proof that you really did know what you were doing and talking about? Sometimes, it's safer that way.

Jack C. Haldeman lives in Florida, and both his science fiction and fantasy have appeared in every major market in the country.

STILL FRAME

by Jack C. Haldeman II

The old man came slowly into focus. Diffused shades of gray gradually became sharp images on the ground-glass screen. Robert framed the picture as the man stared into the camera with dead eyes. The shutter snapped, capturing what was left of his soul on Kodak Tri-X film, ASA 400.

The photographer smiled. He knew a good shot when one fell into his lap.

Robert Whitten was sitting on top of the world. Barely twenty-five years old, he had it all and he knew it. He moved to his left to get a different angle and the old man, bored, looked away. Robert refocused and adjusted his exposure.

The man was sitting in a cane-backed chair and staring out the window of the nursing home where he'd lived for the past ten years. The white curtains shifted in the meager summer breeze. Robert held still for a moment, and as the old man's eyes started to close he pressed the shutter release and fired off three quick shots.

The man turned around sharply and started to say something, but stopped. Instead, he shook his head wearily and turned his face to the wall.

The session was over. Robert let his camera hang on its strap as he jotted a few notes in his worn notebook: the date, shutter speeds, f-stops; all technical information, cold hard numbers, nothing about the man. After all, he'd already picked up the release forms from the nursing home manager. He was legally cleared to photograph the old man. What else did he have to know? The man was old and photogenic. That was all that mattered.

Robert lit a cigarette as he walked out onto the broad front porch of the old wood frame house. A woman, fanning herself as she rocked back and forth, looked up at him and smiled. He looked away from the broken teeth and wrinkled skin and started down the steps to the gravel driveway.

As he reached his car, he noticed two women sitting together on a swing hanging from the far end of the porch. He removed the 50 mm lens from his camera and slipped on the medium telephoto he carried in a case on his hip. He raised the camera and focused. It was as if he were standing beside them. He let his cigarette drop and ground it into the gravel with his heel.

The women wore faded white cotton dresses and they had a sameness about them that could have come from being sisters or it could have come with the equalizing effects of age. Gaunt and white-haired, they were having an animated discussion as the swing slowly moved back and forth. Robert framed them dispassionately as they laughed, concentrating on the shifting light and depth of field.

One woman leaned over and whispered something in the other's ear. They giggled and clapped their hands together like schoolgirls. The expressions on their faces were perfect. Except for the passing of eighty years they could have been children. The chain on the swing was rusted, the paint was cracked and peeling in places. The age splotches on their hands and faces stood out clearly. Liver spots.

Only their eyes held life. It somehow shined through the ruin of the years. Robert snapped the picture and knew he had another winner. He opened the car door and set the camera on the front seat.

As he started his Mercedes, he reached down and flipped on the air conditioner. The face of the woman fanning herself was still fresh in his mind. Slipping the car into gear, he drove down the driveway and turned left, scattering gravel as he spun his wheels getting away from the nursing home as rapidly as possible. Old people depressed him. He felt trapped by them.

It was ironic, of course, since old people had brought him everything he had.

Five years ago Robert had dropped out of college to try his luck at full-time photography. He loved animals and had always wanted to be a wildlife photographer. For several months he lived alone in a cabin deep in the mountains. His days were spent following deer, birds, and bears with his camera. He would stand for hours waiting for the sun to be *just* right, waiting for the perfect picture. His nights were spent working in a makeshift darkroom. When he came back to civilization, he carried a thick portfolio of excellent prints. None of them sold.

In order to support himself, Robert took a job as staff photographer for a small local paper. The rest had been mostly luck as far as he could tell. It started with a shot he'd taken early one morning of an old wino rummaging through a garbage can. The man looked up just as Robert snapped the shutter, and the hopelessness and longing in the man's eyes vaulted Robert to the front page of a hundred newspapers.

Everything had grown from that one photo. Everything.

His editor suggested that he try a feature on the elderly street people in town, and although he didn't think much of the idea, Robert went ahead and shot it. Every bag lady and bum that he encountered depressed him, yet he couldn't deny the appeal the photographs would have. He could see the pathos that other people would see in his pictures, but he couldn't feel it himself. It was as if something was missing deep inside him.

The feature was enlarged and ran every Sunday for a month. Many of the pictures were picked up by the wire services, and UPI ran the shot of two old men sleeping in a doorway in over two hundred papers around the world.

Time and *Newsweek* reprinted part of the series as did several foreign publications including *Paris Match* and *Le Monde*. *Esquire* ran a feature-length article on the young photographer just before his collection *Street People* was published by Doubleday in an oversized limited edition just in time for the Christmas trade.

The book sold well and the paperback edition did even better. Robert quit the newspaper, and with a healthy advance from Doubleday he began shooting the companion edition, *Ancient Eyes*. It was a natural follow-up with a built-in market and he hated every minute. He even hated it the instant he tripped the shutter capturing the old sharecropper leaning against the fence at twilight. That was the one that got him the Pulitzer Prize. It also locked him into photographing old people, seemingly forever.

It was also the time the nightmares started. First came the troubled sleep, the endless series of bad dreams. Then it was little things he started seeing at the edge of his vision, little creepy things with no real shape or form.

The psychiatrists were no help. For two hundred dollars an hour they came up with lots of words and theories, but no cures. He felt trapped by the very things that had brought him success. That much was clear. If he had to live with nightmares in order to live with wealth, he figured he could handle it. Money was a great buffer, the best. It could solve all kinds of problems.

He pulled the Mercedes into the circular drive in front of the condominium he'd bought last year out of royalties from *Ancient Eyes*, leaving the car to be parked by the attendant who opened the door for him. He didn't relax until the elevator let him out in front of the door to his condo, ten floors above and light-years away from the world of the old people.

He threw his jacket over the back of the white sofa and flipped through his mail. Nothing there. His telephone-answering machine held nothing important. Kicking off his shoes, he went to the bar by the balcony and poured himself a drink.

Robert's walls were covered with prints of all sizes. Some were matted, some were framed and covered with glass. They were all photographs of birds and animals. A large color print of a bald eagle dominated one wall, surrounded by smaller prints of hawks in flight. A study of a family of raccoons lined the wall to the bedroom. There were no pictures of people.

He sat for a minute sipping scotch and remembered the old man. The film was in his camera bag and he opened it, taking out the three canisters that held what he'd shot earlier.

For a moment he rolled the film around on the coffee table in front of him, trying to decide if he wanted to work anymore today or not. He faced no deadlines, but a couple of the shots had looked pretty good and he was curious.

Robert took the film into the large darkroom he'd had built off the bathroom and loaded it into the developing tank. While the tank slowly rotated, Robert got down his trays and filled them with chemicals. He took the protective cover off the enlarger and cleaned the lens and negative carrier with a few sprays from a can of compressed air. After the negatives had finished their final rinse, Robert hung them in the drying closet. It would take a few minutes for the film to dry, so he left the darkroom, stripped, and stepped into the shower.

The water felt good, hot and steamy. As Robert soaped himself up, he relaxed and felt the weariness from the nursing home wash away. He closed his eyes and let the hot water rinse him off.

Stepping from the shower, he dried himself and did a few deep knee bends. His body was in good shape and he exercised regularly. No fat, no flab, not so much as a single gray hair. After a day of looking at wrinkled and ruined people, it was good to remind himself of his youth. He touched his toes twice and slipped into a robe.

Walking into the darkroom, Robert's curiosity got the better of him. Rather than taking the time to run contact sheets of the day's work, he went directly to the roll that had the shots of the old man. He held it up to the dim safety light and found his place. There were only ten negatives, but they all looked good. He slipped the first one into the enlarger and pulled out a sheet of 8 by 10 paper.

The exhaust fan whirred softly in the darkened room as he focused the enlarger, cropping the picture as he went along. Blurs of black and gray became sharp lines, defined images. This was the part of photography he liked best. Everything that went before only led up to this final step. The print was all that counted.

He studied the old man carefully, with an eye for detail. Only when preparing the print did he notice the small things: a scar on the man's forehead, a wisp of hair from a small mole on his cheek. All these details were what made the photograph successful, but he never noticed them until this stage, always taking for granted that they would be there and they always were. He estimated the correct exposure and flipped the red filter out of the enlarger.

For seven seconds the black and white image of the old man stared up at Robert from the easel under the enlarger. The man had an intensity in his eyes—a strange mixture of hate and despair —that Robert hadn't noticed when he'd taken the picture. It burned through the milky film of the old man's cataracts with a surprising fierceness.

The man also had a faint area of skin discoloration on the side of his face that had escaped Robert. If he didn't like the effect, Robert could always eliminate the discoloration by dodging it out in the final print. He rubbed the side of his face absently as he stood by the enlarger, staring down at the old man staring back at him from a small square of light in the darkness.

Seven seconds passed, ticked away precisely by the large timer over the enlarger. Robert flipped the red filter back into place and slid the paper into the developer.

Handling it only by the edges with a pair of plastic tongs, he moved the blank paper gently around in the shallow tray, touching it occasionally at the corners to keep it under the fluid. After a few seconds the latent image started to appear; slowly at first, with only the darkest parts of the photograph appearing as a ghostlike outline.

Gradually, the print gained substance, the blacks became a deeper, almost absolute black. The white areas stood out in sharp contrast as the shades of gray supplied the detail. Robert watched the old man's eyes carefully, judging the stage of development by the grain of the print.

When the print was fully developed, Robert transferred it to the stop bath for a few seconds and moved it into the fixer. He swirled the print around for a couple of minutes and dipped it into the running water in the washer. Impatient to get a good look at what he had, Robert took the print out of the water and stepped out of the darkroom into the well-lit bathroom to examine it.

He flattened the print against the large mirror over the double sink, sticking it beneath the strong light. He stepped back to get a general idea of how the cropping had worked. It looked good, and he leaned in close to check the focusing and detail. He still couldn't decide whether or not he should dodge out the man's skin discoloration.

Robert decided it could use a little longer exposure and smoothed down a corner of the print with his finger. As he did, he noticed some small brownish blotches on the back of his hand. They looked almost like developer stains, but that was hardly possible. He'd been in up to his elbows in developer for years and it had never happened before. He rubbed at them, but they didn't go away.

Turning on the water, he rinsed off his hands. It didn't help. He ran the water as hot as he could stand it and scrubbed with soap, but the spots wouldn't go away. Annoyed, he shut off the water angrily. The damn things would have to wear away.

Robert took the print off the mirror and stopped for a second.

Was that a spot of gray hair at his temples? He looked closer, rubbing his hair with his fingers. No, it was nothing. He hated the idea of gray hair, the first sure sign of old age. Gray hair marked the beginning of that inescapable slide into the world of old people, the people he couldn't stand, the people he made both his reputation and living from.

He went back into the darkroom and dropped the photograph back into the print washer. Even though it was a test print, he knew there were people who would pay a lot for it.

He moved the strip of film to the next negative and cropped the picture almost automatically. The old man had been looking away from the camera, his gray hair backlighted by the light from the window.

It would make an effective print. Robert softened the light from the window just a little and brought out the highlights on the man's hair, improving on reality. As he finished moving the print through the trays, he considered making a large one later to display at his upcoming show. It would undoubtedly sell very well.

He took it out to the bathroom to look at it in the light. Details he had missed in the darkroom caught his eye. The man had a cracked thumbnail, an ugly wart half hidden behind his ear. While that only served to make the print more effective, it made Robert feel uncomfortable.

Satisfied with the photograph, he peeled it off the mirror, and as he did, he saw himself reflected in the still-wet glass. It was a distorted image, warped by the rivulets of water as they ran down the mirror. His features twisted as he stared, unable to take his eyes away. It was as if he were watching a wax figure melt in an impossibly hot room. The flesh slid off and was replaced by bone, a gleaming white skull mocking him with vacant eye sockets and a frozen grin.

He grabbed a towel and rubbed the mirror violently. It helped, but not much.

His reflection stared back at him with unbelieving eyes through the musty cloud of cataracts. His hair was solid gray. A patch of skin discoloration spread across his cheek. His hand rose to touch the side of his face and as it did, he looked down and saw the cracked fingernail, the swollen knuckles. He screamed, and it was a violent, hollow sound torn from the depths of his soul. It echoed against the walls of the bathroom and went no farther.

He opened his robe and his body was thin and wasted. His hips jutted out sharply and the flesh hung from his bones in useless folds of dead tissue.

Still clutching the print, he staggered out to the living room. Somehow he managed to punch the proper numbers on the telephone.

"Hillside Nursing Home," said a female voice on the other end.

"This is Robert Whitten," he gasped. "I need . . . I need some information on a patient." His voice was raspy and he couldn't control the tremors in his hands.

"Oh yes, Mr. Whitten. I'm a big fan of yours. We saw you around this afternoon taking pictures. What can I do for you? You'll have to speak up. We seem to have a bad connection."

"An old man. I was taking pictures of him today."

"Most of our clients are elderly, Mr. Whitten. Could you give me a better idea who it is that you're looking for?"

"Front room. Something wrong with his skin." Robert coughed and saw with horror that he was spitting up blood.

"That would be poor Mr. Freeman. It was so sudden."

"Sudden? What do you mean?"

"Just like that. Alive one minute and dead the next. Of course, that happens here. Like I say, many of our clients are elderly and you have to expect—"

Robert hung up the phone and wiped the blood from his mouth. He was slobbering now, a mixture of saliva and blood. His eyes wouldn't focus and his arms and legs shook uncontrollably.

Through his clouded vision, he thought the room was filling up with faces. It could have been his imagination; he could no longer tell. They were all old. They had come to collect what he owed them.

He took the still-wet print in his shaking hands and sat down to wait for the inevitable.

It didn't take long.

Introduction

The writer hunches over a battered table in a cramped attic room, sharpening his quills and staring off into space; the writer strolls through a rainstorm, deep in thought, a scowl upon his face; the writer slips into drug-induced fantasies in which he meets face to face the Muse. Sometimes.

Dennis Etchison works in Los Angeles without quills, and his latest collection is Red Screams.

TALKING IN THE DARK

by Dennis Etchison

In the damp bedroom Victor Ripon sat hunched over his desk, making last-minute corrections on the ninth or tenth draft, he couldn't remember which, of a letter to the one person in the world who might be able to help. Outside, puppies with the voices of children struggled against their leashes for a chance to be let in from the cold. He ignored them and bore down. Their efforts at sympathy were wasted on him; he had nothing more to give. After thirty-three years he had finally stepped out of the melodrama.

He clicked the pen against his teeth. Since the letter was to a man he had never met, he had to be certain that his words would not seem naïve or foolish.

"Dear Sir," he reread, squinting down at the latest version's cramped, meticulously cursive backhand. He lifted the three-hole notebook paper by the edges so as not to risk smearing the ballpoint ink. "Dear Sir . . ."

First let me say that I sincerely hope this letter reaches you. I do not have your home address so I have taken the liberty of writing in care of your publisher. If they forward it to you please let me know.

I am not in the habit of writing to authors. This is the first time. So please bear with me if my letter is not perfect in spelling, etc.

I have been reading your Works for approximately 6 yrs., in

other words since shortly after I was married but more about that later. Mr. Christian, Rex if I may call you that and I feel I can, you are my favorite author and greatest fan. Some people say you are too morbid and depressing but I disagree. You do not write for children or women with weak hearts (I am guessing) but in your books people always get what they deserve. No other author I have read teaches this so well. I can see why you are one of the most popular authors in the world. I have all 6 of your books, I hope there are only 6, I wouldn't like to think I missed any! (If so could you send me a list of the titles and where I might obtain them? A S.A.S.E. is enclosed for your convenience. Thank you.)

My favorite is THE SILVERING, I found that to be a very excellent plot, to tell the truth it scared the shit out of me if you know what I mean and I think you do, right? (Wink wink.) MOON OVER THE NEST is right up there, too. My wife introduced me to your novels, my ex-wife I should say and I guess I should thank her for that much. She left me 2 1/2 yrs. ago, took the kids to San Diego first and then to Salt Lake City I found out later. I don't know why, she didn't say. I have tried to track her down but no luck. Twice with my late parents' help I found out where she was staying but too late. So that is the way she wants it, I guess. I miss the kids though, my little boy especially.

In your next book, THE EDGE, I noticed you made one small mistake, I hope you don't mind my pointing it out. In that one you have Moreham killing his old girlfriend by electrocution (before he does other things to her!) while she is setting up their word processor link. Excuse me but this is wrong. I know this because I was employed in the Computer Field after dropping out of Pre-Med to support my family. The current utilized by a Mark IIIA terminal is not enough to produce a lethal shock, even if the interface circuits were wired in sequence as you describe (which is impossible anyway, sorry, just thought you might like to know). Also the .066 nanosecond figure should be corrected. . . .

And so on in a similar vein. Victor worked his way through three more densely packed pages of commentary and helpful advice regarding Rex Christian's other best-sellers, including *Jesus Had A*

Son, The Masked Moon, and the collection of short stories, *Nightmare Territory,* before returning to more personal matters.

    If you ever find yourself in my neck of the woods please feel free to drop by. We could have a few beers and sit up talking about the many things we have in common. Like our love of old movies. I can tell you feel the same way about such "classics" (?) as ROBOT INVADERS, MARS VS. EARTH and HOUSE OF BLOOD from the way you wrote about them in your series of articles for TV GUIDE. I subscribed so I wouldn't miss a single installment. There are others we could talk about, even watch if we're lucky. I get Channel 56 here in Gezira, you may have heard about it, they show old chestnuts of that persuasion all night long!!
    If you have not guessed by now, I too try my hand at writing occasionally myself. I have been working for the past 1 1/2 yrs. on a story entitled PLEASE, PLEASE, SORRY, THANK YOU. It will be a very important story, I believe. Don't worry, I'm not going to ask you to read it. (You are probably too busy, anyway.) Besides, I read WRITER'S DIGEST so I know where to send it if and when I succeed in bringing it to a satisfactory stage of completion. But you are my inspiration. Without you I would not have the courage to go on with it at all.

He hesitated before the conclusion, as he had when first drafting it four nights ago. On the other side of the window pane the sky was already smoking over with a fine mist, turning rapidly from the color of arterial blood to a dead slate gray. The sea rushed and drubbed at the coastline a mile to the west, shaking and steadily eroding the bedrock upon which his town was built; the vibrations which reached the glass membrane next to him were like the rhythms of a buried human heart.

    There is one more thing. I have a very important question to ask you, I hope you don't mind. It is a simple thing (to you) and I'm sure you could answer it. You might say I should ask someone else but the truth is I don't know anyone else who could help. What I know isn't enough. I thought it would be but it isn't. It seems to me that the things we learned up until now, the really important things, and I can tell we've had many of the same experiences (the Sixties, etc.), when it came time to live them, the system balked. And we're dying. But don't worry, I'm a fighter. I learned a long time ago: never give up.

I live in my parents' old house now, so we could have plenty of privacy. In my opinion we could help each other very much. My number is 474-2841. If I'm not here I'll be at the Blue & White (corner of Rosetta and Damietta), that is where I work, anybody can tell you where to find it. I hope to hear from you at your earliest convenience.

Meanwhile I'm waiting with bated breath for your book of essays, OTHER CEDENTS, they mentioned it on Wake Up, America and I can hardly wait! If you care to let me read the manuscript prior to publication I promise to return it by Express Mail in perfect condition. (Just asking, hint hint.) In any event please come by for a visit on your next trip to the West Coast. I hope you will take me up on it sometime (soon!), I really need the answer. We Horror Fans have to stick together. As you said in your Introduction to NIGHTMARE TERRITORY, "It may be a long time till morning, but there's no law against talking in the dark."

> Faithfully Yours,
> *Victor Ripon*

He sat back. He breathed in, out. It was the first breath he had been aware of taking for several minutes. The view from the window was no longer clear. A blanket of fog had descended to shroud all evidence of life outside his room. The puppies next door had quieted, resigned to their fate. Still, a hopeful smile played at the corners of his mouth. He stacked and folded the pages to fit the already stamped envelope. There. Now there wasn't anything to do but wait.

He stretched expansively, hearing his joints pop like dry bones, and his fingernails touched the window. So early, and yet the glass was chillingly brittle, ready to shatter under the slightest provocation.

With any luck he wouldn't have long to wait at all.

The days shrank as the season contracted, drawing inward against the approaching winter. Trees bared stiffening limbs, scraped the sky and etched patterns of stars as sharp and cold as diamond dust above the horizon. Victor got out his old Army jacket. The main house became dank and tomblike, magnifying the creaking of dry-rotted timbers. He took to sleeping in the guest cabin, though the portable heater kept him tight and shivering night after night.

He pressed bravely ahead with his story, the outlines and preliminary versions of which by now filled two thick notebooks, reorganizing, redrafting, and obsessively repolishing lines and paragraphs with a jeweler's precision.

But it was not good enough.

He wanted the pages to sing with ideas that had once seemed so important to him, all and everything he knew, and yet they did not, and no amount of diligence was able to bring them to life. The story came to be a burden and weighed more heavily in his hands each time he lifted it out of the drawer. After a few weeks he was reluctant to open the desk at all.

He stayed in bed more but slept less, dragging himself up for work each day only at the last possible minute. Nothing except Rex Christian's books held any interest for him now, and he had read them all so many times he believed he knew them by heart, almost as well as his own stillborn effort. Channel 56 exhausted its library of late-night movies and sold out to a fundamentalist religious sect peddling fire and brimstone. The nights lengthened and the long winter closed around him.

Each day, he thought, I die a little. I must. I get out of bed, don't I?

Mornings, he walked the two miles along the creek into town, reexamining the last few years like beads to be memorized in his pocketed fists before they slipped away forever. He walked faster, but his life only seemed to recede that much more swiftly across the dunes and back to the sea. He could neither hold on to nor completely forget how things had once been. Whether or not they had ever truly been the way he remembered them was not the point. The spell of the past, his past, real or imagined, had settled over him like the shadow of giant wings, and he could not escape.

He submerged himself in his work at the shop, a space he rented for small appliance repair behind the Blue & White Diner, but that was not enough, either. For a time he tried to tell himself that nothing else mattered. But it was an evasion. You can run, he thought, but you can't hide. Rex Christian had taught him that.

Some days he would have traded anything he owned and all that he had ever earned to wake up one more time with the special smell of her on his pillow—just that, no matter whether he ever actually set eyes on her again. Other days his old revenge fantasies got the better of him. But all that was real for him now was the numbness of more and more hours at the shop, struggling to penetrate the inner workings of what others paid him to fix, the broken remnants of households which had fallen apart suddenly, without warning or explanation.

When not busy at work, the smallest of rewards kept him going. The weekly changes of program at the local movie theater, diverting but instantly forgettable; the specialties of the house at the Blue & White, prepared for him by the new waitress, whose name turned out to be Jolene; and Jolene herself when business was slow and there was nowhere else to go. She catered to him without complaint, serving something, perhaps, behind his eyes that he thought he had put to rest long ago. He was grateful to her for being there. But he could not repay her in kind. He did not feel it, could not even if he had wanted to.

By late December he had almost given up hope.

The weekends were the worst. He had to get out, buttoned against the cold, though the coffee in town was never hot enough and the talk after the movies was mindless and did not nourish. But he could bear the big house no longer, and even the guest cabin had begun to enclose him like a vault.

This Saturday night, the last week before Christmas, the going was painfully slow. Steam expanded from his mouth like ectoplasm. He turned up his collar against an icy offshore wind. There were sand devils in the road, a halo around the ghost of a moon which hung over his shoulder and paced him relentlessly. At his side, to the north, dark reeds rustled and scratched the old riverbank with a sound of rusted blades. He stuffed his hands deeper into his jacket and trudged on toward the impersonal glow of the business district.

The neon above the Blue & White burned coolly in the darkness.

The nightlife in Gezira, such as it was—Siamese silhouettes of couples cruising for burgers, clutches of frantic teenagers on their way to or from the mall—appeared undiscouraged by the cold. If anything, the pedestrians scissoring by seemed less inhibited than ever, pumping reserves of adrenaline and huffing wraiths of steam as if their last-minute shopping mattered more than anything else in this world. The bubble machine atop a police car revolved like a deranged Christmas tree light. Children giggled obscenities and fled as a firecracker resounded between lampposts; it might have been a gunshot. The patrol car spun out, burning rubber, and screeched past in the wrong direction.

He took a breath, opened the door to the diner and ducked inside.

The interior was clean and bright as a hospital cafeteria. A solitary pensioner dawdled at the end of the counter, spilling coffee as he cradled a cup in both hands. Twin milkshake glasses, both empty, balanced near the edge. As Victor entered, jangling the bell, the waitress glanced up. She saw him and beamed.

"Hi!"

"Hi, yourself."

"I'll be a few more minutes. Do you mind? The night girl just called. She's gonna be late." Jolene watched him as she cleaned off the tables, trying to read his face as if it were the first page of a test. Her eyes flicked nervously between his.

"Take your time," he said. He drew off his gloves and shuffled up to the counter. "No hurry."

"The movie—?"

"We won't miss anything."

She blinked at him. "But I thought the last show—"

"It starts," he said, "when we get there."

"Oh." She finished the tables, clearing away the remains of what other people could not finish. "I see," she said. "Are—are you all right?"

"Yes."

"Well, you don't sound like it." She looked at him as if she wanted to smooth his hair, take his temperature, enfold him in her big arms and stroke his head. Instead, she wiped her hands and tilted her face quizzically, keeping her distance. "How about something to eat?"

"Just coffee," he said. "My stomach's . . ." He sought the precise word; it eluded him. He gave up. "It's not right."

"Again?"

"Again." He tried a smile. It came out wrong. "Sorry. Maybe next time."

She considered the plate which she had been keeping warm on the grill. It contained a huge portion of fried shrimp, his favorite. She sighed.

The door jingled and a tall man came in. He was dressed like a logger or survivalist from up north, with plaid shirt, hiking boots, full beard, and long hair. Victor decided he had never seen him before, though something about the man was vaguely familiar.

Jolene dealt out another setup of flatware. He didn't need a menu. He knew what he wanted.

Victor considered the man, remembering the sixties. That could be me, he thought; I could have gone that way, too, if I had had the courage. And look at him. He's better off. He doesn't have any attachments to shake. He opted out a long time ago, and now there's nothing to pull him down.

Jolene set the man's order to cooking and returned to Victor.

"It won't be long," she said. "I promise." She gestured at the old Zenith portable next to the cash register. "You want the TV on?"

She needed to do something for him, Victor realized. She *needed* to. "Sure," he said agreeably. "Why not?"

She flicked a knob.

The nightly episode of a new religious game show, "You Think That's Heavy?" was in progress. In each segment a downtrodden soul from the audience was brought onstage and led up a ramp through a series of possible solutions, including a mock employment bureau, a bank loan office, a dating service, a psychiatric clinic and, finally, when all else had failed, a preacher with shiny cheeks and an unnatural preoccupation with hair. Invariably, this last station of the journey was the one that took. Just now a poor woman with three children and a husband who could not support them was sobbing her way to the top of the hill.

I hope to God she finds what she needs, Victor thought absently. She looks like she deserves it. Of course, you can't tell. They're awfully good at getting sympathy. . . .

But someone will come down and set things right for her, sooner or later. She'll get what she deserves, and it will be right as rain. I believe that.

But what about the kids? They're the ones I'm worried about. . . .

At that moment the door to the diner rang open and several small children charged in, fresh from a spree on the mall, clutching a few cheap toys and a bag of McDonald's French fries. They spotted the big man in the red plaid shirt and ran to him, all stumbles and hugs. The man winked at Jolene, shrugged, and relocated to a corner booth.

"Whadaya gonna do?" he said helplessly. "I reckon I gotta feed 'em, right?"

"I'll get the children's menus," said Jolene.

"You got any chili dogs?" said the man. "We came a long way. Don't have a whole lot left to spend. Is that okay?"

"Give them the shrimp," suggested Victor. "I can't handle it."

Jolene winked back. "I think we can come up with something," she said.

The pensioner observed the children warily. Who could say what they might have brought in with them? He obviously did not want to find out. His hands shook, spilling more coffee. It ran between his fingers as if his palms had begun to bleed.

Well, thought Victor, maybe I was wrong. Look at the big guy now. He can't run away from it either. But it could be he doesn't want to. He's got them, and they'll stick by him no matter what. Lucky, I guess. What's his secret?

Out on the sidewalk passersby hurried on their way, a look of expectation and dread glazing their eyes. Victor picked up his coffee. It was almost hot enough to taste.

There was another burst of ringing.

He braced himself, not knowing what to expect. He scanned the doorway.

But this time it was not a customer. It was the telephone.

Jolene reached across the counter, pushing dirty dishes out of the way. One of the milkshake glasses teetered and smashed to the floor. At the end of the counter, the pensioner jumped as though the spirit of Christmas past had just lain its withered fingers to the back of his neck.

"What?" Jolene balanced the receiver. "I'm sorry, there's so much—yes. I said yes. Hold on." She passed the phone to Victor. "It's for you," she said.

"It is?"

"Sure is," she said. "I can't tell if it's a—"

"Yes?"

"Victor?"

"Yeah?"

"Vic!" said the reedy voice on the line. "Great to get ahold of you, finally! This is Rex. Rex Christian!"

"Really?" said Victor, stunned.

"Yup. Look, I'll be passing through your town in about, oh, say an hour. I was just wondering. Are you free tonight, by any chance?"

"Uh, sure, Re—"

"Don't say my name!"

"Okay," said Victor.

"I'm on my way from a meeting in San Francisco. Traveling incognito, you might say. You don't know how people can be if the word gets out. So I'd appreciate it if, you know, you don't let on who you're talking to. Understand?"

"I understand." It must be hard, he thought, being a celebrity.

"I knew you would."

Victor cupped his hand around the mouthpiece. The old man from the end of the counter fumbled money from his coin purse and staggered out. Victor tried to say the right things. He wasn't ready. However, he remembered how to get to his own house. He gave directions from Highway 1, speaking as clearly and calmly as he could.

"Who was that?" asked Jolene when he had hung up.

"Nobody," said Victor.

"What?"

"A friend, I mean. He . . ."

"He what?"

"I've got to . . . meet him. I forgot."

Her expression, held together until now by nervous anticipation, wilted before his eyes. The tension left her; her posture sagged. Suddenly, she looked older, overweight, lumpen. He did not know what to say.

He grabbed his gloves and made ready to leave.

She smoothed her apron, head down, hiding a tic, and then made a great effort to face him. The smile was right but the lines were deeper than ever before.

"Call me?" she said. "If you want to. It's up to you. I don't care."

"Jolene . . ."

"No, really! I couldn't take the cold tonight, anyway. I—I hope you have a nice meeting. I can tell it's important."

"Business," he said. "You know."

"I know."

"I'm sorry."

She forced a laugh. "What on earth for? Don't you worry."

He nodded, embarrassed.

"Take care of yourself," she said.

You deserve better, he thought, than me, Jolene.

"You, too," he said. "I didn't plan it this way. Please believe—"

"I believe you. Now get going or you'll be late."

He felt relieved. He felt awful. He felt woefully unprepared. But at least he felt something.

All the way home the hidden river ran at his side, muffled by the reeds but no longer distant. This time he noticed that there were secret voices in the waters, talking to themselves and to each other, to the night with the tongues of wild children on their way back to the sea.

Now he considered the possibility that they might be talking to him.

Victor unlocked the old house and fired up the heater. He had little chance to clean. By the time he heard the car, he was covered with a cold sweat, and his stomach, which he had neglected to feed, constricted in a hopeless panic.

He parted the bathroom curtains.

The car below was long and sleek. A limousine? No, but it was a late-model sedan, a full-size Detroit tank with foglights.

A man climbed out, lugging a briefcase, and made for the front of the house.

Victor ran downstairs and flung open the door.

He saw a child approaching in the moonlight. It was the same person he had seen leave the shadow of the car. From the upstairs window the figure had appeared deceptively foreshortened.

The boy came into the circle of the porchlight, sticking his chin out and grinning rows of pearly teeth.

"Vic?"

Victor was confused.

Then he saw.

It was not a child, after all.

"I'm Rex Christian," said the dwarf, extending a stubby hand. "Glad to meet you!"

The hand felt cold and compressed as a rubber ball in Victor's grip. He released it with an involuntary shudder. He cleared his throat.

"Come on in. I—I've been expecting you."

The visitor wobbled to an overstuffed chair and bounced up onto the cushion. His round-toed shoes jutted out in front of him.

"So! This is where one of my biggest fans lives!"

"I guess so," said Victor. "This is it."

"Great! It's perfect!"

On the stained wall a grandfather clock sliced at the thick air.

"Can I get you something?" Victor's own voice sounded hollow in his ears. "Like something to drink?"

"I'd settle for a beer. Just one, though. I want to keep a clear head."

Beer, thought Victor. Let me see. . . . He couldn't think. He looked away. The small face and the monkey mouth were too much for him. He wanted to laugh and cry at the same time.

"You owe me, remember?"

"What?"

"The beer. In your letter you said—"

"Oh. Oh, yeah. Just a minute."

Victor went to the kitchen. By the time he returned, he had replayed his visitor's words in his mind until he recognized the rhythm. Everything the dwarf—midget, whatever he was—had said so far fit the style. There was no doubt about it. For better or worse, the person in the other room was in fact Rex Christian. The enormity of the occasion finally hit him. Setting the bottles on the coffee table between them, he almost knocked one over.

My time has come, he thought. My problems are about to be over. My prayers have been answered.

"This must be pretty far out of the way for you," Victor said.

"Not at all! Thanks for the invitation."

"Yeah," said Victor. "I mean, no. I mean . . ."

And in that instant he saw himself, this house, his life as it really was for the first time. He was overwhelmed with self-consciousness and shame.

"Did . . . did you have any trouble finding the place?"

"Nope. Followed your directions. Perfect!"

Victor studied the virgules in the carpet, trying to find his next words there.

Rex Christian leaned forward in his chair. The effort nearly doubled him over.

"Look, I know what it's like for you."

"You do?"

"Believe me, I do. That's my business, isn't it? I've seen it all before."

Rex sat back and took a long pull from the tall bottle. His Adam's apple rolled like a ball bearing in his throat.

"You must know a lot about people," said Victor.

"Never enough. That's why I take a trip like this at least once a year." He chortled. "I rent a car, visit folks like you all over the country. It's a way of paying them back. Plus it helps me with my research."

"I see." There was an awkward pause. "You—you said you were in San Francisco. On business. Was that part of this year's trip?"

"Right. Nothing beats the old one-on-one, does it?"

So he didn't come all this way just to see me, thought Victor. There were others. "From your writing, well, I thought you'd be a very private person."

"I am! Somebody wants a book, they have to climb the mountain. But when it comes to my fans, it's a different story. They're raw material. I go to the source, know what I mean?"

"I used to be a people-person," said Victor, loosening up a bit. He drained his bottle. He thought of going for two more. But the writer had hardly touched his. "Now, well, I don't go out much. I guess you could say I've turned into more of a project-type person."

"Glad to hear it!"

"You are?"

"It just so happens I've got a project you might be interested in. A new book. It's called *A Long Time Till Morning.*"

"I like the title," said Victor. "Excuse me."

He rose unsteadily and made a beeline for the stairs. The beer had gone through his system in record time. When he came out of the bathroom, he gazed down in wonderment from the top of the landing. Rex Christian was still sitting there, stiff and proper as a ventriloquist's dummy. I can't believe this is happening, he thought. Now everything's changed. There he is, sitting in my living room!

His heart pounded with exhilaration.

Let me never forget this. Every minute, every second, every detail. I don't want to miss a thing. This is important; this matters. The most important night of my life.

He bounded down the stairs and snagged two more beers and an opener from the kitchen, then reseated himself on the sofa.

Rex Christian greeted him with a sparkling grin.

"Tell me about your new book," said Victor breathlessly. "I want to hear everything. I guess I'll be the first, won't I?"

"One of the first." The author folded his tiny hands. "It's about an epidemic that's sweeping the country—I don't have the details yet. I'm still roughing it out. All I gave my editor was a two-page outline."

"And he bought it?"

Rex Christian grinned.

"What kind of epidemic?"

"That's where you can help, Vic."

"If it's research you want, well, just tell me what you need. I used to do a lot of that in school. I was in premed and—"

"I want to make this as easy as possible for you."

"I know. I mean, I'm sure you do. But it's no sweat. I'll collect the data, Xerox articles, send you copies of everything that's ever been written on the subject, as soon as you tell me . . ."

Rex Christian frowned, his face wrinkling like a deflating balloon. "I'm afraid that would involve too many legalities. Copyrights, fees, that sort of thing. Sources that might be traced."

"We could get permission, couldn't we? You wouldn't have to pay me. It would be an honor to—"

"I know." Rex Christian's miniature fingers flexed impatiently. "But that's the long way around, my friend."

"However you want to do it. Say the word and I'll get started, first thing in the morning. Monday morning. Tomorrow's Sunday and—"

"Monday's too late. It starts now. In fact, it's already started. You didn't know that, did you?" Rex's face flushed eagerly, his cheeks red as a newborn infant's. "I want to know *your* feelings on the subject. All of them." He pumped his legs and crept forward on the cushion. "Open yourself up. It won't hurt. I promise."

Victor's eyes stung and his throat ached. *It starts here,* he thought, awestruck. The last thirty-three years were the introduction to my life. Now it really starts.

"You wouldn't want to know my feelings," he said. "They—I've been pretty mixed up. For a long time."

"I don't care about what you felt before. I want to know what you feel tonight. It's only *you,* Vic. You're perfect. I can't get that in any library. Do you know how valuable you are to me?"

"But why? Your characters, they're so much more real, more alive. . . ."

Rex waved his words aside. "An illusion. Art isn't life, you know. If it were, the world would go up in flames. It's artifice. By definition." He slid closer, his toes finally dropping below the coffee table. "Though naturally I try to make it echo real life as closely as I can. That's what turns my readers on. That's part of my mission. Don't you understand?"

Victor's eyes filled with tears.

Other people, the people he saw and heard on the screen, on TV, in books and magazines, voices on the telephone, all had lives which were so much more vital than his own wretched existence. The closest he had ever come to peak experiences, the moments he found himself returning to again and again in his memory, added up to nothing more significant than chance meetings on the road, like the time he hitchhiked to San Francisco in the summer of '67, a party in college where no one knew his name, the face of a girl in the window of a passing bus that he had never been able to forget.

And now?

He lowered his head to his knees and wept.

And in a blinding flash, as if the scales had been lifted from his eyes, he knew that nothing would ever be the same for him again. The time to hesitate was over. The time had come at last to make it real.

He thought: I am entitled to a place on the planet, after all.

He lifted his eyes to the light.

The dwarf's face was inches away. The diminutive features, the taut lips, the narrow brow, the close, lidded eyes, wise and all-forgiving. The sweet scent of an unknown after-shave lotion wafted from his skin.

"The past doesn't matter," said the dwarf. He placed the short fingers of one hand on Victor's head. "To hell with it all."

"Yes," said Victor. For so long he had thought just the opposite. But now he saw a way out. "Oh, yes."

"Tell me what you feel from this moment on," said the dwarf. "I need to know."

"I don't know how," said Victor.

"Try."

Victor stared into the dark, polished eyes, shiny as a doll's eyes.

"I want to. I—I don't know if I can."

"Of course you can. We're alone now. You didn't tell anyone I was coming, did you, Vic?"

Victor shook his head.

"How thoughtful," said the dwarf. "How perfect. Like this house. A great setting. I could tell by your letter you were exactly what I need. Your kind always are. Those who live in out-of-the-way places, the quiet ones with no ties. That's the way it has to be. Otherwise I couldn't use you."

"Why do you care what I feel?" asked Victor.

"I told you—research. It gives my work that extra edge. Won't you tell me what's happening inside you right now, Vic?"

"I want to. I do."

"Then you can. You can if you really want it. Aren't we all free to do whatever we want?"

"I almost believed that, once," said Victor.

"Anything," said the dwarf firmly. "You can have anything, including what you want most. Especially that. And what is it you want, Vic?"

"I—I want to write, I guess."

The dwarf's face crinkled with amusement.

"But I don't know what to write about," said Victor.

"Then why do you want to do it?"

"Because I have no one to talk to. No one who could understand."

"And what would you talk to them about, if you could?"

"I don't know."

"Yes, you do."

"I'm afraid."

"Tell me, Vic. I'll understand. I'll put it down exactly the way you say it. You want me to relieve your fear? Well, in another minute I'm going to do that little thing. You will have nothing more to fear, ever again."

This is it, Victor thought, your chance. Don't blow it. It's happening just the way you had it planned. Don't lose your nerve. Ask the question—now. *Do it.*

"But where does it come from?" asked Victor. "The things you write about. How do you know what to say? Where do you get it? I try, but the things I know aren't—"

"You want to know," said the dwarf, his face splitting in an uproarious grin, *"where I get my ideas?* Is that your question?"

"Well, as a matter of fact—"

"From you, Vic! I get my material from people like you! I get them from this cesspool you call life itself. And you know what? I'll never run out of material, not as long as I go directly to the source, because I'll never, ever finish paying you all back!"

Victor saw then the large pores of the dwarf's face, the crooked bend to the nose, the sharpness of the teeth in the feral mouth, the steely glint deep within the black eyes. The hairs prickled on the back of his neck and he pulled away. Tried to pull away. But the dwarf's hand stayed on his head.

"Take my new novel, for instance. It's about an epidemic that's going to sweep the nation, leaving a bloody trail from one end of this country to the other, to wash away all of your sins. At first the police may call it murder. But the experts will recognize it as suicide, a form of *hara-kiri*, to be precise, which is what it is. I know, because I've made a careful study of the methods. Perfect!"

The underdeveloped features, the cretinous grin filled Victor with sudden loathing, and a terrible fear he could not name touched his scalp. He sat back, pulling farther away from the little man.

But the dwarf followed him back, stepping onto the table, one hand still pressing Victor in a grotesque benediction. The lamp glared behind his oversized head, his eyes sparking maniacally. He rose up and up, unbending his legs, knocking over the bottles, standing taller until he blocked out everything else.

Victor braced against the table and kicked away, but the dwarf leaped onto his shoulders and rode him down. Victor reached out, found the bottle opener and swung it wildly.

"No," he screamed, "my God, no! You're wrong! It's a lie! You're . . . !"

He felt the point of the church key hook into something thick and cold and begin to rip.

But too late. A malformed hand dug into his hair and forced his head back, exposing his throat and chest.

"How does *this* feel, Vic? I have to know! Tell my readers!" The other claw darted into the briefcase and dragged forth a blade as long as a bayonet, its edge crusted and sticky but still razor-sharp. "How about this?" cried the dwarf. "And this?"

As Victor raised his hands to cover his throat, he felt the first thrust directly below the rib cage, an almost painless impact, as though he had been struck by a fist in the chest, followed by the long, sawing cut through his vital organs and then the warm pumping of his life's blood down the short sword between them. His fingers tingled and went numb as his hands were wrapped into position around the handle. The ceiling grew bright and the world spun, hurling him free.

"Tell me!" demanded the dwarf.

A great whispering chorus was released within Victor at last, rushing out and rising like a tide to flood the earth, crimson as the rays of a hellishly blazing sun.

But his mouth was choked with his own blood and he could not speak, not a word of it. The vestiges of a final smile moved his glistening lips.

"Tell me!" shrieked the dwarf, digging deeper, while the room turned red. "I must find the perfect method! *Tell me!*"

Introduction

Courtship ought to be romantic, when each side learns to overlook the flaws of the other and concentrate on those things which caused and supported the attraction in the first place. But first you have to find what you're looking for.

Parke Godwin's latest is a collection of fine stories, The Fire When It Comes, *which includes his World Fantasy Award-winning novella.*

A MATTER OF TASTE

by Parke Godwin

Mediocrity lives in a crowded house. Perfection dwells alone. For Addison Solebury life was lonely at the top. Even in the upper reaches of gastronomy his tastes were so lofty that no restaurant in the world could hope for his continued custom. In the main, he prepared his own meals, a process of considerable labor and research that only added zest to anticipation, feasts so rarefied in their reflection of taste that few could share, let alone cater them.

His standards were arcane but not inflexible. On an off night he could squeak by with properly aged filet mignon and *vin ordinaire,* but for the most part, Solebury's antipathy to the ordinary was visceral and had been all his life. He turned even paler than normal at the sight of margarine, fled a block out of his way to avoid the effluvium of pizza, and often woke whimpering from nightmares of canned tomato soup.

Food—his ecstatic, almost sexual vision of it—was an art he could not see coarsened; therefore, integrity exacted its price. The absence of sharing, of a woman, was the minor mode of Solebury's male lament. After all, not even the nightingale sang for the hell of it, but Solebury, through overspecialization, labored and dined for the most part alone. Time and again, he girded himself and went woman hunting, but with his intolerance of the mundane, his quest was akin to a majestic elk bugling for a mate in the city pound.

Many were called, none were chosen. He despaired of finding a woman of similar refinement. Even those for whom Solebury had the highest hopes revealed a gullet of clay. His fragile expectations would inevitably dampen as she attacked her salad, flickered as she swallowed garlic *escargots* with vulgar relish, guttered with the entrée, and died over brandy and cheese. Failure upon failure, until the coming of Pristine Solent.

From the first tentative conversation in the library reference room where he worked, Solebury felt right about Pristine. When he peered over her shoulder, he found her scanning just those sources he ferreted out in his pursuit of perfection. An exploratory dinner was even more promising. Craftily, he suggested the Four Seasons and was heartened when Pristine answered her door in sensible clothes rather than the coronation gown an ordinary woman might have worn for the occasion. Clothes were not important. The key, the subtle clue to the unerring rightness of his choice was in the way Pristine addressed herself to food. Looks counted for something, to be sure. Pristine was short and robust, with a pale but infinitely well-nourished complexion, a square face with faintly critical brows, and a wide, ready smile that displayed 90 percent of her perfect teeth. For his own appearance, she seemed tacitly to approve of him: pallid as herself with a clear skin, perhaps a small roll of flesh around his fortyish middle that only attested to many years of choosy but ample diet.

But her address to the food—ah, that was exquisite. Her fork balanced in a firm hand, Pristine studied the entrée, turned it this way and that in the manner of an inquisitive coroner, then, resigned that the chef could come no closer to her ideals, speared, chewed, and reluctantly swallowed. Solebury's lips parted in silent admiration. He dared to hope.

"The best is none too good, is it?" he winked at her, then applied the test. Would she join him soon again in a dinner of his own preparation? "I'm something of an expert on dining. In a small way."

"Small way" was the code phrase that separated *cognoscenti* from the uninitiated. He was instantly gratified.

"Why don't we?" Pristine touched her white hand to his, strong fingers curving around intimately to touch his callused palm. She wrinkled her upturned nose at him. "It sounds memorable."

Solebury leaned forward and their eyes met over the forgotten trout almandine. "I think it could be. You know what it means to meet someone you can truly share with?"

"Yes, yes. I know." Pristine stroked the back of his slightly trembling hand. "So seldom. So rare."

A bubble of happiness swelled in Solebury's chest. "You're very beautiful."

"I feel beautiful tonight," said Pristine Solent.

They got out of the taxi a few blocks before her apartment, not wanting the evening to end, holding hands, heads close together. Solebury kissed her with clumsy ardor at her outside door. Pristine swayed into him, then threw back her head to the night sky with a little mew of contentment.

"What an evening. Oh, Addison, I hope there'll be a moon next time. I'm so damned romantic about these things. And a moon is part of it."

"It is. So important." Solebury positively quivered with joy.

"And what's a romantic dinner without moonlight?" Pristine squeezed his hand. "G'night."

If there was a sidewalk under him, Solebury didn't feel it. He floated to the corner and let three cabs approach, slow tentatively, and pass on before remembering he wanted one.

Like Lancelot, Solebury's love quest lay through great deeds. Such a dinner could not be conjured for the next evening or even within a week. Pristine would consider that careless. This called for his full mastery. Since the bone of genius is discipline, Solebury went back to basics, to research.

His own office, the library reference room, was his usual start. All the dailies were searched, torrents of fine print skimmed for the form of his menu. All professionals have their secrets; one of Solebury's lay in his insistence on a slightly pungent spice overlooked by all but a few masters and not commonly used for centuries. Only one establishment, Whittakers, still used it in their prepared seasonings. Just a tiny dollop, but to Solebury it was *sine qua non,* adding an overtaste delicate as it was incomparable.

At length his entrée was found. In a rising fever of concentration Solebury turned his attention to the treacherous but crucial matter of wine.

Only a tyro considered geriatric vintages automatically best. Like any living thing, the grape had its youth, prime, and declining age. Of recent years he gave serious consideration to only one:

'76 of course—but '76 what? Even within the confines dictated by a white-meat entrée, there were nuances of choice. Some masters —and Pristine could well be one—preferred a *demi-sec* where he would choose a drier variety. A blunder here, one false step, could shadow Pristine's judgment. She'd be kind, but Solebury would feel a door closing behind her charity, and successive evenings would find her otherwise engaged.

He let instinct guide him, recalling a champagne he'd chosen not two months back, a superb Chardonnay *brut*. His usual shop produced one remaining bottle at a larcenous price, but Solebury's heart sang as he hurried home. He knew all this was preamble, part of the labor of love. A great deal of delving remained.

One more choice awaited him: the time, more of a gamble than all the rest. Pristine wanted a moon, but though Solebury scanned the papers and the skies, one promised nothing and the other remained perversely overcast. At last came an evening when the early autumn moon entered like a diva from a proscenium of fleecy cumulus clouds. Solebury turned from his window and reached for the phone, at once stabbed to the heart and uplifted by Pristine's throaty greeting.

"Hel*lo*, Addison. I was just thinking of you."

He choked on his ecstasy. "You were?"

"Must be ESP. I was looking at the moon and thinking tonight might be—"

"Yes. Perfect. That's why I called. You wanted a romantic moon. Shall we dine? Something *very* special?"

"In a small way. Love to," Pristine whispered over the wire. "I'm famished for something special."

A world of promise throbbed in her honeyed contralto.

Solebury always dined late. Pristine was not surprised by the hour or the address, neither that fashionable.

"It's a perfect time, Addison. I'm never hungry much earlier than that. I'll be there."

Solebury hung up in a soft rush of joy. Here was a mate for all reasons.

Humming with busy pleasure, Solebury twirled the '76 down into the waiting ice. Even now, before Pristine arrived, there was spadework. He miscalculated slightly and was only half ready with final preparations when she appeared. If her first dinner costume had been sensible, her clothing tonight was downright utilitarian —jeans and boots and a windbreaker against the cool. She gave Solebury a cheerful little peck and surveyed his labors.

"Can I help?" she asked politely.

"Oh no, really. There's just a little further—"

"No, let me. You've already worked so hard."

It flattered Solebury to see Pristine pitch in. She was very sturdy, but no dining of this caliber was ever accomplished without hard physical labor. At length Pristine paused, wiping her brow with the back of one white hand, and drew the champagne from its bucket to browse the label with admiration.

"Lovely year, Addison." She turned again briefly to the last shovel work, then stepped aside for her host. "You'll want to open up and carve."

"Of course. You are a dear, Pristine." Descending into the grave, Solebury wielded his implement with a practiced economy of movement. Three deft snaps with the crowbar broke the casket seals. With a gustatory flourish, he threw it open for her approval.

"Bon appetit, darling."

He hovered waiting under the October moon for the sunbeam of her approval, but he saw only a frown of disappointment.

"Beautifully aged," he assayed against her silence. "Buried Thursday."

Pristine sat down on the freshly turned earth. "Oh, Addison. Oh dear . . ."

"What—what's wrong?"

"Everything!" she wailed.

He felt a premonitory chill. "But he's perfect. Buried from Whittaker's last Thursday. I use them exclusively, the only undertakers who still use myrrh in their preparation. You must know that."

Pristine's disappointment turned brittle. "Of course I know that. There is Whittaker's and only Whittaker's. But as you see, the entrée is hardly Caucasian."

True, the entrée was decidedly dark. There was no mention of that in the obituary. He'd assumed white meat; a minor variant and trivial. Solebury vaulted out of the grave to sit facing Pristine like a teacher. "Pristine, that doesn't really matter. Expertise is one thing, ivory tower another."

"Doesn't matter?" Pristine corrected him like an errant child.

"Surely you know non-Caucasian flesh doesn't take the myrrh flavor well at all. It cancels it out."

"I *beg* to disagree." Solebury's pride was at stake, and she was dead wrong. "A difference, yes. A subtle piquance, if you will, but hardly canceled."

"Even if that were true," Pristine countered in a voice cool as the churchyard dark, "it completely negates champagne."

Solebury began to feel a bit waspish despite himself. "Oh, really! The principle is the same as dark meat on fowl. I took days choosing that champagne. I am not an amateur."

But her pretty head wagged back and forth through his protestations. "Cold Duck, Mister Solebury. Nothing else."

He went falsetto at the sacrilege. "Cold *Duck?* It's so bloody common!"

"But," Pristine riposted with a raised forefinger, "the *un*common choice." Her assertiveness quavered and broke. "I'm sorry, Addison, but I—"

"Oh, please, Pristine. I worked so hard."

"I know, but it's all so *wrong.*"

"Please stay. I adore you."

"Oh, go to hell. Go to McDonald's—no. No, please, dear Addison, I didn't mean that. That was filthy. Just—" Her voice caught and shattered on a sob. "Just that I was looking for someone, too, someone to share with. It's so lonely being the best. And I thought you . . ."

"I am, Pristine, darling. We could share so much."

"No, not with differences as wide as these. Don't say anything, just goodbye. I'm leaving. I won't look back. Don't call me. Oh, my dear Addison. You were so close to perfection."

Solebury choked out something in farewell and admission of his sins, following Pristine with the eyes of tragedy as she receded forlornly through the cemetery gate. He slumped down on the turned earth, working without relish at the champagne cork. The *pop* was hollow as his hopes.

"So close to perfection," she had said. All right. He raised the glass to his better, though it cost him a love to learn. Life was still lonely near the top. The moon went down and the wind before dawn was desolate.

He could barely pick at supper.

Introduction

It's curious how success often breeds paranoia—they're out to get you, you see, because you're on top and they don't want you there. It's seldom explained, however, who "they" are. Often, it's just as well you don't know.

Chelsea Quinn Yarbro's latest novel is Nomads, *and her collection from Scream Press should be in print by the time you read this.*

DO NOT FORSAKE ME, O MY DARLIN'

by Chelsea Quinn Yarbro

Ben crumpled the telegram in his fist, smiling weakly at Heather. "It's just . . . some kind of joke."

She reached out to take the wadded yellow paper from him, not quite frowning as she did. "What on earth, then—"

He snatched it away from her and began to tear at it, so that bits of it fluttered down onto his half-eaten poached eggs. "It's nothing," he said more vehemently. "Don't make such a big thing about it." He put the shredded telegram next to his spoon. "Somebody at the office, I guess. They get prankish about the time summer comes."

Now Heather was definitely curious. "But what *was* it, honey? If it's just a prank, why not let me in on it?" She automatically poured more coffee for him. "Do you want me to be on the alert for more . . . pranks?"

His head jerked up. "More?" There was a pale line around his mouth and the muscles in his jaw worked. "There won't be any more," he promised her as he reached for his mug.

"All right. If you're sure." She could tell that he was still irritated, so she tactfully changed the subject. "I'll be working late at the library. Denise has both her boys home with measles and I said I'd fill in for her for the rest of the week."

"Oh—yeah," Ben said distractedly. His eyes were still on the remains of the telegram, and he was not paying much attention to her.

Heather knew that look well and accepted it philosophically. She would have time enough later to examine the telegram and find out what it was that had disturbed Ben.

When he had finished his eggs, he got up from the table. "Gotta run," he told her, as he did every morning before going to work. He reached down and took the torn paper, and without a word went and dropped it in the trash. "I'll call you if I'm going to be late."

"At the library," she reminded him, hoping he would remember.

She retrieved the telegram half an hour after Ben had left the house. With care she smoothed it out on the kitchen counter and began the painstaking task of putting it back together. She stared at it as the words took shape:

YOU ARE CORDIALLY INVITED TO ATTEND THE FUNERAL OF BENEDICT TURNER SATURDAY JUNE 23 4 PM

There was no signature, and the date was ten days away.

With hands that were not quite steady, Heather put the telegram back in the trash, handling it carefully, as if she feared it would explode. "A joke?" she asked the air, her voice shriller than usual. What kind of idiot, she wondered, made light of inviting a man to his own funeral? As if to rid the house of vermin, she closed the plastic sack that held the trash and carried it out to the curbside before gathering together her purse and notebook and leaving for work. As she double-locked the front door, she worried for the first time in over a year about the risk of leaving their home unattended.

"You got a moment, Carl?" Ben asked from the door of the vice-president's office. He had been debating for the better part of the morning if he should speak to his superior about some of the company clowns.

Carl Hurley looked over the rims of his glasses. He was neatly barricaded behind his desk, but still gave the impression of peering out at a dangerous world. "Sure. What is it, Ben?"

"I was . . . curious about Tim Hoopes. What's he up to these days?" It was a safe beginning, a way to approach his question without being obvious.

"Tim's been on leave, you know," Carl said cautiously.

Ben made a gesture showing he knew that. "When's he supposed to come back?"

"Not for a while yet. His doctors have been hedging their bets about him. It might be a couple more months yet." He waited a second. "Why?"

"Oh, nothing. It's been a little dull around here without him, is all." He hoped that Carl would give him a chance to expand on this notion.

"The way Tim can be, that's not such a bad thing." Carl put aside the contracts he had been examining. "What's the matter? Have you been hearing the rumors too?"

This startled Ben. "Rumors? No." He tried to conceal his anxiety. "What are the rumors?"

Carl chuckled, which was rare, and indicated to Ben that he should sit down, which was rarer. "Well, it isn't likely that Tim will be able to resume his old job. He isn't up to managing an office any longer, or won't be for some time. We can't have this company going rudderless for that long. So there has been some speculation about who will be promoted. Are you *sure* you haven't heard any rumors about this, Ben?"

Ben had never known Carl to be impish, but that was the only word that suited the vice-president now. "No, I haven't," he said, taking the chair nearest Carl's enormous desk.

"Well, it's better you don't admit it, even if you have," he said. "Nothing is final yet and it could still fall in the cracks." He leaned back in his padded leather chair. "Let's just say that you might get the chance you've been looking for. Nothing is final. Keep that in mind."

"Of course," Ben nodded, feeling stunned. Was Carl trying to tell him that he would be Tim Hoopes' replacement?

"They've narrowed it down to two; I'll say that much. Harry Riverford's a good man. His office runs well." He narrowed his eyes, watching Ben for his reaction.

"He does very good work," Ben managed to say, thinking of the rough humor of the man. Could it be that the telegram was nothing more than putting him on notice that it was Harry and not himself who would be promoted into Tim Hoopes' job?

"Something the matter?" Carl demanded.

Ben recovered himself. "Uh . . . no. I've got my mind on too many things. That machine tool plant that burned—I still don't like the way the reports look. The damn thing's too neat." It was true enough that the case was a troublesome one, and it let him account for his lapse of attention.

"Was that why you came in here? Tim started that claim investigation, didn't he?" Carl knew full well that it had been Tim Hoopes' case, but preferred to let the men under him explain themselves without his help.

"He started it. We're still not quite through. The cops are not committing themselves, and I think that warrants further investigation on our part. You'd be surprised how many questions are hanging on this one." He glowered down at his knees. "Is Tim at home yet, or is he still in the hospital?"

"He's been at home for three days," Carl said colorlessly.

"Three days? Do you think it would be okay if I gave him a call? I mean, do you think it would upset him?" If Tim had been at home and bored, he might take it into his head to send such a telegram to a man he feared would get his job. It made sense.

"I'll phone Lilah and ask her when would be a good time," Carl offered, not smiling at all.

"Sure, if you think that would be best." He started to get up, not wanting to appear to be soliciting Carl's good opinion. "If anything clear turns up, I'll let you know."

"I'd appreciate that," Carl said, making no attempt to stop him. "You can check with me this afternoon and I'll tell you what Lilah said."

"Thanks." He started toward the door, then paused. "How much have you said to Harry about these . . . rumors?"

"About as much as I've said to you. Leave it alone, Ben. I've told Harry the same thing." He said it coldly.

Ben responded at once. "Right."

The next day coming back from lunch, Ben found a note tucked under his windshield wiper:

THE FAMILY OF BENEDICT TURNER

ARE GRIEVED TO ANNOUNCE

HIS UNTIMELY DEATH

ON THURSDAY, JUNE 21

He was about to tear it up when he decided that he might need this as evidence. Handling it as if it had poison on it, he folded the paper three times and slipped it into his wallet. He was not quite certain what he planned to do with it, but he had a vague sense of strategy building up within him. Whoever it was that was doing this to him, he was not prepared to suffer the outrage in silence. He looked down the street, but all he saw was the meter maid puttering along in her little cart, pausing now to write a ticket. He wanted to run after her, to find out if she had seen anyone put the note on his windshield, but he could not bring himself to move, for that might require an explanation.

"Damn!" he whispered, as if any stronger word would lend an importance to the incident that he did not want it to have. He walked back to the office in a thoughtful funk, not sure how best to proceed.

"I had a phone call this afternoon," Heather said during a commercial on the evening news. She had been fidgety since she got home but had not been willing to say why. "About half an hour before closing, there was a call at the library."

"Anything important?" Ben asked, not paying too much attention. He was still thinking about the hostage bargaining crisis that the last story had covered. It had been three minutes long. Three minutes, with eighteen lives at stake. He had never been bothered by that brevity until now.

Heather started to tell him, but the jingle for fast foods gave way to the crisp tones of the local newscaster and Ben waved Heather into silence for another twelve minutes while a possible new treatment for AIDS was speculated on—cautiously and technically by the researcher, more enthusiastically by the reporter; a multicar collision on the largest local freeway was shown; there was a report on a hearing for a utilities increase; and the fire marshal discussed what hazards were to be watched for in the coming dry months of summer, with the reporter doing her best to make a sense of order out of the man's rambling discourse. "Now," Ben said while three handsome, rugged young men praised an imported beer, "what were you saying about a phone call?"

"Can you imagine another increase in the electric bill?" Heather said, her indignation making her cheeks redden.

"Was the phone call about that?" Ben asked, avoiding sarcasm by the barest margin.

Heather cleared her throat, becoming more subdued at once. "No. No, it wasn't about that. It was . . . it was a condolence call."

Ben gave her his full attention for the first time. "A *what?*"

"You heard me," she snapped. "A man called and asked for me, and then said he was very sorry about your death. He wanted to know if he was to send flowers or a donation to a charity." She choked on the laugh she attempted.

"That's ridiculous," Ben said apprehensively. "Who'd do a thing like that?"

"The same person who sent you the telegram, perhaps?" she suggested, then flushed as he stared at her. "All right. I read it. You were so upset, well, what would you have done?"

Ben was about to upbraid her when a name on the news caught his ear.

"The suicide of Mister Hoopes was the result of depression following open-heart surgery. His wife of twenty-three years, Lilah, discovered the body when she returned from shopping. The Haymarket Insurance Group has issued a request that all those clients dealing with Mister Hoopes contact company vice-president Carl Hurley at their earliest convenience, as the destruction of files in Mister Hoopes' possession was extensive and it appears that he deliberately destroyed many of the computer records before he took his life."

"Je-*sus!*" Ben burst out. "Did you hear *that?*"

"Yes," Heather answered. "That poor woman."

"Destroyed computer files and . . . he must have been in worse shape than anyone guessed." Secretly, he thought that his several annoyances might now come to an end. It was tragic, but with Tim Hoopes dead there would be no more notes, no more phone calls, no more telegrams. The worst was over and he could let himself feel pity for the man. "There's gonna be hell to pay at the office."

"What ever possessed him?" Heather wondered aloud, staring at Ben. "What made him do it?"

"Who knows?" Ben answered. "A man does all kinds of crazy things if he wants to kill himself. I guess you better call Lilah in a while, let her know that we're sorry." He cleared his throat.

"Don't say anything about the pranks, though. It wouldn't be right to mention it."

Heather was silent for a moment, and when she spoke, it was with unusual reserve. "If that's what you want, Ben."

"Thanks," he said, his mind already on the problems they would face at the office with the files in disorder. "You're a good kid, honey."

INSURANCE EXECUTIVE KILLED IN CRASH

Benedict Turner, newly appointed vice-president of the Haymarket Insurance Group, was one of four victims when a late-model Mercury collided with an ambulance near the emergency entrance to Southside General Hospital. Also pronounced dead were ambulance driver George D. Bellman, paramedic Kevin Chmura, and Evelyn Hayward . . .

Ben read the newspaper clipping and swore with more feeling than he had shown all through the exasperating morning.

"Something the matter, Mister Turner?" his secretary asked as she put down a stack of files and peered at him over her glasses.

He forced himself to be calm. "Nothing. Nothing really. Someone with a ghoulish sense of humor and very bad taste," he said, attempting to laugh. "You know what some of our people can be like. Coming now . . ." He let her finish his thought for herself. "With Hoopes dead, and all."

"Very tragic," she said, shaking her head and clicking her tongue in disapproval.

Ben was about to throw the clipping away, when he read it over. It said that he was a vice-president of Haymarket Insurance Group, and that was not the case. It also said that there had been . . . would be an accident between an ambulance and a late-model Mercury. His Cougar was three years old and might still qualify for that description. "It's easy," he said to himself.

"What was that, Mister Turner?" Rosalind inquired, speaking more sharply. "I'm trying to get some order here, Mister Turner."

"Nothing, Rosalind. Just thinking out loud. Don't mind me." He smiled. Whoever was pulling these stunts had gone too far this time. It said that he would be killed outside the emergency entrance to Southside General. He already knew it was supposed to happen next Thursday. All he had to do was be somewhere else on

Thursday and there would be no problem. He would even let Heather take his car to work, and that would take care of everything. He folded the clipping neatly and put it in his wallet with the note that had been left on his windshield.

"Do you want me to work overtime, Mister Turner?" Rosalind cut into his thoughts.

"Um?" He looked up with a start, then glanced at the clock. More than an hour had slipped away from him. "Oh. No, I don't think it will be necessary. I'll put in a couple hours tonight and that should give you enough to do tomorrow. Monday is no day to work late, Rosalind."

"All right, Mister Turner," she said prissily. "I imagine that you will want me to come in early tomorrow?"

He frowned. Obviously, she had said something that he had not caught. "Yes, I suppose so, if you think you ought to."

"Very good, Mister Turner." She was already prepared to leave, slipping her summer-weight cardigan over her beige shirtwaist dress. "I hope it's good news."

This puzzled him even more, but he did not permit himself to question her. "So do I, Rosalind," he called after her. Why, he wondered, would he be driving near Southside General, anyway? There was always the remote chance that he would have to visit a client in the hospital, but he could think of no one who was ill or old enough to require an emergency visit. With a sigh he shrugged it off. Another time he would work it out, sometime next week, or the week after.

"Hector Wyland called," Heather told Ben as he came in the door. "He would like you to call him back." She could not disguise the excitement she felt; Hector Wyland was the chairman of the board of the Haymarket Insurance Group.

"Wyland?" Ben asked, startled. "Did he say what he wants?"

"No. Of course not." She looked closely at him. "Do you know why he'd want to talk to you?"

Ben did not hear the suspicion in her voice, nor notice the pointed way she watched him. "It's probably something to do with Hoopes' files. It's a mess the way he left things." He smiled at her. "Fix me a drink, will you? I might as well get this over with."

Heather did as he told her, trying to decide how she would react to any bad news. She took her time in the kitchen, dawdling over the ice tray and impulsively setting out cheese and crackers, so that she would not have to listen to what Ben said to his boss. By the time she heard him put down the phone, she was ready to listen to him.

"Hey!" he beamed at her. "How did you know it was a celebration?" He pointed to the cheese and crackers.

"Oh . . ." She gave a flustered giggle. "Woman's intuition, I guess."

He took the drink from her and tasted it. "Great! Just great."

She put the cheese and crackers on the coffee table. "And what are we celebrating?"

Ben swaggered the length of the living room. "We are celebrating my promotion. You, my darling wife, are looking at the new vice-president of Haymarket In—"

"Haymarket Insurance Group?" she finished for him when he broke off in some bewilderment.

His enthusiasm left him. "Yeah," he muttered, and took a long pull on the drink.

Heather was perplexed by this change in him, but she said, "Ben, that's just wonderful. You've wanted this for so long."

"Un-huh," he said, thinking of the clipping in his wallet, that had identified him as the newly appointed vice-president of Haymarket Insurance Group. "I just didn't think it would be because of Tim Hoopes killing himself." The words sounded lame to him, but apparently they satisfied Heather, who came to his side and put her arm around him.

"You shouldn't feel that way, Ben. You've deserved promotion for a long time. It's very . . . sad about Tim Hoopes, but you had nothing to do with it, and you mustn't think of your advancement as some kind of grave robbing." She patted him affectionately. "Come on. Have some cheese. And then, let's think of a nice place to have dinner out."

His mouth was dry and there was a vaguely sick feeling south of his stomach, but he smiled at her. "Sounds great."

This time she was not fooled. "Are you all right?"

"Sure. A goose must have walked on my grave, is all." He drained his glass hoping that the alcohol would relieve the dread that had awakened within him.

Lunch the next day was a festive affair, with half the office accompanying Ben to the Golden Calf for their most sumptuous fare. Men who ordinarily had little to say to Ben now sought him out to offer effusive good wishes for his success; only a few were unable to conceal their envy of his promotion, but they were wise enough to mask their jealousy in banter. Rosalind never moved more than six paces away from him, simpering whenever he spoke to her.

When the meal was almost over, a waiter brought in a large bouquet of white mums and yew boughs, his expression sheepish. "They were delivered, Mister Turner," he told the gathering who stared at the funereal display.

"Must have been some kind of mistake at the florist's. They probably thought it was because of Hoopes." Carl Hurley had started to reach for the card as he said this, but Ben snatched it out of his hand.

"In Sincere Sympathy" said the silver-scrolled letters on the front of the card. Inside was a typewritten note. "In memory of Benedict Turner."

"Oh, shit," Ben whispered. It was not funny anymore, he thought. It had been eerie at first, but this was definitely not amusing.

"It's a foul-up, Ben," Carl said, doing his best to smooth over the awkward moment. "I'll call the florist when we get back to the office; they'll straighten it out for you."

Ben waved this suggestion away. "No. Don't bother."

"But . . ." He cleared his throat. "They might have sent . . . a different arrangement to Lilah. I'd better find out what happened."

This was met with a chagrined silence. Slowly, Ben nodded. "Sure. It wouldn't be right for her to get . . ." He shrugged.

Most of the Baked Alaska went uneaten.

When Ben moaned in his sleep, Heather woke. She lay still, uncertain of what had disturbed her. She had almost drifted off when Ben cried out and turned over abruptly, no longer entirely asleep.

"It's a lie," he mumbled angrily.

"Ben?" Heather said, propping herself on her elbow so that she could watch him. "What is it?"

He did not answer her. His arms thrashed, catching the sheet and pulling the bedding into disorder. The muscles of his jaw worked and sweat ran down the side of his ear.

"Ben!" Heather was growing alarmed. Against her better judgment, she reached over and gave him a timid shake. "Wake up, Ben."

"What!" It was a shout and it startled them both. He shook his head and looked about wildly, as if expecting to see something frightening. "I thought I saw an ambulance coming," he said, as much to himself as to her.

"It was a dream, Ben." She wanted him to reassure her by agreeing, but he did not do this.

"God, I hope so. It was so real . . . I could have sworn that . . . Well, it didn't happen, did it?" At last he looked at her as if he knew where they were. "Sorry, honey. I didn't mean to upset you."

"But what was it?" She was becoming distressed, her fear magnified by the darkness and the late hour. Only emergencies happened at three-forty in the morning.

He attempted to chuckle. "A dream. That's all. I guess . . . I'm spooked by the new work. Probably, I'm afraid that it will all go wrong." He knew that this was not a lie, but he did not want to explain more.

Heather touched his arm. "That isn't all of it."

He did not answer her. "It's late. Get some sleep. I'll be fine in the morning. Chalk it up to the extra brandy."

She was not placated, but she knew it was useless to insist. "All right. But if you're worried, I wish you'd talk to me about it."

"I'm not worried," he said, drawing the blankets up to his chin in spite of the warmth of the night. "I'm fine." As he tried to relax, he decided that the first thing to do when he got to the office would be to get rid of those two scraps of paper in his wallet.

"We're having trouble with the branch office," Carl Hurley said to Ben on Thursday morning. "Are you willing to fly down this afternoon and have a talk with Bryant and his people, to find out what the trouble is?"

Ben almost leaped out of his chair in his hurry to accept the offer. "I'll call Heather at work and tell her I'll be gone tonight," he said, speaking so quickly that the words were slurred. "What time do you need me to leave?"

"There's a plane at two-thirty. That'll give you time to go home and put a few things in your bag and collect your shaving gear." He regarded Ben as he leaned back. "You know, I wasn't certain you were the right choice at first, but if you're going to be this dedicated, I know you'll work out for us."

"Thanks," Ben said, not quite sarcastically. "Do you need me any more this morning?"

"There's a meeting in fifteen minutes, but I don't think you have to sit in, not with a plane to catch." He extended his hand across his enormous desk. "Good to see you so active, Ben."

It was tempting to say that he would have accepted any assignment that would get him out of town, away from Southside General Hospital, before the hour on the most recent card, which he had found that morning inserted in his Rolodex. With any luck he would be at the airport by one forty-five, which was the time announced. "Well, I want the Board to be satisfied with my performance," he said as he took Carl's hand. "I want to get off on the right foot; you know how it is."

"Yes, I do." His smile remained fixed, full of good humor and completely without warmth. "Have a good flight. The tickets will be waiting for you at the airport."

"Great. I'll call you from Bryant's office?" It had been the usual procedure, but this time he knew it was proper to ask.

"When you've had a chance to evaluate the situation, yes. But use your initiative, Ben. You go in there and have a look around; you decide what has to be done, and then you report. If you manage this as well as you have other problems, we'll back you to the hilt. It shows us how you'll do when you're in charge." Carl made friendly movements with his hands, but Ben was not deceived: he was being tested, and if he failed now, he would never rise one notch higher in Haymarket as long as he worked there.

"Thanks," he said, trying to keep from sounding irritated.

"My pleasure." The hands now indicated that Ben ought to leave the office. "Look forward to hearing from you."

Ben went through the departing ritual, his mind already racing, taking him away from the hazard that waited for him near Southside General Hospital. He went back to his office to pick up his briefcase and to take one last look at the card, which purported to be part of the autopsy results:

. . . massive burns over the entire body, in some cases reducing the flesh completely and blackening bone. Identification was confirmed by dental charts. Benedict Turner died within seconds of the fatal collision when the double explosion from both gas tanks occurred . . .

God*damn,* he was glad to be getting out of town.

At home he called Heather at the library and gave her the news. "So there's nothing to worry about, honey."

"I guess you're right," she said, a bit of a shake in her voice. "You have a good trip. I'll expect a call tonight."

"You'll get it," he promised her, pleased to be able to do this for her, since she had been so good this last week. "You're great, Heather. I want you to know that. I don't always say it, but it means a lot to me, the way you stick by me . . . you know."

Her chuckle was more than half a sigh. "Thanks. I love you, too. It's good this is finally over."

"It sure is," he agreed fervently. "It had me spooked there for a while. If I ever find out who did it to . . ."

When he did not elaborate, she said, "I almost forgot: Dave Wheeler from Valley called. He wants to talk to you."

"Why? Did he say?" It was rare for the competition to make personal calls.

"Only that it was fairly urgent." She hesitated. "I'll miss you. But you'd better call Wheeler and then get going. I heard on the radio there's a real traffic mess at the Fourth Street Bridge—only one lane opened westbound."

"Oh, shit. I'll leave right after I call Wheeler. See you in a day or so." He made a kissing noise at the receiver as he hung up and reached for his pocket directory.

"That you, Turner?" Dave Wheeler demanded when he came on the line.

"Yeah. What's the trouble, Dave?" He had recently tried to persuade one of Dave's clients to switch companies, but that was not so uncommon that it merited a phone call.

"Who's in charge of dirty tricks at your office, anyway?" he demanded without preamble.

"We don't do dirty tricks, Dave, and you know it," Ben answered, affronted.

"Well, someone sure as hell is trying to be funny, but I'm not amused. You find whoever it is who sent this damned clipping and you tell them that if I get any more of this crap, I'm going to talk to my lawyer." His voice had risen from an angry hush to a near shout.

"What are you talking about?" Ben asked, his voice faltering; he was afraid he knew. "What kind of clippings?"

"You *know* what kind—don't deny it!" Behind his anger there was panic. "*Obit*uary clippings. For me." He paused. "It's not funny, not at all, and you better tell the joker over there that if anything like this happens again, I'm going to sue you for every cent in your company coffers. Got that?"

"But why tell me? Why not call Carl Hurley?" It was a sensible question, one he should have asked at first.

"Because I thought you and I had a little rapport. My mistake!" He slapped the receiver down and left Ben standing, listening to the dial tone.

For a minute he pondered what he ought to do—phone Carl, or his secretary? Call Dave back? A glance at his watch told him he did not have the luxury of time. He reached for his carry-on bag.

In the airport parking lot Ben tripped and stumbled in his rush for the terminal. He swore at the pain that lanced up his leg with every step he took. "Must've sprained it," he said to the sky, determined to ignore it. He was almost inside the vast building when he collapsed.

He came to in the ambulance, the siren in his ears.

"Lie still, Mister Turner," said the young paramedic as Ben began to thrash. "We're almost to the hospital." There was a tag on his left breast pocket: K. CHMURA it said.

"What?" Ben demanded, his voice rising. His mouth felt woolly.

"You've been given a sedative and a painkiller. Your right leg is broken. It beats me how you were able to walk on it at all." He spoke soothingly.

"Where . . . ?" Ben cried out, trying to deny what he saw.

"At the airport. Do you remember that?" He smiled. "Ordinarily, we'd take you to Mercy, but there's a traffic tie-up in that direction. We're being sent to Southside General."

"*No!*" he screamed, straining at the belts that held him on the gurney.

"Mister Turner, relax. We're almost there," K. Chmura assured him.

"God, no. Nononono," Ben whispered. Not this way. He had assumed it was his car that had struck the ambulance; he had never thought that he would be riding in it, a patient on his way to the emergency room for a stupid broken leg.

"We'll call your office for you, and your wife," the paramedic assured him.

"Slow down. You've got to slow down." He was panting with fear but strove to be calm and steady.

"Don't worry, Mister Turner. This is one of the best ambulances built. Hell, George could take this thing on a Grand Prix course." He smiled at Ben. "We'll take good care of you, Mister Turner. Don't you worry about it."

"Please slow down," Ben begged in a whisper.

"Almost there," the driver called out.

"Oh God," Ben muttered as despair flooded through him.

From the front, the driver said, "Will you look at that?"

K. Chmura glanced over his shoulder. "What is it?"

"That crazy—"

"*No!*" Ben shrieked.

"—broad must be going sixty mi—"

Introduction

The good life, as depicted in commercials and in the memories of hunters, campers, and hikers, is filled with loving Nature, soft sunsets, and tranquil lakes. Sure, there are occasional moments of stormy weather and hard climbing and discomfort, but it's always worth it, just to get back in tune with our ancestor's roots. Sometimes, though, the tune isn't exactly the way we recall it.

Jere Cunningham is the author of a number of fine Dark Fantasy novels, among them The Abyss, The Legacy, *and* The Visitor. *He doesn't often do short stories, but he does always remind us.*

DECOYS

by Jere Cunningham

She peered miserably through the rough wood planks of the duck blind. Swamp mud under her cold aching knees was frozen in patches; crackling starbursts erupted at her slightest squirm, jagged sounds appallingly loud in the fading stillness. And she could feel the eyes of the two men, her husband and her brother, angrily on her from the opposite blind. Their eyeholes were slits.

The decoys sat on the glassy pond like dark spots on an old mirror. They were lure. The wooden blinds were shields, deceptions to conceal men from creatures of the sky. She felt as much *ashamed* now as anything else.

And it was so strange, all of it. . . .

Dusk was destroying the afternoon with such slowness; she could not perceive the fading of the light, no matter how hard she tried to focus, no matter what individual thing she stared at—an ice-sparkling log shaped like a dead troll, a patch of shaggy black leaves alone on a naked tree. The whole day had been a stupid waste, except for this.

Because if night were a spell, it was terrifyingly wondrous to watch. One never did, not in the city; during this forced male ritual called hunting one did little else.

One lay in wait to kill, thought Helen.

Yet she tried harder to be still. Somehow it was a matter of pride.

Her own idiocy had brought her out here today, after all. Some shred, some last particle of desire to see something in her man, anything worth admiring. And, God knew, this wasn't filling the bill.

It would be fully dark soon. She would have her hot shower and emerge, steamy-naked. She would demand the divorce with a sweet smile. The camouflage clothes would disappear, mud and ice, boots too; the trash compactor was forever.

And you'll be alone all over again. . . .

Blocking thought, not allowing data to collate into words that would laugh at her like some spy within herself, she stared ferociously at the lifeless luster of the fading pond. The two clusters, fifteen plastic ducks each, wiggled with her own eye exertion.

Staring long enough at a rock made it creep toward you. Or maybe things did creep, except we never watched long enough to realize, she thought. Believing stupid things had always been a problem. Her husband called her a romantic. He smirked when he said it, not without contempt.

Like you talk to a bright but stubborn child. . . .

Her name was Helen and she wanted to stand up and scream now. Yes, she was going to make a hell of a lot of noise and stand up, right this minute.

Her heart sneaked into her throat.

God, they'll be just furious!

If anyone was ridiculous, Helen knew that it was herself. Her body wouldn't move. She just did not dare. And maybe part of it too was the trancelike suspension of time and reality—the pond itself, its dying silver luster, its stunned and pale wintry colors that somehow calmed her deeply, though her clenched teeth wanted to chatter like ice in a drink.

Bob's black Lab was in the other blind with them. Even the dog had abandoned her.

Probably curled up warming their goddamned boots. . . .

If she had any brains or guts, she would jump up and yell or do anything. She would stomp and demand to be taken back to the city. If she had any courage, she wouldn't mind looking silly, she would not be here at all, she would be in a hot tub somewhere trying for the fourth orgasm, she would make herself get up

right now go on and get up you ninny!

Helen started to stand up. She was going to get up and go slog and slip over to her brother's new Jeep and start the engine and turn on the heater.

And I hope to God they bitch about it. . . .

Something honked.

She had half risen, knee joints popping, a grin on her face because of the way her brother and husband would howl at her noise. She stopped rising. Hearing that strange honking sound, she looked into the pinkish sky, scanning the black crowns of treeless oaks and sweetgum.

It honked again.

Looking up now, Helen heard a flapping of heavy wings that beat the cold air, somewhere high above.

The air made a whispering, shifting sound.

Helen gasped. With incredible grace, a large shape was wheeling round against the deep purple-pink dusk. Still high but sliding downward, it came arcing back toward the pond. Her nape was electrified by the sheer majesty of the thing.

"A *goose!*" she heard her husband's voice hiss.

Ducks were hard to lure in, her husband always said. But geese were legendary, once-in-a-lifetime. The shape turned and its wingspan caught the horizon glow. Now she saw the sleek body and incredibly long neck. Its beauty was sensuous, its motions hypnotic.

The powerful wings dropped like great knives as the creature sank swiftly toward the far end of the pond.

Helen was stunned.

It wasn't gray like a goose at all. Its neck was *so* long. She stared because it was like a thing out of a fairy tale book, here in this awful place, coming in. It was white as snow, she saw. It wasn't a goose at all. It was a—

"A . . . *swan?*" came her brother's faint whisper from the opposite blind.

Helen, crouched and peering numbly through the planks and thatch, felt a wave of inner heat. The great bird was more than merely lovely; like a regal being, it swept onto the water. She watched it circle, neck looping and wings folding, swimming toward the duck decoys with their painted eyes.

It honked at the plastic objects and Helen heard a *click*, metallic on the frigid dusk air. She realized what was about to happen. The thought hit her like a little spurt of madness.

"NO!" She screamed, rising awkwardly, twisting; one foot was asleep and she fell and waved in horror: "NOOO!"

With a powerful thrust of wings it lifted. The twin blasts of shotguns boomed. Ears ringing, Helen fell forward out of the blind as if they'd shot her.

"Hey!" shouted Bob, her husband.

"Where'd it *go?*" yelled her brother Harry.

"Shit!" said Bob, running toward the pond.

Helen stood up. The front of her camouflage jumpsuit was heavy with frozen mud. Astonished, in sudden joy, she saw no bleeding white corpse on the water, no feathers floating in air. Not a trace of the swan or even the sound of beating wings.

The plastic ducks, bobbing on consecutive ripples, were hardly more than black splotches. Night was falling. The Labrador retriever stood between the cursing men while the decoys were hauled in. Helen watched the dog gaze up at the trees; it was shivering, just as she was, and her body was not reacting to the cold.

"Let's haul ass," said Bob.

"Thanks a lot," Harry said, glaring at her. The dog stayed close beside Bob's leg, constantly sneaking looks at the pond behind it.

A few minutes later Helen sat with the dog in the back jumpseat of the Jeep.

"I hope to hell you're happy," bitched Bob. He was pouring Bourbon and Coke in plastic cups, spilling it on his lap. "I just hope you're damn satisfied, Helen."

She said nothing, filled with an inexplicable wonder. She *was* happy, but not satisfied: she wanted to see the swan again.

Beside her the black dog whined, shuddering badly. Muddy ruts leaped up and down in the yellowish cones of the headlights. Naked trees passed in clusters like ancient pillars.

"If you're such a goddamned bird lover," Bob said, "you should've stayed home."

"What's wrong with the dog?" asked Harry, as if that would be the last straw.

Helen didn't answer them; her mind was too full of the sensual majesty of the swan. The strange excitement of being so near it was unlike anything she'd ever felt before, and she tried to hold on to the sensation. The two men up front seemed bestial, crude; the reflections of their faces glowed on the inner glass, greenish with panel light. She had saved the great bird from their savagery, she thought.

"We'll *never* see another one," griped Harry, who was a CPA. Bob was a tax attorney, like Helen.

"Nobody'll ever believe us, either," said Bob.

"You know?" said Harry. "I could *swear* I hit him."

"Man, I had my bead right *on* that sucker," agreed Bob.

Helen thought she saw a blur of motion far off in the dark. The big Lab stiffened, hackles rising; he growled.

"He's about as frustrated as me," said Bob.

Harry said, "Hit that bastard *twice* with my 12-gauge, and number-four shot ought to penetrate. Shit, and then I kind of just didn't . . . see it."

"Maybe it went right down."

"Sink?" Harry laughed angrily. "Get serious. The big bastard outsmarted us, that's all, thanks to Lady Jane back there. Ducked into the trees carrying our shot loads. Probably some plowboy'll find it frozen like a rock on his back forty in the morning. I *know* I hit it."

The big dog barked, jarring Helen. The men jerked in their seats at the explosive loudness inside the tight Jeep. Bob reached back and slapped the animal's nose. Helen peered into the black trees where the Labrador kept staring.

"How big was that sucker?" said Harry. "To me it looked nearly as big as a man, almost."

"The one that got away," said Bob. "But I'd swear it was huge. There's a five-grand fine for nailing a swan, if you ever see one. That's how big a chance we blew today."

Helen saw a whitish motion disappear behind a black tree. A growl curdled in the Labrador's throat. The dog pushed against Helen and she felt its violent shivering.

"What the hell's wrong with him?" groaned Bob.

"Blue-nuts," suggested Harry. "Wanted that big bird."

The vehicle bounced sharply through a twist of muddy trees. Under Helen's feet some of the duck decoys looked up at her with those lifeless eyes. Suddenly, the Jeep was grinding to a stop, so abruptly that Helen had to grab the dog and the seat, thrown violently forward.

"Look!" whispered Bob.

Harry said something Helen couldn't decipher. To their left she saw a glow. Dimly through icy trees she saw that it was a campfire.

"Damn," said Harry angrily.

Two hunters sat at the campfire on folding camp chairs. A new Jeep the same color as Bob's was parked behind the fire. A bottle of Bourbon gleamed in one hunter's hand and the other held a shotgun. The scene was like something out of an L. L. Bean catalog except for one thing—across the hood of the Jeep, glimmering gorgeously in the periphery of the campfire's radiance, was a large white shape. Even from here she saw what it was. The great white wings were spread open, trophylike, nearly covering the whole hood and fender of the Jeep. A sick heat soured in her chest.

"Damn," repeated Harry.

Bob said, "That's our bird!"

The Labrador made no sound now. It was pressed so hard against Helen's side she could hardly breathe. Her fingers clenched the seat top as the Jeep gunned abruptly at a hard angle toward the campfire.

The two hunters there sat undisturbed, gazing serenely into their fire, not even looking up as the vehicle roared up to a halt.

Bob was blustering but Harry grabbed his gun. They piled out of the Jeep. Helen squeezed out behind them. The dog refused to move at all; she saw its baleful eyes full of the glow of the fire. Its fangs were bared and a string of drool hung from its trembling chin.

But she didn't care about the dog. No more than she cared what happened between Bob and Harry and those two men at the fire. Helen forced herself to breathe, her eyes fixed upon the majestic whiteness that seemed to lounge massively across the front of that Jeep. The shapely white head seemed turned toward her, as if watching her with those noble obsidian eyes. Her boots scraped the frozen ground.

"Quite a bird there," said Bob at the fire.

"How you boys doing?" said Harry, beside Bob.

"Find the bird dying, did you?" asked Bob.

Helen stopped and for some reason turned to look at her brother and husband, hearing the odd tone in their voices. The two hunters still sat implacably gazing into their fire, eyes not meeting Bob or Harry.

"Hey," said Bob darkly.

Harry said, "You boys kidding us or what?"

Past a brother she hadn't liked for years, past a husband she loathed, Helen stared directly at the two seated hunters. Bob reached for the one closest to him. Helen saw how clean and crisp the hunter's clothes were, how his skin looked so perfectly smooth and how his eyes weren't looking up as Bob's hand reached tentatively toward his shoulder. Helen looked at the other one and saw an ember that swirled from the fire. It landed on the hunter's unblinking eyeball.

At the edge of the clearing the Labrador yowled and skittered into the dark, baying as it fled.

Harry screamed and Helen gave a giddily crazy little laugh, but Bob made no sound at all, running for the open door of his Jeep.

But a huge white shape was there; Helen saw it descend upon Bob with a beating of wings. Harry staggered backward with a bleating sound in his throat. Helen vaguely heard him fire his shotgun once; she hardly cared.

She had stepped backward toward the fire.

She bumped one of the hunters and he toppled out of his chair. She twisted to look. Still folded in the sitting position, he fell forward uncomplaining into the fire. His serenely gazing face sank into the orange coals, the unblinking eyes and silent lips beginning to burn.

Silvery masses moved in the black trees just beyond the light. Harry and Bob no longer yelled, but she was aware of the faint and distant howling of the fleeing dog.

A silvery shape loomed over her.

The eyes that looked deep into hers were like black living glass. There was nothing on the hood of the Jeep behind it. The great white head swayed on the looping, silken neck and a velvety bill moved with alien curiosity, softly across her face. A flash of heat poured through her body and she knew she would scream now. But she didn't.

Great satin wings enfolded her with the strength of steel cords. Around her in the dying firelight the camp scene was withering, shriveling like skins of deflating balloons, and she saw the face of the fallen hunter melting in the coals like plastic.

The velvety bill probed her collar and found the throat of her blouse and she let herself be silently pressed into the dark.

Introduction

Love is an obsessive emotion, and an overwhelming one. Once you're caught up in it, you can think of little else but the object of your affection. Back then, if memory serves, it was wonderful and miserable at the same time—now, it's simply miserable. Especially when your lover returns the favor.

Melissa Mia Hall is a poet and photographer from Texas, and she has just completed her first novel.

RAPTURE

by Melissa Mia Hall

He knew what she was not long ago. The discovery came upon him with a thrill of thanksgiving, of joy, of release. He dreams of the moment when he will tell her he knows. He lives for that moment. And she will share with him her life.

His hands grip the beer mug unsteadily. He sets it down on the counter and looks at her in the fern-enshrouded corner. Her protruding upper lip gives her a perpetual childlike sweetness. Her wide empty eyes are avoiding his.

She touches her current companion's hand and shakes her head slowly. She laughs and the stranger drinks the rest of his bourbon in one hasty gulp. She murmurs something deliciously low. The companion nods.

David looks at the popcorn kernels in the bowl before him. He cups a few in his palm restlessly. The waiting tonight has become too long and too tense. He glances at them again. Tonight her name is Willo, on other nights it has been Lara, Christine, and others. Tonight her blond hair swings loose around her face, faintly curled and fragrant. Pale, icy, fragile, tall. Her legs cross and re-cross. The stranger will know them but maybe nothing else. Or he will know everything. David burns with a sudden flame of jealousy. But the stranger doesn't know what she is. And David does. He knows. She only wears gold jewelry. He's never seen her near a cross or a mirror, or during the day when the sun shines hard and bright.

The popcorn kernels are bullets biting into the flesh of his closed fist. He grimaces and throws them back into the bowl. He wishes she'd get it over with. He finishes his third beer and slips down from the barstool. The bar swims with smoke and businessmen afraid to go home. A fern twirls above him and he ducks his head awkwardly. A drunk swipes at him merrily, thinking him a compadre.

"Had a little too much, fella, well, let me tell you . . ."

David feigns a laugh and moves toward the door. He goes outside and checks the sky nervously. Still night, no sign of dawn. Of course, he knows it can't be that late. A loving couple jostles him accidentally on their way inside. The woman winks at him and smiles, "Hey, baby." Her boyfriend jerks her closer. David hates them. He stares at the parking lot. Her Mercedes is parked near his Volkswagen. It's more convenient that way.

She must hurry.

As David returns to the bar he sees that they are standing. He leans against a wall and sucks his breath in tightly as they go past, creating an enormous heat inside his gut. Perspiration breaks out all over his body. He follows them, shivering when the night air touches his skin.

A saxophone wails and cries out as he leaves the bar.

His car sputters and dies twice, but he manages to catch up to them at the light at the intersection right past the bar. He smiles with relief. If she doesn't know he knows what she is, she does know that he's been following her for the last couple of weeks. It's become a game of sorts.

Just now she's looking over her shoulder at him, her face an oval of obscurity. He imagines her red lips smiling. The light changes. The two cars charge into what remains of the night.

David turns the radio up for the drive out to her secluded house half-embedded in the earth, a trendy house with the focus on saving energy and blending into the environment without disturbing it. A rich house for a rich woman. David starts singing and their cars pass and repass each other. He almost drives too fast, singing too loudly about being tied to a mast and of rocks and of home, singing much too loudly. He lapses into silence as they arrive. The stranger can go into the house but he cannot. He parks the Volkswagen out of sight and waits.

He stirs sleepily in the early sun. Birds scream out overhead, pinwheeling and diving. David snatches at the fading dream of blood in a chalice spilled over a soft, naked torso. Willo/Lara/ Christine. He staggers out of the car and views the house mournfully. The Mercedes sits in the circular driveway, shining red and knowing. He's made a ritual of going to the door each morning after one of her feedings. He likes to touch the stained glass circle and brush the pewter handle with a kiss. It's always locked.

But not today.

David gapes at the slender opening. The stranger must have forgotten to close it when he left her side, if he left her side. She may have drunk too much. She may have killed him.

He enters the house, passes through the rooms in a daze, following what he imagines to be her scent. It will lead him to the bedroom. He descends deeper and deeper into the heart of her house. He passes many pictures and book-lined walls. He feels the darkness of the colors she has chosen to live among, deep browns, blues, and other dusky, nameless colors. Finally, he comes to what must be her room. A door made of walnut is open an inch. He goes through the doorway and closes the door quietly behind him. He turns to regard the blackness.

Blood drips from the air, cloying and sweet.

Suddenly, light enflames a lamp in a corner and he can see the room dimly, the bed enclosed by a black canopy and drapes, the naked man on the floor and the naked woman sitting in a blue velvet chair, the ice princess, the beloved, her.

"I did not know if you would come. I didn't know if I wanted you to. But since you have, please do me a favor and take away this bastard. I cannot stand it. It's made me sick. I am so"—she hunched over her stomach—"sick."

David starts to speak and she shakes her head, begging for silence. "Please, just get him out of my house and lock the doors behind you, especially the front door."

"Is he dead?"

She shakes her head again. David's stomach rises to his throat. The thought of that stranger making her ill was overwhelming.

"Can I do anything for you?"

Her form hurts his eyes. He cannot have her yet; they cannot share. He has to look away.

He hears her move toward the bed. When he looks again, the

curtains of the bed have closed around her white body. The smell of blood has also gone. He wonders if he imagined it.

He listens to Boz Scaggs and stretches his lanky frame. He needs to eat something, a steak rare and juicy, oysters on the half shell, caviar, something, but all he has on hand is hamburger. He broils it quickly, heats some leftover squash, and eats alone just as he lives alone, sleeps alone. The stranger had been heavy to unload, an athlete from the looks of the muscles, and a newly turned junkie. He can't imagine why she made such a mistake choosing someone like that, so unclean.

He calls the office. His secretary's frantic. He was supposed to be in court this morning. David had forgotten. He'd never done that before. He tells her it won't happen again if he can help it. It was just that he was sick, still is sick, and hopefully, he'll be in the next day. His secretary oozes sympathy. He hangs up gratefully.

The rent will be due soon. He needs more clients. He wants to do better.

He goes to the bathroom and looks at his unshaven face. He does *not* want to do better. He does *not* need more clients. All that matters is her and the blood in the chalice. His blue eyes are rimmed with red. Sleep surges upward through his body. He sways on his feet. With effort he finds his unmade bed and strips his body of its wrinkled white shirt and jeans.

Night.

He awakens, his body revitalized and ready. He brushes his teeth after a hot shower. He shaves carefully and sings along with a Doobie Brothers album. He belts out, "Do you know that I love you? Do you know that I need you?" and laughs uncontrollably, feverish with anticipation. He has been a thrall to her, a servant; he has indeed served her. He will be rewarded. Then he wonders if she has left her house. It's been an hour since sunset. He has dawdled away precious time.

His heart pushes to get out of his chest. He looks down and imagines the skin bulging outward.

The needle is stuck on "You belong to me," but he hasn't time to fix it. He must run; he must hurry.

He pulls up to her house and parks his car behind hers. The front door is open and a yellow patch of light extends welcome. She expects him.

This may be the night of communion.

His hands clench and unclench as he walks into the house.

"Hello? Anybody home?" he says, hating the quaver in his tone and the inept choice of words.

She sits in a high-backed chair done in alternating stripes of green and burgundy. Her hair is done in two long, silky braids. She wears a simple violet shift with a boatneck and wide, loose sleeves. She gazes at him with an expectant but severe expression.

Wordlessly, he sits on a stool at her feet and waits raptly.

Her lips part and he sees the teeth he has dreamed about, the two canine points so often misunderstood. She speaks.

"I don't know what you want from me. I do know you've been watching me, have been following me for many nights. I don't even want to know why. Do you understand?" She folds her hands and looks at a nearby sculpture of a woman giving birth to a beast. She sighs. "I don't want to know why." The repetition startles her. She leans forward slightly and whispers, "I don't want to know what you want, understand?"

"I know what you are," he says, almost whining.

She shakes her head and sits back. He reaches forward, one hand wanting to grab the end of a braid. She slaps at him. He withdraws.

"Can I call you Willo or Lara or Christine?"

Her mouth purses.

"Well, can I call you something?"

"No, I have no name," she says sharply.

"But you are a vampire," he says, amazed he's finally done it, that it came out so easily.

"You go too far."

"I want you. I want you to—" He is unable to finish his request. He does not need to.

Her hands search out her ears. Her fingers flash with golden rings. She tucks her head down.

"I want you to go, please." There is a petulance, a childish sulkiness. "You make me mad."

"I won't go."

She sits up and changes her voice into a steel instrument. Her blue-gray eyes watch him closely.

"When you were silent, when you asked nothing, when you

were my shadow, then you were love, protection, and fear. I enjoyed you. Now you are a thousand voices, asking, always asking. Beware. You may be answered. Then what will you do?"

He begins unbuttoning his shirt. He takes it off and folds it neatly. Then he makes her touch his chest and her fingers are like frost upon grass. She regards this without emotion. He makes her fingers go to his throat.

"Please?" he says urgently.

She does not answer. Her lips remain fixed and rose-colored. She takes back her hands. He finishes undressing, then sits motionless, waiting.

The hours of the night dissipate around them. He waits and watches. She stares.

Toward dawn, David's heart flutters like a trapped bird's. He can no longer sustain the unknowing. She must free him. He reaches for her, kisses her marble mouth. Her eyes are like opals.

"Blood," he whispers.

She seems to laugh or cry softly, her face toward the open door.

"Morning comes, please hurry . . ."

She unbraids her golden hair and slips off her shift. David springs to his feet in hope. She takes his hand and guides him toward the door, where the dawn rolls in on a wave of pearly light. He pulls back, afraid for her.

"Blood," he says longingly.

She smiles as the sun rises and the pearls take fire. He screams, afraid she will die. The light pours over her smooth body. She glows with health.

David falls to the floor in extreme pain and disbelief. She kneels at his side, bends over him, her breasts brushing his bleeding, cracking chest.

"You are dying," she says.

"Why?" he groans, his mouth a charred pit her tongue enters with a kiss.

"It is what you wanted, isn't it?"

Introduction

I can remember, when I wasn't so prone to catching colds, thinking how great it was to walk in the rain, or to view a massive storm over the ocean or mountains, or sit with a book in the living room while thunder and lightning play games with the lights. It was great fun, and not at all frightening.

David Morrell, author of The Totem *and* First Blood, *lives in Iowa City, where he teaches English at the University of Iowa. His latest is the best-selling* Brotherhood of the Rose. *He eats bark and berries.*

THE STORM

by David Morrell

Gail saw it first. She came from the Howard Johnson's toward the heat haze in the parking lot where our son Jeff and I were hefting luggage into our station wagon. Actually, Jeff supervised. He gave me his excited ten-year-old advice about the best place for this suitcase and that knapsack. Grinning at his sun-bleached hair and nut-brown freckled face, I told him I could never have done the job without him.

It was 8 A.M., Tuesday, August 2, but even that early, the thermometer outside our motel unit had risen to eighty-five. The humidity was thick and smothering. Just from my slight exertion with the luggage, I'd sweated through my shirt and jeans, wishing I'd thought to put on shorts. To the east, the sun blazed, white and swollen, the sky an oppressive, chalky blue. This'd be one day when the station wagon's costly air conditioning wouldn't be a luxury but a necessity.

My hands were sweat-slick as I shut the hatch. Jeff nodded, satisfied with my work, then grinned beyond me. Turning, I saw Gail coming toward us. When she left the brown parched grass, her brow creased as her sandals touched the heat-softened asphalt parking lot.

"All set?" she asked.

Her smooth white shorts and cool blue top emphasized her tan.

She looked trim and lithe and wonderful. I'm not sure how she did it, but she seemed completely unaffected by the heat. Her hair was soft and golden. Her subtle trace of makeup made the day seem somehow cooler.

"Ready. Thanks to Jeff," I answered.

He grinned up proudly.

"Well, I paid the bill. I gave them back the key," Gail said. "Let's go." She paused. "Except—"

"What's wrong?"

"Those clouds." She pointed past my shoulder.

I turned—and frowned. In contrast with the blinding, chalky, eastern sky, I stared at numbing, pitch-black western clouds. They seethed on the far horizon, roiling, churning. Lightning flickered like a string of flashbulbs in the distance, the thunder so muted it rumbled hollowly.

"Now where the hell did *that* come from?" I said. "It wasn't there before I packed the car."

Gail squinted toward the thunderheads. "You think we should wait till it passes?"

"It isn't close." I shrugged.

"But it's coming fast." She bit her lip. "And it looks bad."

Jeff grabbed my hand. I glanced at his worried face.

"It's just a storm, son."

He surprised me, though. I'd misjudged what worried him.

"I want to go back home," he said. "I don't want to wait. I miss my friends. Please, can't we leave?"

I nodded. "I'm on your side. Two votes out of three, Gail. If you're really scared, though . . ."

"No. I . . ." Gail drew a breath and shook her head. "I'm being silly. It's just the thunder. You know how storms bother me." She ruffled Jeff's hair. "But I won't make us wait. I'm homesick, too."

We'd spent the past two weeks in Colorado, fishing, camping, touring ghost towns. The vacation had been perfect. But as eagerly as we'd gone, we were just as eager to be heading back. Last night, we'd stopped here in North Platte, a small, quiet town off Interstate 80, halfway through Nebraska. Now, today, we hoped we could reach home in Iowa by nightfall.

"Let's get moving then," I said. "It's probably a local storm. We'll drive ahead of it. We'll never see a drop of rain."

Gail tried to smile. "I hope."

Jeff hummed as we got in the station wagon. I steered toward the interstate, went up the eastbound ramp, and set the cruise control at fifty-five. Ahead, the morning sun glared through the windshield. After I tugged down the visors, I turned on the air conditioner, then the radio. The local weatherman said hot and hazy.

"Hear that?" I said. "He didn't mention a storm. No need to worry. Those are only heat clouds."

I was wrong. From time to time, I checked the rearview mirror, and the clouds loomed thicker, blacker, closer, seething toward us down the interstate. Ahead, the sun kept blazing fiercely though. Jeff wiped his sweaty face. I set the air conditioner for DESERT, but it didn't seem to help.

"Jeff, reach in the ice chest. Grab us each a Coke."

He grinned. But I suddenly felt uneasy, realizing too late he'd have to turn to open the chest in the rear compartment.

"Gosh," he murmured, staring back, awestruck.

"What's the matter?" Gail swung around before I could stop her. "Oh, my God," she said. "The clouds."

They were angry midnight chasing us. Lightning flashed. Thunder jolted.

"They still haven't reached us," I said. "If you want, I'll try outrunning them."

"Do *something*."

I switched off the cruise control and sped to sixty, then sixty-five. The strain of squinting toward the white-hot sky ahead of us gave me a piercing headache. I put on Polaroids.

But all at once, I didn't need them. Abruptly, the clouds caught up to us. The sky went totally black. We drove in roiling darkness.

"Seventy. I'm doing seventy," I said. "But the clouds are moving faster."

"Like a hurricane," Gail said. "That isn't possible. Not in Nebraska."

"I'm scared," Jeff said.

He wasn't the only one. Lightning blinded me, stabbing to the right and left of us. Thunder actually shook the car. Then the air became an eerie, dirty shade of green, and I started thinking about tornados.

"Find a place to stop!" Gail said.

But there wasn't one. The next town was Kearney, but we'd already passed the exit. I searched for a roadside park, but a sign said Rest Stop, Thirty Miles. I couldn't just pull off the highway. On the shoulder, if the rain obscured another driver's vision, we could all be hit and killed. No choice. I had to keep on driving.

"At least it isn't raining," I said.

As I did, the clouds unloaded. No preliminary sprinkle. Massive raindrops burst around us, gusting, roaring, pelting.

"I can't see!" I flicked the windshield wipers to their highest setting. They flapped in sharp, staccato, triple time. I peered through murky, undulating, windswept waves of water, struggling for a clear view of the highway.

I was going too fast. When I braked, the station wagon fishtailed. We skidded on the slippery pavement. I couldn't breathe. The tires gripped. I felt the jolt. Then the car was in control.

I slowed to forty, but the rain heaved with such force against the windshield, I still couldn't see.

"Pull your seatbelts tight," I told Gail and Jeff.

Though I never found that rest stop, I got lucky when a flash of lightning showed a sign, the exit for the next town, called Grand Island. Shaking from tension, I eased down the off-ramp. At the bottom, across from me, a Best Western motel was shrouded with rain. We left a wake through the flooded parking lot and stopped under the motel's canopy. My hands were stiff from clenching the steering wheel. My shoulders ached. My eyes felt swollen, raw.

Gail and Jeff got out, rain gusting under the canopy as they ran inside. I had to move the car to park it in the lot. I locked the doors, but though I sprinted, I was drenched and chilled when I reached the motel's entrance.

Inside, a small group stared past me toward the storm—two clerks, two waitresses, a cleaning lady. I shook.

"Mister, use this towel," the cleaning lady said. She took one from a pile on her cart.

I thanked her, wiping my dripping face and soggy hair.

"See any accidents?" a waitress asked.

With the towel around my neck I shook my head.

"A storm this sudden, there ought to be accidents," the waitress said as if doubting me.

I frowned when she said *sudden*. "You mean it's just starting here?"

A skinny clerk stepped past me to the window. "Not too long before you came. A minute maybe. I looked out this window, and the sky was bright. I knelt to tie my shoe. When I stood up, the clouds were here—as black as night. I don't know where they came from all of a sudden, but I never saw it rain so hard so fast."

"But—" I shivered, puzzled. "It hit us back near Kearney. We've been driving in it for an hour."

"You were on the edge of it, I guess," the clerk said, spellbound by the storm. "It followed you."

The second waitress laughed. "That's right. You brought it with you."

My wet clothes clung cold to me, but I felt a deeper chill.

"Looks like we've got other customers," the second clerk said, pointing out the window.

Other cars splashed through the torrent in the parking lot.

"Yeah, we'll be busy, that's for sure," the clerk said. He switched on the lobby's lights, but they didn't dispel the outside gloom.

The wind howled.

I glanced through the lobby. Gail and Jeff weren't around. "My wife and son," I said, concerned.

"They're in the restaurant," the second waitress said, smiling to reassure me. "Through that arch. They ordered coffee for you. Hot and strong."

"I need it. Thanks."

Dripping travelers stumbled in.

We waited an hour. Though the coffee was as hot as promised, it didn't warm me. In the air-conditioning, my soggy clothes stuck to the chilly chrome-and-plastic seat. A bone-deep, freezing numbness made me sneeze.

"You need dry clothes," Gail said. "You'll catch pneumonia."

I'd hoped the storm would stop before I went out for the clothes. But even in the restaurant, I felt the thunder rumble. I couldn't wait. My muscles cramped from shivering. "I'll get a suitcase," I said and stood.

"Dad, be careful." Jeff looked worried.

Smiling, I leaned down and kissed him. "Son, I promise."

Near the restaurant's exit, one waitress I'd talked to came over. "You want to hear a joke?"

I didn't, but I nodded politely.

"On the radio," she said. "The local weatherman. He claims it's hot and clear."

I shook my head, confused.

"The storm." She laughed. "He doesn't know it's raining. All his instruments, his radar and his charts, he hasn't brains enough to look outside and see what kind of day it is. If anything, the rain got worse." She laughed again. "The biggest joke—that dummy's my husband."

I remembered she'd been the waitress who joked that I'd brought the storm with me. Her sense of humor troubled me, but I laughed to be agreeable and went to the lobby.

It was crowded. More rain-drenched travelers pushed in, cursing the weather. They tugged at sour, dripping clothes and bunched before the motel's counter, wanting rooms.

I squeezed among them at the big glass door, squinting out at the wildest storm I'd ever seen. Above the exclamations of the crowd, I heard the shriek of the wind.

My hand reached for the door.

It hesitated. I really didn't want to go out.

The skinny desk clerk suddenly stood next to me. "It could be you're not interested," he said.

I frowned, surprised.

"We're renting rooms so fast we'll soon be all full up," he said. "But fair is fair. You got here first. I saved a room. In case you plan on staying."

"I appreciate it. But we're leaving soon."

"You'd better take another look."

I did. Lightning split a tree. The window shook from thunder.

A scalding bath, I thought. A sizzling steak. Warm blankets while my clothes get dry.

"I changed my mind. We'll take that room."

All night, thunder shook the building. Even with the drapes shut, I saw brilliant streaks of lightning. I slept fitfully, waking with a headache. Six A.M.; it still was raining.

On the radio the weatherman sounded puzzled. As the lightning's static garbled what he said, I learned that Grand Island was suffering the worst storm in its history. Streets were flooded, sewers blocked, basements overflowing. An emergency had been declared, the damage in the millions. But the cause of the storm seemed inexplicable. The weather pattern made no sense. The front was tiny, localized, and stationary. Half a mile outside Grand Island—north and south, east and west—the sky was cloudless.

That last statement was all I needed to know. We quickly dressed and went downstairs to eat. We checked out shortly after seven.

"Driving in this rain?" the desk clerk said. He had the tact to stop before he said, "You're crazy."

"Listen to the radio," I answered. "Half a mile away, the sky is clear."

I'd have stayed if it hadn't been for Gail. Her fear of storms—the constant lightning and thunder—made her frantic.

"Get me out of here," she said.

And so we went.

And almost didn't reach the interstate. The car was hubcap-deep in water. The distributor was damp. I nearly killed the battery before I got the engine started. The brakes were soaked. They failed as I reached the local road. Skidding, blinded, I swerved around the blur of an abandoned truck, missing the entrance to the interstate. Backing up, I barely saw the ditch in time. But finally, we headed up the ramp, rising above the flood, doing twenty down the highway.

Jeff was white-faced. I'd bought some comics for him, but he was too scared to read them.

"The odometer," I told him. "Watch the numbers. Half a mile, and we'll be out of this."

I counted tenths of a mile with him. "One, two, three . . ."

The storm grew darker, stronger.

"Four, five, six . . ."

The numbers felt like broken glass wedged in my throat.

"But Dad, we're half a mile away. The rain's not stopping."

"Just a little farther."

But instead of ending, it got worse. We had to stop in Lincoln. The next day, the storm persisted. We pressed on to Omaha. We could normally drive from Colorado to our home in Iowa City in two leisured days.

But *this* trip took us seven long, slow, agonizing days. We had to stop in Omaha and then Des Moines and towns whose names I'd never heard of. When we at last reached home, we felt so exhausted, so frightened we left our bags in the car and stumbled from the garage to bed.

The rain slashed against the windows. It drummed on the roof. I couldn't sleep. When I peered out, I saw a waterfall from the overflowing eaves trough. Lightning struck a hydro pole. I settled to my knees and recollected every prayer I'd ever learned and then invented stronger ones.

The hydro was fixed by morning. The phone still worked. Gail called a friend and asked the question. As she listened to the answer, I was startled by the way her face shrank and her eyes receded. Mumbling "Thanks," she set the phone down.

"It's been dry here," she said. "Then last night at eight the storm began."

"But that's when we arrived. My God, what's happening?"

"Coincidence." She frowned. "The storm front moved in our direction. We kept trying to escape. Instead, we only followed it."

The fridge was bare. I told Gail I'd get some food and warned Jeff not to go outside.

"But Dad, I want to see my friends."

"Watch television. Don't go out till the rain stops."

"It won't end."

I froze. "What makes you say that?"

"Not today it won't. The sky's too dark. The rain's too hard."

I nodded, relaxing. "Then call your friends. But don't go out."

When I opened the garage door, I watched the torrent. Eight days since I'd seen the sun. Damp clung on me. Gusts angled toward me.

I drove from the garage and was swallowed.

Gail looked overjoyed when I came back. "It stopped for forty minutes." She grinned with relief.

"But not where I was."

The nearest supermarket was half a mile away. Despite my umbrella and raincoat, I'd been drenched when I lurched through the hissing automatic door of the supermarket. Fighting to catch my breath, I'd fumbled with the inside-out umbrella and muttered to a clerk about the goddamn endless rain.

The clerk hadn't known what I meant. "But it started just a minute ago."

I shuddered, but not from the water dripping off me.

Gail heard me out and gaped. Her joy turned into frightened disbelief. "As soon as you came back, the storm began again."

The bottom fell out of my soggy grocery bag. I found a weather station on the radio. But the announcer's static-garbled voice sounded as bewildered as his counterparts through Nebraska.

His report was the same. The weather pattern made no sense. The front was tiny, localized, and stationary. Half a mile away, the sky was cloudless. In a small circumference, however, Iowa City was enduring its most savage storm on record. Downtown streets were . . .

I shut off the radio.

Thinking frantically, I told Gail I was going to my office at the university to see if I had mail. But my motive was quite different, and I hoped she wouldn't think of it.

She started to speak as Jeff came into the kitchen, interrupting us, his eyes bleak with cabin fever. "Drive me down to Freddie's, Dad?"

I didn't have the heart to tell him no.

At the school the parking lot was flecked with rain. There weren't any puddles, though. I live a mile away. I went into the English building and asked a secretary, though I knew what she'd tell me.

"No, Mr. Price. All morning it's been clear. The rain's just beginning."

In my office I phoned home.

"The rain stopped," Gail said. "You won't believe how beautiful the sky is, bright and sunny."

I stared from my office window toward a storm so black and ugly I barely saw the whitecaps on the angry churning river.

Fear coiled in my guts, then hissed and struck.

The pattern was always the same. No matter where I went, the storm went with me. When I left, the storm left as well. It got worse. Nine days of it. Then ten. Eleven. Twelve. Our basement flooded, as did all the other basements in the district. Streets eroded. There were mudslides. Shingles blew away. Attics leaked. Retaining walls fell over. Lightning struck the hydro poles so often the food spoiled in our freezer. We lit candles. If our stove hadn't used gas, we couldn't have cooked. As in Grand Island, an emergency was declared, the damage so great it couldn't be calculated.

What hurt the most was seeing the effect on Gail and Jeff. The constant chilly damp gave them colds. I sneezed and sniffled too but didn't care about myself because Gail's spirits sank the more it rained. Her eyes became dismal gray. She had no energy. She put on sweaters and rubbed her listless, aching arms.

Jeff went to bed much earlier than usual. He slept later. He looked thin and pale.

And he had nightmares. As lightning cracked, his screams woke us. Again the hydro wasn't working. We used flashlights as we hurried to his room.

"Wake up, Jeff! You're only dreaming!"

"The Indian!" He moaned and rubbed his frightened eyes.

Thunder rumbled, making Gail jerk.

"What Indian?" I said.

"He warned you."

"Son, I don't know what—"

"In Colorado." Gail turned sharply, startling me with the hollows the darkness cast on her cheeks. "The weather dancer."

"You mean that witch doctor?"

On our trip we'd stopped in a dingy desert town for gas and seen a meager group of tourists studying a roadside Indian display. A shack, trestles, beads and drums and belts. Skeptical, I'd walked across. A scruffy Indian, at least a hundred, dressed in threadbare faded vestments, had chanted gibberish while he danced around a circle of rocks in the dust.

"What's going on?" I asked a woman aiming a camera.

"He's a medicine man. He's dancing to make it rain and end the drought."

I scuffed the dust and glanced at the burning sky. My head ached from the heat and the long oppressive drive. I'd seen too many sleazy roadside stands, too many Indians ripping off tourists, selling overpriced inauthentic artifacts. Imperfect turquoise, shoddy silver. They'd turned their back on their heritage and prostituted their traditions.

I didn't care how much they hated us for what we'd done to them. What bothered me was behind their stoic faces they laughed as they duped us.

Whiskey fumes wafted from the ancient Indian as he clumsily danced around the circle, chanting.

"Can he do it?" Jeff asked. "Can he make it rain?"

"It's a gimmick. Watch these tourists put money in that so-called native bowl he bought at Sears."

They heard me, rapt faces suddenly suspicious.

The old man stopped performing. "Gimmick?" He glared.

"I didn't mean to speak so loud. I'm sorry if I ruined your routine."

"I made that bowl myself."

"Of course you did."

He lurched across, the whiskey fumes stronger. "You don't think my dance can make it rain?"

"I couldn't care less if you fool these tourists, but my son should know the truth."

"You want convincing?"

"I said I was sorry."

"White men always say they're sorry."

Gail came over, glancing furtively around. Embarrassed, she tugged at my sleeve. "The gas tank's full. Let's go."

I backed away.

"You'll see it rain! You'll pray it stops!" the old man shouted.

Jeff looked terrified, and that made me angry. "Shut your mouth! You scared my son!"

"He wonders if I can make it rain? Watch the sky! I dance for you now! When the lightning strikes, remember me!"

We got in the car. "That crazy coot. Don't let him bother you. The sun cooked his brain."

"All right, he threatened me. So what?" I said. "Gail, you surely can't believe he sent this storm. By dancing? Think. It isn't possible."

"Then tell me why it's happening."

"A hundred weather experts tried but can't explain it. How can I?"

"The storm's linked to you. It never leaves you."

"It's . . ."

I meant to say "coincidence" again, but the word had lost its meaning and smothered in my lungs. I studied Gail and Jeff, and in the glare of the flashlights I realized they blamed me. We were adversaries, both of them against me.

"The rain, Dad. Can't you make it stop?"

I cried when he whispered "Please."

Department of Meteorology. A full professor, one associate, and one assistant. But I'd met the full professor at a cocktail party several years ago. We sometimes met for tennis. On occasion, we had lunch together. I knew his office hours and braved the storm to go to see him.

Again the parking lot was speckled with increasing raindrops when I got there. I ran through raging wind and shook my raincoat in the lobby of his building. I'd phoned ahead. He was waiting.

Forty-five, freckled, almost bald. In damn fine shape though, as I knew from many tennis games I'd lost.

"The rain's back." He shook his head disgustedly.

"No explanation yet?"

"I'm supposed to be the expert. Your guess would be as good as mine. If this keeps up, I'll take to reading tea leaves."

"Maybe superstition's . . ." I wanted to say "the answer," but I couldn't force myself.

"What?" He leaned forward.

I rubbed my aching forehead. "What causes thunderstorms?"

He shrugged. "Two different fronts collide. One's hot and moist. The other's cold and dry. They bang together so hard they explode. The lightning and thunder are the blast. The rain's the fallout."

"But in *this* case?"

"That's the problem. We don't have two different fronts. Even if we did, the storm would move because of vacuums the winds create. But this storm stays right here. It only shifts a half a mile or so and then comes back. It's forcing us to reassess the rules."

"I don't know how to . . ." But I told him. Everything.

He frowned. "And you believe this?"

"I'm not sure. My wife and son do. Is it possible?"

He put some papers away. He poured two cups of coffee. He did everything but rearrange his bookshelves.

"Is it possible?" I said.

"If you repeat this, I'll deny it."

"How much crazier can—?"

"In the sixties, when I was in grad school, I went on a field trip to Mexico. The mountain valleys have such complicated weather patterns they're perfect for a dissertation. One place gets so much rain the villages are flooded. Ten miles away another valley gets no rain whatsoever. In one valley I studied, something had gone wrong. It normally had lots of rain. For seven years, though, it had been completely dry. The valley next to it, normally dry, was getting all the rain. No explanation. God knows, I worked hard to find one. People were forced to leave their homes and go where the rain was. In this seventh summer they stopped hoping the weather would behave the way it used to. They wanted to return to their valley, so they sent for special help. A weather dancer. He claimed to be a descendent of the Mayans. He arrived one day and paced the valley, praying to all the compass points. Where they intersected in the valley's middle, he arranged a wheel of stones. He put on vestments. He danced around the wheel. One day later it was raining, and the weather pattern went back to the way it used to be. I told myself he'd been lucky, that he'd somehow read the signs of nature and danced when he was positive it would rain, no matter if he danced or not. But I saw those clouds rush in, and they were strange. They didn't move till the streams were flowing and the wells were full. Coincidence? Special knowledge? Who can say? But it scares me when I think about what happened in that valley."

"Then the Indian I met could cause this storm?"

"Who knows? Look, I'm a scientist. I trust in facts. But sometimes 'superstition' is a word we use for science we don't understand."

"What happens if the storm continues, if it doesn't stop?"

"Whoever lives beneath it will have to move, or else they'll die."

"But what if it follows someone?"

"You really believe it would?"

"It does!"

He studied me. "You ever hear of a superstorm?"

Dismayed, I shook my head.

"On rare occasions, several storms will climb on top of each other. They can tower as high as seven miles."

I gaped.

"But this storm's already climbed that high. It's heading up to ten now. It'll soon tear houses from foundations. It'll level every-thing. A stationary half-mile-wide tornado."

"If I'm right, though, if the old man wants to punish me, I can't escape. Unless my wife and son are separate from me, they'll die, too."

"Assuming you're right. But I have to emphasize—there's no scientific reason to believe you are."

"I think I'm crazy."

Eliminate the probable, then the possible. What's left must be the explanation. Either Gail and Jeff would die, or they'd have to leave me. But I couldn't bear losing them.

I knew what I had to do. I struggled through the storm to get back home. Jeff was feverish. Gail kept coughing, glaring at me in accusation.

They argued when I told them, but in desperation they agreed.

"If what we think is true," I said, "once I'm gone, the storm'll stop. You'll see the sun again."

"But what about you? What'll happen?"

"I wish I knew. Pray for me."

We kissed and wept.

I packed the car. I left.

The interstate again, heading west. The storm, of course, went with me.

Iowa. Nebraska. I spent three insane, disastrous weeks getting to Colorado. Driving through rain-swept mountains was a night-mare. But I finally reached that dingy desert town. I found that sleazy roadside stand.

No trinkets, no beads. As the storm raged, turning dust to mud, I searched the town, begging for information. "That old Indian. The weather dancer."

"He took sick."

"Where is he?"

"How should I know? Try the reservation."

It was fifteen miles away. The road wound narrow, mucky. I passed rocks so hot they steamed from rain. The car slid, crashing in a ditch, resting on its drive shaft. I ran through lightning and thunder, drenched and moaning when I stumbled to the largest building on the reservation. It was low and wide, made from stone.

I pounded on the door. A man in uniform opened it, the agent for the government.

I told him.

He stared suspiciously. Turning, he spoke a different language to some Indians in the office. They answered.

He nodded. "You must want him bad," he said, "if you came out here in this storm. You're almost out of time. The old man's dying."

In the reservation's hospital, the old man lay motionless under sheets, an I.V. in his arm. Shriveled, he looked like a dry, empty cornhusk. He slowly opened his eyes. They gleamed with recognition.

"I believe you now," I said. "Please, make the rain stop."

He breathed in pain.

"My wife and son believe. It isn't fair to make them suffer. Please." My voice rose. "I shouldn't have said what I did. I'm sorry. Make it stop."

The old man squirmed.

I sank to my knees, kissed his hand, and sobbed. "I know I don't deserve it. But I'm begging. I've learned my lesson. Stop the rain."

The old man studied me and slowly nodded. The doctor tried to restrain him, but the old man's strength was more than human. He crawled from bed. He chanted and danced.

The lightning and thunder worsened. Rain slashed the windows. The old man danced harder. The frenzy of the storm increased. Its strident fury soared. It reached a crescendo, hung there—and stopped.

The old man fell. Gasping, I ran to him and helped the doctor lift him in bed.

The doctor glared. "You almost killed him."

"He isn't dead?"

"No thanks to you."

But I said, "Thanks"—to the old man and the powers in the sky.

I left the hospital. The sun, a common sight I used to take for granted, overwhelmed me.

Four days later, back in Iowa, I got the call. The agent from the government. He thought I'd want to know. That morning, the old man had died.

I turned to Gail and Jeff. Their colds were gone. From warm sunny weeks while I was away, their skin was brown again. They seemed to have forgotten how the nightmare had nearly destroyed us, more than just our lives, our love. Indeed, they now were skeptical about the Indian and told me the rain would have stopped, no matter what I did.

But they hadn't been in the hospital to see him dance. They didn't understand.

I set the phone down and swallowed, sad. Stepping from our house—it rests on a hill—I peered in admiration toward the sky.

I turned and faltered.

To the west, a massive cloudbank approached, dark and thick and roiling. Wind began, bringing a chill.

September 12. The temperature was seventy-eight. It dropped to fifty, then thirty-two.

The rain had stopped. The old man did what I asked. But I hadn't counted on his sense of humor.

He stopped the rain, all right.

But I knew the snow would never end.

Introduction

No matter how much you travel, nothing can ever compare to the first time you set eyes on something you've only read about in books or have seen in the movies; and nothing can compare with the thrill of discovering that your own favorite niches in history are as impressive as you'd imagined. They were, of course, never as terrifying.

Alan Ryan lives in the Bronx, travels often to England and Ireland, and has the world's largest collection of unwatched video tapes. His newest novel is Cast A Cold Eye.

I SHALL NOT LEAVE ENGLAND NOW

by Alan Ryan

I shall not leave England now.

I cannot.

It is true that there are but few ties that keep me here. But those that bind me hold me in their grasp firmly and forever.

The most powerful of them is the memory of an old man named Robert Clairthorpe, a name rather more elegant than his background, his poverty, and his humble station in life would suggest as suitable for him. But we grew very close in the short time we spent together, and I knew him for a man of bold and questing spirit. That is an awfully old-fashioned expression, "a man of bold and questing spirit," but it is just the sort of description, has just the right sort of flavor and implication, that Robert Clairthorpe would have liked. He would never have applied such words to himself, of course, but they are true of him, nevertheless. Could he have heard them in life, he would have smiled, I am certain, and shaken his head at the folly of the speaker.

I wish I could see my old friend smiling now. It would ease the passage of time for me. My days have grown long and wearisome, and the nights are even worse.

Insofar as these things may be said to have a beginning, I must start my story there.

Robert Clairthorpe was born in the second decade of this century and, according to his own account, abandoned when he was no more than twelve hours old. The infant, wrapped in a single thin blanket, was left by the side of a road, half a mile from the nearest cottage, in a remote part of the Isle of Wight. Fortunately, the weather was fair, but the passerby who found him and the local doctor who examined him had no way of judging how many hours the child had lain there. The local authorities were informed, of course, and discreet inquiries were made in the vicinity, paying close attention to serving girls employed in the better houses, but no indication, not even a likely possibility, of his parentage was ever discovered.

Through the intercession of the local clergyman, the infant was taken in and raised by a childless couple in the parish. Samuel and Margaret Coombes were poor—he was a wheelwright whose one skill was in ever-decreasing demand with the coming of the automobile—but they gave the child their home, their love, and their name.

Robert Coombes was a quiet child, not at all athletic, and not much suited to life in the countryside, but he was a good student and loved reading above all else in the world. In his youth, the hero of his favorite book of boys' adventure stories had been named Robert Clairthorpe, and in his eighteenth year, upon his arrival in London following the deaths of both his foster-parents, he changed his name to Clairthorpe.

But, though he was dazzled by the wonder and variety of London, the world had not intended a life of adventure for young Robert. The only success he had was in finding a place as a clerk in a small bookstore in an almost hidden back street of Bloomsbury, near the British Museum. Wealth had never been one of his goals, so he was satisfied where he was.

And he was satisfied to remain there. Six years after his arrival, the old proprietor of the shop passed away. Without children or family himself, he left the shop to his young assistant. Robert, absolved from all military service by his weak eyesight and generally frail physical condition, spent all the rest of his life in the bookshop, keeping it open six days a week and living alone, always surrounded by his beloved books, in the small dark room just behind it.

He was still there fifty years later when a lashing rainstorm drove me in at his door.

It seems odd now, with the memory of Robert Clairthorpe so vivid in my mind, to recall that I came to London that time seeking relief from memories.

I must state this part as simply as grief permits. Elizabeth, my beloved wife of forty years, had passed away very suddenly. As we had never been blessed with children, we were perhaps even more dependent on each other for love and support than other long-married couples. Neither of us had other living relatives, and hardly any other friends, and her death left me totally alone in the world. What is more, I had just retired from my position with the bank and purchased a home for us near Woodstock, in the Catskills, an area we both loved immensely and where we had been looking forward to spending our last years, away from the city, in each other's constant company, and pursuing together the interests for which there had never been adequate time before. So I was all the more alone, living by myself in an empty house, more than adequately supplied with income, but with all our happy plans crumbled to dust in my heart.

I had to leave. I had to get away.

I had always, through the years, loved London, loved all of England, and coming here seemed the best thing to do. Here I could find pleasure, entertainment, relaxation, perhaps a few new friends among my British banking acquaintances: here I could find distraction.

My career in banking had left little time for hobbies and other interests. Even so, I had done a fair bit of traveling, often combining business trips with vacations, and had occasionally contributed a minor travel article to several magazines. I loved music and had amassed an extensive library of recordings. And I collected books.

As it turned out, my tastes in reading were virtually identical to those of Robert Clairthorpe. It was that likeness of mind and sensibility that drew us so close so very quickly in our acquaintance, and that accounted for what happened to us after.

I came crashing into the shop that day, dripping wet and quite out of breath.

I was staying at a very comfortable bed-and-breakfast house in

Bedford Place, just around the corner from the British Museum in Great Russell Street. My situation would have permitted a finer hotel, at least for a short stay, but I preferred Bedford Place above all else. Completed in the first quarter of the eighteenth century, it is quiet, sedate, and pretty, only one elegant street long, with the trees of Bloomsbury Square at one end and the trees and roses of Russell Square at the other. On this particular day, I was exploring the narrower, less often traveled streets of the vicinity, when suddenly the heavens seemed to open and a moment later the rain was pounding down violently. I was in Little Russell Street, just behind the church that fronts on Bloomsbury Way, and there seemed no escaping the rain.

I was instantly soaked. I looked around for a shelter and saw the dark and dusty little bookshop. An elderly gentleman, perhaps ten years older than myself, stood in the doorway with his hand on the knob. Perhaps he had been watching the skies, or perhaps the sudden crashing noise of the rain had drawn him to the door. In any case, we saw each other at the same moment. He beckoned, and I dashed to the dry safety he offered.

It began so haphazardly, the product, in part, of all the circumstances of our lives up to the moment when we found ourselves together in that street. Then it needed only a sudden, chance spattering of rain, and we were both of us trapped.

"Come in, come in!" he said. "Oh dear, you're wet already!"

He instantly closed the door behind me, for the wind was driving the rain hard against the glass of the windows. As soon as it was firmly shut, we both breathed a little sigh of relief, as if we had just succeeded in rescuing ourselves from a band of ravening wolves. And a moment later we both laughed a little at ourselves, just a bit self-consciously. It was right then—we spoke about it a few days later and agreed—that each of us began to sense a kindred spirit in the other.

I thanked him for his kindness and told him, a little breathlessly, how glad I was that he'd been standing there just then. He shrugged away my gratitude. We stood for a moment, looking at the rain and listening to it clatter against the glass.

"It's a little like the start of a nineteenth-century novel, isn't it?" he said, but he murmured the words so softly that I wasn't quite sure if he'd spoken them aloud or if I'd had the thought myself.

"Here," he said, "you must have that coat off and warm up a bit. Will you take a cup of tea? I was just about to fix some."

Naturally, I hesitated, but as I looked around for the first time at the shop, and incidentally had my first good look at the kind face of Robert Clairthorpe, he said, "Do," and added, "You shall have to wait out the storm anyway."

The bookshop certainly suggested, to my way of thinking, at least as warm a welcome as its owner was offering to provide. The walls were lined from floor to ceiling with sagging shelves of books, and I could see at a glance that his stock ranged from used copies of recent bestsellers to yellow piles of *National Geographic* to fine older books and sets of classics. On a shelf near the door I recognized a complete set of Joseph Conrad, the edition signed in Volume I shortly before his death, for I had the same set on my own shelves in the now empty house in Woodstock. On an immense center table almost filling the floor space of the tiny shop were teetering piles of more books, of all ages, sizes, and conditions, apparently waiting there to be catalogued. Best of all—and only true booklovers will understand this—the shop *smelled* so right, with the familiar and comforting scent of old paper and bindings.

"Well, all right," I said. "Thank you very much. I'd be glad of a cup of tea. In fact," I added, looking around more carefully at the shop and its contents, "if I'd known your shop was here, I would have come by before now."

I had nothing to do in London, of course, no plans, no agenda, and a quiet, rainy afternoon spent in a little bookshop like this would let me lose myself for hours. Now it also held out the prospect of a hot cup of tea and, I anticipated, a pleasant conversation with the owner.

We introduced ourselves and, with only mild embarrassment but, I think, the mutual hope of several pleasant hours together, shook hands. We were two strangers, sealing a bargain of which neither of us was aware. If things had turned out differently in the end, I might have added here that Robert Clairthorpe had a better idea than I—at least an inkling of the possibility—of what was to follow from this meeting; for he was the one who proposed, only a week later, the course of action we were to take, and that would have such frightening results for both of us. But he assured me afterward that, at our first meeting, the thought of sharing his secret with me had not once entered his mind, so long had he held it close, away from the sight of the world, away even from his own conscious thoughts.

But a week later, all of that was changed.

Our friendship grew quickly. We were of similar ages. We were both completely alone in the world. And, most important of all, we shared our love for the whole world of books. What is more, we liked the same kinds of books. No effete academic novels for us, no ephemeral or faddish books, no cynical best-sellers by renegade priests writing about trashy sex, not for us. What we loved, and what had been an intimate part of all our lives, both a formative and an ever-present part, was the literature of fantasy and adventure, books that made the heart beat faster, tales that could sweep the reader away to lands that never were, among characters who were far larger than life and passionate in seeking their goals.

And best of all we loved the literature of what is known as dark fantasy, those tales that explore the darker regions of the mind, the monsters of the night, the blackest passions that inhabit the human soul, stories that use as their ruling metaphor an overwhelming image of evil. That was what we'd always loved best.

I spent almost four hours in the shop that first day, and when Robert Clairthorpe and I parted, we parted as friends, each of us aware that our lives had been enriched by this chance meeting.

I can see him in the doorway now, saying goodbye as I left. He was a small man, somewhat shrunken by age, I suppose, as I may be myself or will be as the slow years pass. He had extremely fair skin that appeared very soft, so that the wrinkles only gentled the lines of his face. A crown of white hair ringed his head. An ordinary person would not have noticed him in the street, I am sure, but that person would have missed seeing the bright blueness of his eyes, startling in his otherwise pale face. There was life in those eyes; they were the eyes of a young man, for whom the dawn held only promise and the night no threat of death. When I looked into his eyes, I saw a promise for my own future.

We shook hands, lingering for a moment, reluctant to part, reluctant to end the afternoon.

"Come back again," he said.

"I will," I said.

I was holding in one arm a parcel of books I had purchased from his enormous stock. The price he had asked was, I knew, far below their real value, but he would hear not a word of protest from me.

"I must help you empty more of your shelves," I said, indicating the parcel.

"Oh, do," he said. "I should be glad of another chat."

"Well, I'll see you again, then," I said.

I went back the next day. I must admit that I returned with some trepidation, fearing that my welcome would be less warm than it had been. After all, this man and I did not really know each other, and perhaps I was presuming too much. Several days a week, I imagined, he must have other customers like myself wandering into the shop. Indeed, he must have many regulars, oldtimers like himself—or like myself, I had to admit—who came by, perhaps on a regular schedule, to sort through the books, to chat, and to drink tea with him. I was assuming too much, yes, and I was also self-conscious about my own, seemingly obvious, need for a friend.

But I need not have worried. Robert Clairthorpe was visibly as happy to see me as I was to be welcomed warmly once again. We spent another four hours together, talking about books, reminding each other and ourselves about old favorites and scenes we'd particularly enjoyed. Over and over again, one or the other of us would say, "Oh, and do you remember the part where . . ." We had a grand time. When I left, I said, "Well, I suppose I'll see you tomorrow."

"I'll be looking forward to it," he said happily, those bright blue eyes beaming with pleasure.

It was only when I'd eaten some dinner and returned to my room in Bedford Place that I realized today was Sunday and that the shop would normally have been closed.

On that Sunday, the day of our second meeting, Robert Clairthorpe had six days left to live.

And I must now continue in the knowledge that, had it not been for my arrival in his shop and in his life, my friend would still be alive today.

I went to the shop every day that week. On Tuesday, the day of my fourth visit, I tried to coax him out of the shop to a local restaurant for dinner, but he would not come with me. He was, he said, a creature of long habit, and he would not be comfortable eating in a restaurant.

The next day, Wednesday, he insisted that I stay and let him prepare the meal. He had, he told me, already been out to the butcher around the corner and purchased lamb chops for both of us. Although I protested that he must, in return, accompany me to a restaurant, I was touched by his invitation, and of course I agreed to stay. I could not remember the last time I had had the simple pleasure of a quiet meal with a friend, where the exchange of the evening was nothing more than mutual interest and friendship. And I am certain that he felt the same.

It was that evening, while he prepared the simple meal, refusing to let me help in any way, that I first saw the back room of the shop where he lived, a single, small room, dark and cramped, that served him as sitting room, bedroom, and kitchen, all in one. This too was cluttered with books, books that had the look of good companions about them, books that had been read recently, or were being read now, or that were waiting to be read very shortly. The helter-skelter way they littered his living quarters made me think that the books were almost alive, each one jostling the others in friendly rivalry for the privilege of being the next one read. Even in the man's private quarters, where I had not before been admitted, I immediately felt at home.

Other than the books, there was nothing at all remarkable about this little room, except for a very handsome showcase against the wall. It was perhaps four feet high and two feet square, its sloping glass top covered in green baize. I could see from the carvings of its legs and the ornamentation on its sides that it was a very fine piece of furniture and, presumably, quite valuable. Possibly it might once have stood in a very elegant private library.

I remarked on it and felt free enough to lift the cover, curious to see what treasure was so carefully and lovingly preserved beneath the glass. The showcase was empty. When I looked curiously at Robert Clairthorpe, he said only that the showcase was an old thing and that he didn't use it. I assumed from the way he spoke that it must have had some sentimental meaning for him, perhaps something unpleasant or painful to recall, and I said nothing else about it.

I tried again the next evening, Thursday, to bring him out to a restaurant for the evening meal, but he would not. He was long past that, he said; he had lived so long in the world of fiction that he would be a stranger anywhere but in his own little shop. No amount of urging could convince him.

It was on that Thursday evening, I believe, as our visit drew to a close, that I first detected a change in his eyes when he looked at me, a subtle veiling of his expression, and an unwillingness to meet my gaze directly. At the same time, and this struck me as very odd, I thought I noticed him looking at me very closely, as if examining me intently, when he thought my attention was drawn elsewhere. It made me slightly uncomfortable, and later, back at Bedford Place, although we had agreed to meet again the next day as usual, I began to wonder if perhaps I had overstayed my welcome and was making a pest of myself, taking up too much of his time. Unschooled as I was in the ways of friendship, I worried about this all the rest of the evening and did not sleep well that night.

But I was quite wrong. It was not a lack of friendship that had made my new acquaintance act strangely. Rather, it was his own lack of familiarity with feelings of closeness to another person that made him hesitate and mistrust his own judgment, just as I was mistrusting mine.

When I arrived at the shop on Friday, my arms were filled with parcels from the local shops. I was determined that, if I could not treat my friend to dinner in a restaurant, I would repay the debt by providing all the ingredients of a pleasant dinner to be fixed at home. It was this gesture on my part that settled the doubt in both our minds and, in the course of our conversation that afternoon, made us both admit the slight awkwardness we'd been feeling, and admit further how glad we both were to have made such a congenial friend.

Perhaps if I had not thought to buy that piece of meat and those greens and potatoes, Robert Clairthorpe would not have taken me into his confidence. And in that case, he would not have lost his life and I would not have lost my only friend. Perhaps. Or perhaps some other set of irresistible circumstances would have brought us together anyway and, together, carried us off into the darkness that awaited. I am inclined to believe the latter. I would prefer to believe it, for it would make the long days and the longer nights easier for me now.

As it happened, no customers came into the shop that afternoon and our long, pleasant conversation was uninterrupted for hours. We were enjoying ourselves, freed of all doubt that each was imposing on the other's time, and looking forward to prolonging the visit through a nice dinner and well on into the evening. At about six o'clock we rose from our seats near the window at the front of the shop. Robert Clairthorpe locked the door and drew down the shades on the windows, and we retired together to the little room at the back to share the work of preparing our meal. It is a terrible thing to be alone in the world—I had known it for months before this and I know it again now—but, to such a person, the joy of a new friend's company is beyond all measure.

While we fixed the meal—it was nothing very special, to be certain, but I think we both looked forward to it as to a regal repast —I was thinking that I really must draw my friend out, convince him that he should come with me to restaurants and to see some West End shows. There were currently three plays, at least, that I knew would carry him away to the world of make-believe we both loved.

During dinner we talked about the novels of Thomas Hardy, recalling where and when we had first discovered his world. Robert asked which of the novels was my favorite and I replied that it was *Tess of the D'Urbervilles,* perhaps because that had been the first I'd read. He smiled gently and told me that had been his own experience. We spoke of Dickens in the same way, agreeing on *The Pickwick Papers* as our favorite. Then something in the conversation—I wish I could recall now what it was, but perhaps, as it seemed to me after, this was part of his plan—made him mention *The Monk* by Matthew Gregory Lewis. This was much more in line, of course, with our particular taste in fiction, and we talked about it for some while, recalling favorites from among its dark and dreadful scenes. And somewhere in this part of the conversation, as pleasant and relaxed as it was, I began to feel that Robert Clairthorpe was putting me to a test.

We had finished our meal and cleared the table, then returned to our chairs. When I seated myself and looked across at my friend, he was staring at me intently and biting his lower lip. I shall never forget his face at that moment, the last moment before he took me into his confidence. He was a man about to set out on an adventure, the outcome of which could not be predicted, because its direction and ending could not be settled by courage and determination alone, an adventure in which a man could only try his best against forces beyond his knowing and which would determine his fate for him. It was all in his face as he looked at me then.

"What is it, Robert?" I said. "What's wrong?"

He dropped his gaze to the table and would not look up at me for some minutes as he spoke, as if he feared that a doubtful or scornful look from me would sap his courage.

"I want to share something with you," he said, so softly that I could barely hear him. "The showcase," he added, even more quietly.

I glanced across the room at it. It stood as before and appeared not to have been touched since I had lifted its covering and looked inside a couple of days before.

"I don't understand," I said. "What do you mean?"

He was obviously nervous, even embarrassed, and I tried to make my voice as neutral as I could. Of course, I was intrigued by all the mystery in his manner. And it occurred to me that, if in fact I had been given a test, apparently I had passed.

"The showcase," he said again. "It's . . . It's quite special."

And then he told me what most people—perhaps every person in the world with the exception of the two of us—would consider a fantastic story. But Robert Clairthorpe was telling the truth. I know he was telling the truth. My friend had lived through the experiences he described, and I could hear the truth of it in his voice.

I know I must tell this part as simply as I can manage.

The showcase had belonged to the previous owner of the shop, the man for whom Robert had clerked when he first came up to London. Where the showcase had been before that, or what were its origins, Robert did not know. When, in his final illness, the old man had felt the approach of death, he had taken young Robert into his confidence.

The showcase had—I should say, has—the ability to transfer a person into the world of the book it contains.

That is what the old man told Robert, that is what Robert found to be true, that is what he told me, and what I myself can vouch for. The reader of these pages may choose not to believe it, but it is true, nevertheless.

"Tell me," I said. "Tell me about it. How does it work?"

My tone of voice, devoid of all mockery and filled with a desire to know more, made my friend look up at me then. His eyes were glistening with excitement and the pleasure of sharing his secret at last.

"I don't know how it works," he said. "But it does. Oh, it does. I know it."

He explained quickly that all one had to do was select a book, open it to the passage desired, place the open book in the showcase, and lower the glass cover into place. That was all. Instantly, one was transported to the scene described on the open pages of the book.

He was watching my face eagerly as he spoke, waiting for signs of doubt or a conviction that he was mad.

But of course I believed him. I had to believe him. I could hear the truth in every word he spoke. And there was another thing. Already I was beginning to long to share his knowledge.

"Have you done it?" I asked. "Gone somewhere?"

He nodded.

"Where?"

He mumbled something, stopped, swallowed, cleared his throat. *"The Pickwick Papers,"* he said.

I stared at him.

"I have," he said. "I swear to you, I have."

"Tell me."

He had owned the showcase for thirty years after the death of his benefactor before he had the nerve to put the showcase to the test. He had chosen *The Pickwick Papers* in part because it was a favorite and in part because its world seemed to pose fewer dangers than other books he might have chosen. He had selected a very innocent passage in which Mr. Pickwick and his companions were journeying by carriage along a country road. The book was opened to that scene and carefully placed into the showcase. Then he closed the top.

And instantly found himself standing, not in his living quarters but behind some bushes at the side of a lonely country road. And, just down the road to his right, a carriage was rattling toward him.

Could it be real? Could it all be real? The ground beneath his feet was solid. A breeze was cooling his brow and rustling the bushes in front of him. The carriage was moving ever closer, sending up a little cloud of dust behind it. And then the carriage was jouncing past. Robert was so frozen with wonder that he did not even duck out of sight, but he was glad of that afterward. He could not make out the faces of the men rushing past him, but he definitely caught sight of Sam, Mr. Pickwick's servant. In fact, their eyes even met for a second. Sam's gaze seemed to linger briefly and then, his face still impassive, he turned away and was carried off by the coach.

And a moment later, Robert Clairthorpe was back in his room behind the bookshop.

He stared at me a long while, his eyes pleading with me to believe him.

"Did you go again?" I asked.

He had gone again and, emboldened by his first successful trip, had chosen a different sort of world to enter, that of *The Monk*. He had studied the book with great care and finally selected a passage that was purely descriptive.

The result was the same. The instant he closed the top of the showcase, he was transported to the world described in the open pages. He found himself standing—and shivering—in a dank corridor that, he knew, was far underground. Feeble candlelight flickered in the distance, off to his left. Water dripped down the gleaming walls and startled rats scurried past his feet. The air was stale and unpleasant. Down the corridor to his left, he could hear singing but could not make out the words. Then suddenly, from his right, he heard a woman's high-pitched scream, its sound caroming off the wet, stone walls of the passageway. He jumped, his skin crawling at the back of his neck.

And found himself back in his warm and familiar room.

After that—and it was nearly twenty years ago now—he'd been afraid to venture off again.

My hands were trembling. I turned my head and looked over at the showcase where it stood against the wall.

"Where shall we go?" I said.

Robert Clairthorpe reached across the table and squeezed my hand.

"There is one book I've always longed to know better," he said. "Where I've always longed to go." He was breathing hard. "The best of them all."

I was sure I knew what he meant.

"Dracula," he breathed.

I was too excited to speak and could only nod my agreement.

Back in Bedford Place, I was awake most of the night.

My room was at the front of the building, a lovely Georgian townhouse, and had two immensely tall arched windows. After changing for bed, and with the lights turned out, I had pulled back the heavy draperies. In recent months, I had found myself more comfortable with a little light while I slept. The window was open six inches at the bottom, against the floor, and a bit at the top, and the breezes of the night stirred the white curtains continually. After a while, with sleep evading me, I rose up on one elbow and watched their languid, lacy movements. But my heart was racing, and my thoughts were carrying me away.

Outside, I heard in the quiet street the occasional growling of a taxi, a sound so distinctive and characteristic of modern London. The houses of Bedford Place are now all bed-and-breakfast establishments, and several times I heard the slow footsteps of residents returning home, and laughter once or twice. Lorries passing nearby in Great Russell Street and, less often, the rumble of a bus making its way around Russell Square—all these sounds of ordinary London reached me in the silence of the night, as if floating on the soft *swish swish* of the curtains on the floor.

Could I really be going off, my friend and I, just tomorrow afternoon, to a world that had never been? Could we? Would we dare?

I listened to a distant bus, tried to picture where it was: coming up Southampton Row from Kingsway, barely slowing as it made its swaying left turn into Russell Square, halting for a moment at the request stop, then continuing on. The sound was so real, so very casually real. The lights would be on in the lobby of the Russell Hotel. The roses in the square would be swaying in the breeze. In the underground car park beneath Bloomsbury Square, couples returning late from the theater would be starting their cars. In Great Russell Street, late strollers might be looking in the shop windows at ancient coins and packets of stamps, books in the windows of Souvenir Press, Shetland wool sweaters in the windows of Westaway and Westaway. In Coptic Street, the Pizza Express was probably still open.

But Robert Clairthorpe and I were going away to a world that had never been. I felt—and I am not at all embarrassed to admit it, at least here, on paper, and now, when nothing in the world can cause me embarrassment—that I felt like a little boy who has been forced to settle in a new city, far from school and playmates, but who has just found a new best friend with marvelous toys to share.

Oh, yes. Robert Clairthorpe and I were definitely going.

We had a copy of Bram Stoker's *Dracula* on the table between us. It was a beautiful copy, a first edition, first impression, and of course very rare, especially in this nearly mint condition. Under ordinary circumstances, one would not actually open and read such a copy—it was Robert Clairthorpe's most prized volume—but this occasion, we both felt, justified it.

We talked for a very long time, discussing the advisability of selecting various scenes, weighing and considering which passage in the entire novel would best suit us. At long last, we settled on one. It was an outdoor scene, since we did not care to be trapped indoors anywhere in that book. And it was in England, as we thought that safer than a Transylvanian scene. Once the top of the showcase was closed, we would find ourselves, we trusted, in the road that bordered Carfax.

"All right, then," Robert said quietly, his breath coming short with excitement.

"All right," I said. "Let's do it."

And then Robert shocked me with what he said. I was so taken aback that I hardly knew how to react, whether with mere surprise, with disappointment, with concern for him, with anger, or with an expression of love and gratitude.

He would not let me come with him, he said, because he feared the danger. He would go first, alone, and if he returned safely, then the two of us would go together.

We argued, as friends argue when each would outdo the other in expressions of love and concern, but he would not hear of anything but his own plan. He would not, he insisted, allow me to place myself in any danger on account of him.

I tried, again and again, but I could not convince him otherwise. Reluctantly, I was forced to yield.

And found myself more anxious about my friend's safety than I had been about my own.

Robert lifted the book from the table and marked the place with his finger. We moved across the room and stood before the showcase. I reached out and lifted back the cloth that covered the glass.

"The wood never needs polishing," he whispered. "The glass never grows dusty or cloudy."

We looked at each other for a long moment, each of us seeking to penetrate into the other's mind and thoughts.

"Come back," I said, and Robert nodded. But it was a foolish thing to say out loud, because it only crystallized the fear we both felt, gave form to the danger that we now felt lurked before us.

Robert looked at the showcase. "All right," he said.

Using both hands, I lifted the wood-framed glass top. Robert took a step closer and placed the open book in the center of the space inside. Then he raised his hands and grasped the wooden frame of the top himself. I released it and stepped back.

"Robert . . ." I said.

"I promise you," he said, and now it was my turn to nod.

Slowly, holding his breath, he began to lower the top. With it only halfway down, he stopped and raised it again.

"You'll wait here?" he said, not looking at me. He was staring at the book.

"Of course," I said instantly. "I'll be here."

"Thank you," he said. "I must do this quickly, or I shall lose my nerve."

With a firm, quick movement he lowered the glass top into place. At the instant it touched the body of the showcase, my friend vanished from before me.

And in almost the same instant, after the fraction of a second it took me to react to what I'd seen, I was shouting, "No! No! Robert!"

But it was too late.

The pages of the book had not been lying fully flat. The heavy Victorian paper was rather stiff and this, combined with the book's seldom, if ever before, having been opened, and its tightly bound spine, had caused the pages to drift upright a little. And then the movement of the glass top must have created a tiny current of air, just enough to make the pages flutter and resettle themselves, with a different passage from the one we'd selected now open in the book.

My friend was gone and I did not know where.

I have been alone again ever since that night.

I waited, of course. I waited there all the rest of the evening and well into the night, never once taking my eyes from the pages of the book in the showcase.

After a while, although my heart cried out that *this must not happen,* I knew he would not be coming back. Something had happened to him . . . wherever he had gone. And it had happened a century before.

Until I moved at last, I was hardly aware of the pain and stiffness in my legs and back from standing still for so many hours. I approached the showcase cautiously, scarcely daring to breathe, but at the same time I knew it held no danger for me. Robert, my friend, had himself suffered the danger he had insisted on sparing me.

I studied the pages of the book in the showcase, as this was the only chance I had—if there were any chance at all—of locating him or helping him. I sobbed aloud once before gaining control of myself.

Without once taking my eyes from the exposed pages, I slowly lifted the top of the showcase. As soon as it was high enough, I reached in with one hand and took hold of the book, pressing open the stiff pages that were uppermost. Holding my breath, I read the passage.

He was in Whitby, on the west coast, on the very night when Dracula, ravening with thirst after his long sea voyage, first arrived in England.

It is not easy to travel from London to Whitby late on a Saturday night. I can recall now none of the details of my trip, only the dread and the loss and the loneliness that I felt that night. By Sunday afternoon, chilled and wet from a ceaseless rain, I was in the tiny, gray port town of Whitby.

I was unable to think very clearly, I must admit, but by the time I reached my destination, I had come to one sad conclusion. Whatever fate had befallen my friend, he must be long dead by now.

Before leaving his bookshop, I had replaced the book, open to the same passage, in the showcase, so that he would be able to return—so that the doorway would be open to him, as it were—whether I was there or not. Even so, I had no expectation of ever seeing him again. He was lost to me forever.

And why did I not go after him? No. Had he been able to return, he would have. He would have *had* to; it was in the nature of the way the showcase worked. Also, I knew with absolute certainty that were I to follow him, I would arrive in the exact place and time where he had arrived, and would have suffered the same fate, whatever it was. That is what he had spared me. No, I could not follow him. At least, now, I do not have to regret that.

Whitby did not welcome me. The cold rain would not let up and the cobbles of the street, perhaps the same cobbles that Robert Clairthorpe had trod, were slippery in the wet. I walked and walked, going nowhere, and seeing only a few bedraggled figures like myself, hunched over against the rain.

There was no one I could go to see, no one whom I could ask, no one to whom I could tell my tale. I must remain silent, with the secret, and the pain, locked tight and hard within me.

I took a room in a bed-and-breakfast house at the outskirts of the town. I paid the landlady in cash for two weeks, and she looked less suspicious then and was immediately concerned for my health in this wet weather. She kindly fixed me a cup of tea and I could have wept in gratitude. In my room I pulled off my wet clothes and slept for three hours.

When I awoke, the rain had eased off to a drizzle and the sky was black. Although my clothes were still wet, I dressed and went out to walk again in the empty dark streets of Whitby.

My mind was clearer now, and the instant I stepped out the door and started along the pavement, I saw the very place where I knew I would find my friend. From the steps of the house I could see the leaning iron railings of the graveyard.

I went back inside and climbed up to my room at once. I rushed to the window, opened it, and looked out. It faced the graveyard, I could see that much, but there was too little light to see anything else.

I could get a flashlight, a torch, from the landlady, I thought desperately. I could . . . Wearily, I sat back on the edge of the bed to try to think things through carefully. The next thing I knew, I had slept through the night and the gray light of morning was coming through the window.

I ate the breakfast the landlady fixed for me without tasting a bite of it. I knew I must eat, and so I ate. As I was finishing, she inquired casually if I had come to Whitby for business or pleasure.

I told her I had come on business and might be staying awhile. She seemed satisfied at that and asked me nothing further.

I was stiff and uncomfortable from sleeping in my damp clothes all night, and of course my clothing was in a sorry state. But I had no time for that now; when the opportunity offered, I would buy new clothes. I thanked Mrs. Williams for breakfast and, feeling a little more fortified for what lay ahead, ventured out into Whitby once more.

The rain had ceased, but shimmering pools still lay on the uneven flags of the pavement, their rippled surfaces reflecting the gray tumult of clouds overhead. The wind was brisk, fresh with the smell of salt from the sea, and its dampness cut to the bone. I walked steadily toward the graveyard. I could see the gates ahead.

Shock and exhaustion had combined to numb my thoughts, but now it all came rushing back to me as the sharp breeze touched my face and cleared my mind. Had Robert Clairthorpe breathed this air the night before, I wondered; had the same rain chilled my friend? Was there a chance he might still be among the living? If I returned at once to London, would I find him in the warm, familiar bookshop, waiting for me, worrying about me, wondering where I'd gone? No. He was not there, I was certain of it. He was here, in Whitby, and I was beginning to think—with the most terrible dread I had felt up to that day—that I knew what had happened to him, what his fate had been.

I pushed back the gate—the black-painted iron was cold and wet and rough against my hand—and walked into the cemetery.

It is on a hillside and one can see the ocean while walking among the stones. The chilling winds come in here, cold and determined, and lay flat the straggly grass, polish the stones and push them over. The narrow paths are wet and weedy. A few brave trees, bent by the wind, struggle for life in this place of death. I was the only living person in the graveyard.

It was less than an hour before I found it. Just a very simple gravestone, little more than a marker, certainly not a memorial. The letters carved into it were shallow and a little uneven, and nearly obscured by the work of wind and rain: only his name and the year of his death. There would be no more, of course; he had been a stranger here. No one in Whitby knew him and he had been alone when he died.

I knelt on rough stones, in wet grass, with the wind flapping the collar of my coat, and murmured a prayer for the friend I had known so briefly, who had kept me from lying here in Whitby's graveyard myself. That thought chilled me and made me shudder. I stood up. And, looking down at the worn and leaning gravestone, I realized that my obligation was not ended, would never end. There was more I had to do for Robert Clairthorpe, a task that I was bound, by ties of love and friendship and human decency, to perform. The wind from the sea was cold but I did not feel it, for a colder wind moved within me.

It was still early in the day. I still had plenty of time to prepare.

I returned to the cemetery in the late afternoon. I had purchased a new raincoat and I concealed beneath it the other things I had bought. The grave was on the slope facing the sea, away from the fence of the cemetery and the street that ran along it, and visible only to one or two of the highest windows of nearby houses, one of which, I thought, must be my own. No one would see me digging, but I had not wanted to take the chance of doing it in full daylight. I did not fear being arrested—I had no room in my thoughts for such a fear—only that I would be prevented from doing what I must do. And it must be done, the whole task completed, before the gray of evening turned into the black of night.

I am not accustomed to the work of digging. I had to stop often to catch my breath and to ease the pain of cramped muscles. I prayed that my heart would not fail me before I finished here; if it failed me afterward, I would welcome the end. As for the rest of it, I tried not to think of it, tried not to picture what I would find at the bottom of the grave, tried not to think of what I had to do, tried to think only of taking out one more shovelful of dirt, and then another, and another, and another. I prayed in gratitude now for the nasty weather that kept ships and pleasure craft from the water and so prevented anyone there from seeing me digging up a grave.

The coffin—it did not surprise me—was of the thinnest, cheapest sort, and had almost rotted back into the earth. My shovel struck it and went right through the wood. I stopped and threw my head back up to the heavens to draw air into my aching lungs. And to spare myself another moment before having to look at the thing beneath my feet. But my heart almost stopped then, for only the tiniest glimmer of gray daylight remained in the sky. In another moment the graveyard would be swallowed by night.

I had laid the other implements at the edge of the hole. I grabbed them now and, with the pick, pried up what remained of the coffin's lid. It was a pauper's grave, the grave of a stranger alone in the world, and the body had not been dressed, only wrapped in a heavy winding sheet and laid in the box. The sheet was as fresh and white as it was the last day human hands had touched it. Not permitting myself to stop and think of what I was doing, fearing I would fail in the task I'd set myself, I slit the sheet open with a knife.

I was looking at the face and the naked chest of Robert Clairthorpe. Time and the earth had worked no horrors on his body. He was pale, but otherwise looked exactly as I had last seen him the night before in London, the same kind face, with the same promise of gentleness in it. My hands were shaking violently. I had to bite my lower lip to keep from crying.

The stake was actually a small fence post. I had bought four of them. I reached for it at the edge of the hole, dropped it from trembling fingers, scrabbled around and found it again. And took the heavy mallet in the other hand. For a moment, I thought I could not do it. I looked at the sky. At most there might be a couple of minutes left before it would be too late. My hands were shaking so badly that I could barely hold the stake and mallet. My mouth was open but I could not get enough air into my burning lungs. And this was my friend. Had been my friend. Would always be.

I poised the stake above his chest where I imagined the heart to be. I feared to touch him with it until the final instant, for fear the touch would wake him from his temporary sleep.

I poised myself, forced myself to keep my eyes open, rested the tip of the stake against his skin, sobbed "Robert!" and slammed the mallet against the head of the stake.

In the same instant, the bloodless face beneath me, a moment ago so deeply at rest, was transformed. It flushed red—red that I could see even in the dark—and the eyes flew open, burning at me in venomous hatred. His fingers curled and the hands twitched upward, but the stake had been driven through his heart and he could not rise up to stop me.

Sobbing, my face wet with tears, I took the ax and braced myself once again. My knees threatened to topple me, but I somehow found solid footing. It was so difficult, standing deep in a grave. This was the worst part of all I had dreaded.

I swung the ax as best I could. It sliced into his shoulder and the whole body surged beneath me. I swung again, this time cutting into the neck where I had aimed. The darkness and my tears prevented me from seeing clearly. I swung the blade again and missed entirely. I was crying out loud now. His eyes kept rolling and spewing hatred at me. The hands clutched feebly at my legs and made my flesh crawl. In the end, I had to stop swinging and hold the handle of the ax near the blade, chopping and chopping madly until Robert Clairthorpe's head was entirely severed from his body.

And then, at the instant of true death, I saw my friend's kind face again for just a moment. The hatred faded from the eyes, which seemed to cloud over, then grow clearer again, and look at me as they had in life, filled with kindness and warmth, perhaps even with love. And then they clouded once again, the features relaxed, and my friend was gone forever.

I bent down and reversed the head, finding that touching the body was not nearly so bad as what I'd done already. Then I settled the sheet once again and climbed out of the hole. I was so exhausted that it took almost as long to fill it in again as it had taken me to dig it.

When I reached home, Mrs. Williams called out from the kitchen that she'd be glad to fix a little dinner for me. I called back from halfway up the stairs that I was going to bed and did not wish to be called for breakfast.

In my room, I went at once to the window. I thought I could see the very place where my friend's body lay in the earth. Then I went to bed and slept until noon the next day.

I am still here. I have been here ever since, except for one brief trip up to London.

I accomplished a great deal that day. I contacted a solicitor and gave him instructions for dealing with my own attorney at home, whom I instructed to dispose of all my property in the United States, my bank accounts, everything. I had already visited the bookshop and found everything intact, and the London solicitor was given instructions about that too. I am moved now again when I report what I found in the shop. On a shelf, in the very spot

036

where the *Dracula* volume had rested, was a white envelope. It contained Robert Clairthorpe's last will and testament, dated the morning of that terrible Saturday, and left the shop and all its contents to me. No mention was made of the showcase, which was careful thinking on Robert's part. Had it been mentioned there specifically, I could not have removed it that very day, as I intended. I made arrangements for that too, and rode all the long way to Whitby in the lorry, never once letting the showcase out of my sight.

It is here with me now in my room. Its wood still gleams as it did before. I keep the glass covered, as Robert did. Inside it, I keep the book, open to the page.

I am staying here with Robert. I can see his grave from the window. I think he would be glad to know that I am here. His grave might have been my own, so, in a way, I share that with him.

Mrs. Williams cooks my meals and looks after me a bit, and my room is filled with books, so the time goes by for me. It will not be so very long. I am old, and growing older.

I think sometimes that it would be nice to see my old home again, the places where I grew up, where Elizabeth and I lived, even the house where I lived so very briefly. But the feeling passes. This is my home now. This is where my friend is. I shall not leave England now.

I cannot.

CHARLES L. GRANT is one of the most respected writers and editors in the fields of horror and fantasy. He is the winner of two Nebula Awards for science fiction writing, a World Fantasy Award as the editor of the original *Shadows* anthology, and at the most recent World Fantasy Awards he emerged as the winner in the categories of Best Novella and Best Collection (for *Nightmare Seasons*, an anthology of his own horror fiction). His most recent novel is *Night Songs*. In addition to the popular *Shadows* series, he is also the editor of the anthologies *Terrors* and *Nightmares*. He lives in New Jersey.